The Case of the Kidnapped Orphans

A Stu Fletcher, PI novel

By

Jeff Ridenour

Publisher: Karlsbad Middleford Press KMP
Seattle, Washington

ISBN-13: 979-8595206617

For: Maureen & Lon

Acknowledgement:

Again I would like to my wife, Ronda Lynn Ridenour,
For her skillful, patient editing, without which… blech!

An ounce of mother is worth a pound of clergy.
                                    -- a Spanish proverb

1941 Ford Woody Station Wagon

1

Wednesday
October 30, 1968

Agnes Sullivan still bore smudges of white paint on the tips of her thumbs and index fingers when she finally joined me in her modest office. She was Mother Superior at the Convent of Santa Franchesca Ornella, in the foothills northeast of the city of Santa Julietta, on the Central California coast and I had come to speak to her about two young orphan girls who had been kidnapped from her convent's school grounds two months earlier, at the beginning of the school term. They were eight-year-old Melissa Hargrove and ten-year-old Eileen Sanchez. The young girls had yet to be found.

Even the FBI remained baffled, much to their chagrin. Hoover's men muscled in on the case immediately, as they were entitled to do ever since the Lindbergh kidnapping back in 1932, when Charles Lindbergh's 20-month-old son was abducted in New Jersey and soon found dead. The Federal Kidnapping Act became law that same year.

That the FBI had achieved no success in finding the girls did not surprise me. I firmly believe the claim allegedly made by an old Texas Ranger that the three most overrated things in the world are young pussy, Mack trucks, and the FBI. The attribution may be apocryphal, but that didn't stop most cops, and ex-cops like me, from believing the claim. My own past experiences with the FBI bore out the fact that they are glorified bunglers. So, as a PI licensed by the state of California I was confident I could do better.

"Sorry to keep you waiting, but the children come first, Mr. Fletcher. They all do *so* get excited when they line up to have their faces painted as skeletons."

Mother Agnes smiled as she spoke, but I sensed she felt less enthusiasm than she tried to convey.

"Why are you painting them today?" I said. "All Souls' Day is not until Friday."

"Tomorrow, of course, is Halloween, when we will take our children out and around the nearby neighborhood. Tomorrow night we will allow them two pieces of candy before bedtime. On Thursday they will be permitted to have more. Naturally we expect them to feel ill all weekend long, some of them too queasy even to march in the downtown *Dia* parade."

Over many decades the convergence of All Souls Day and *El Dia de los Muertos*, The Day of the Dead, has left the Catholic Church in a bind. Although for the Church Satan must never ultimately prevail, in this part of the New World many Aztec traditions have infiltrated Christian rituals. One such Aztec tradition calls for Mictlantecuhtli & Mictecacihuatl, the Aztec husband-and-wife God and Goddess of the Underworld, to capture and protect the souls of the dead. That obviously is not what Christians have in mind when they speak of Satan and of his Underworld, full of fire and brimstone, triggering weeping and wailing and the gnashing of teeth.

A woman named Wendy Ellen Sheldon had acted as foster mother to both Melissa and Eileen for two years, until, a year and a half ago, the local branch of the Child Protective Services took the children away from Wendy Ellen and placed them in the convent, because a curtain-twitching neighbor of Wendy Ellen had spied her pouring herself a drink from a bottle of what appeared to contain gin or vodka. A recovering alcoholic who had been clean for six years, Wendy Ellen had been granted foster-mother status on condition that she continue to stay clean. Such was the shortage of volunteer foster mothers on the Central California coast.

When two CPS workers searched Wendy Ellen's modest house, in a shabbier section of Santa Julietta, they found no alcohol and Wendy Ellen denied having gone off the wagon. But "just to be safe", the two children were removed from Wendy Ellen's care. Both foster mother and children were devastated. Beginning this school year, after much wrangling, Wendy Ellen had finally been granted a visiting privilege, one agreed upon by CPS, Mother Agnes, and a reluctant, despondent Wendy Ellen. Once a month, for fifteen minutes. Blessed are the magnanimous.

Following the kidnappings, when she hired me to find the girls, she described to me CPS's taking *her* children as "legalized kidnapping". I didn't dispute that description. My dealings with CPS over the years had been few and depressing. I had come to the conclusion that women who lack the wits to teach elementary school end up working for the State of California's Child Protective Services. Now here I sat, waiting to interview the latest woman from whom children were ripped away. Only this time not by CPS but by a person or persons unknown.

From local articles I had unearthed at my local library, I knew that Mother Agnes was sixty-four years old. She hailed from Traverse City, Michigan and had served as a nurse on the USS Comfort, a hospital ship during the Battle of Okinawa in the summer of 1945. A Japanese kamikaze plane hit the Comfort amidships, killing twenty-eight people, including six nurses. So the abbess was a resilient old bird. She not only had watched enormous pain and suffering by others, but she also had barely survived that particular moment of her God's perpetual wrath. But now, perhaps to try to make amends for some of her deity's malice, she had become an expert at meting out love and kindness to the younger nuns of the Sisters of Mercy under her tutelage, and especially to the children in her convent's school.

She pulled up a chair next to me, rather than sit at her desk, and brushed away a non-existent speck of dust from the lap of her habit as she sat. I wanted to be amused, but then I reconsidered. Mother Agnes felt at ease in reaching out to flick away imaginary specks of dust, I judged, because she was accustomed to acknowledging other non-existent entities on a habitual basis – pardon my flippant pun - creatures such as angels, saints, and her morally amorphous God.

"As I explained to you on the phone, Mr. Fletcher, I told the police everything I know about the girls' disappearance."

"Yes, Mother Agnes. But the police, the sheriff, and especially the FBI do not share their information with me."

"You are working for the foster-mother, Wendy Ellen, from whom the girls were taken away due to her discovered negligence toward the poor creatures."

"I am. Wendy Ellen admits her errors. Sins of omission, I believe you call them. But reverting to intemperance wasn't one of those sins. She tells me she still really cares deeply about the girls and wants them to be found. She wants *me* to find them, given that the sheriff's people, the police, and even the vaunted FBI have come up empty-handed."

"Oh, posh. Miss Sheldon misses the money that the state paid her more than she misses those girls."

I couldn't argue with Wendy Ellen's 's missing the money, so I said, "It *is* possible to miss both."

"Nonsense. The level of neglect Child Protective Services discovered is not compatible with any sense of passionate caring."

"She was not abusive toward them," I said.

"Of course, she was. She failed to feed them for days on end."

One of the downsides of being unemployed. Wendy Ellen hadn't fed *herself* either during that time – and for longer. But I knew when I was routed.

"Okay then, let's just say *I* care about what has happened to them."

"Who's paying you? Wendy Ellen Sheldon doesn't have two nickels to rub together," Mother Agnes said.

"Sorry. I'm not permitted to divulge who is footing the fee for my services. Let's just leave it at: Fletcher works in mysterious ways."

"If you are trying to provoke me, Mr. Fletcher, you'll not succeed."

"No offense intended, Mother Agnes," I said, even though both of us knew my intention was indeed to provoke her and do so by using her Church's all-too-frequent defense of this or that indefensible, inexplicable event by proclaiming: *God works in mysterious ways.*

"Very well, Mr. Fletcher, I'll grant you a five-minute summary of what transpired when those two unfortunates were hijacked from my care. Five minutes. No more," she said, her tone indicating that, should she stray into a sixth minute of narrative, God might grab her by her throat and shake her violently, as punishment for the sin of conveying too much useful information.

I took a hard look at my watch.

When Mother Agnes finished -- with thirty-eight seconds to spare -- her account amounted to little improvement on local news articles.

As if on cue, an attractive young woman named Sister Melda knocked on the office door and announced, "Something urgent has come up, Mother Agnes."

Before I rose to leave I was sorely tempted to peer underneath Mother Agnes' chair to see if I could spy a little buzzer, one that signaled Sister Melda to come rushing to the rescue, saving the Mother Superior from having to answer more upsetting questions.

The girls had been kidnapped from the convent's school playground on the afternoon of Tuesday, August 26th. Sister Melda and Sister Carmen were herding the school's twenty-seven elementary-age children back into the schoolhouse at the end of an outdoor recess period when, from beyond the schoolyard, the two nuns heard a loud squeal. Sister Carmen later described it as a "squeal of delight". Sister Melda disagreed, calling it a "cry of fright". Both nuns, however, agreed the sound came from Melissa Hargrove.

As both nuns ran toward Melissa, they watched helplessly as a green automobile carried both Melissa and Eileen away. They described the car as a model known widely as a "Woody". That name came from the practice by some auto manufacturers of making the exterior trim of the passenger compartment portion of such vehicles in hardwood. The Woody had been produced mostly as either a station wagon or a convertible and, my research told me, that, as time passed, models were primarily manufactured as third-party conversions of assembly line vehicles.

I left Mother Agnes's office, stepped outside into a chilly breeze blowing down from the north, then turned to my right and walked toward the playground from which the two girls departed. From the east side of the main building a seven-foot-high chain-link fence ran parallel to the sidewalk for some two hundred yards, all the way down where the street turned turn because a low bluff ran from north to south.

At the bluff the fence turned left and ran for a hundred yards or so before turning west and continuing on until it stopped at the back of a red brick building topped by a cupola and cross. The convent's chapel. Through the fence, just beyond the eastside exit from Mother Agnes's office, from which I now saw that the Abbess could look out on, was a typical children's playground, with two see-saws, a slide, and a set of what, when I was a kid, we called monkey bars and others called a jungle gym.

Farther east, as I walked, I saw a dirt softball diamond. The bases appeared to be made of painted plywood anchored into the ground. Home plate was near the end of the fence. To capture foul balls the fence rose and curled, like a nun's headpiece, a coif I believe it's called, and the fence on either side of the head piece rose to twelve feet. I am six-foot-two and it seemed to be twice my height.

Between the classroom building and where the fence turned south were two entry gates. The first one I came to was padlocked. The second one, near where the fence was higher, was not. Mother Agnes had pointed out to me that the absence of a lock on the gate nearer   home plate was because sometimes the twelve-foot fence was not enough to stop a batted softball from flying out into the street. It was through this unlocked gate that the two missing girls passed through and entered the Woody. Sister Carmen, according to her abbess, had reached first-base, out of breath, when the car sped away.

The two manufacturers of Woody-style autos were Ford and Chrysler. Ford's model was called a Sportsman, Chrysler's a Town and Country. Both Ford and Chrysler sent orders for a custom Woody to reputable coachbuilding firms, most of which were owned and operated by small Amish businesses in northern Indiana. The police eventually narrowed the vehicle the nuns saw down to one of those two models of cars, but, because the Ford and Chrysler Woodies are very similar, that was the limit of the police's determination.

However, Sister Melda assured police that the first letter of the California license plate was either "K" or "R", the second 'F' or 'P', and the third 'Z'. Our state's license plates thankfully are easy to read from a distance. And she was certain the first two numbers were both '8'. Plates are issued with three yellow numbers followed by three yellow letters. The plate's background is black. Unfortunately, having run those combinations of letters and numbers through the State Bureau of Vehicle Registrations in Sacramento, local police found no car having those sets of letters and numbers turning up on a Woody of any model. Sister Melda stood by her eyewitness claim.

In any event, local police issued a statewide bulletin asking for other law enforcement agencies to be on the lookout for a Woody with the letters 'KFZ', 'KPZ', 'RFZ, or 'RPZ' and '88' for the first two numbers. As part of that search, police began examining car lots, airport parking lots, parking garages, and even auto junkyards. By the middle of October no one had reported any useful sighting.

Subsequently, police expanded their searches to looking into private garages, even when their inquiries were unrelated. Such practice only ceased when too many criminal defense attorneys began to complain, including the woman I do contract research for, Amanda Reynolds. And, even though she was not involved with the search for the missing girls, Amanda had the idea, rejected by the police, that a search be made of country clubs' parking lots, given that the Woody was in all other respects a luxury car model.

Because police refused to drive even their *unmarked* vehicles through country club parking lots, I had found myself performing that task. But alas, I came up empty-handed, which literally, drove me further afield. I found myself scouring parking lots at Central Coast yacht harbors, once again in the belief that the abductor may come from a wealthy family. In addition to putting lots of miles on my '61 Chevy Biscayne, I ended up using my police connections as a former cop on the Burbank force to obtain a list of purchases and sales of Woodies in Santa Julietta County from the time when Ford and Chrysler Woodies were first made, 1932. Thankfully, that list of owners was reasonably short but, proving Amanda right, the list led me to making drive-by examinations of the license plates of Woodies parked in driveways belonging to the rich and richer. Those quick peeks, however, proved fruitless, too.

2

I'm as envious of the idle rich as anyone else, except I'm glad I don't have to make their mortgage payments. I barely manage to make my own. And, from what I saw, my house appears to be smaller than many of the guest houses in the flossier foothills suburbs of Santa Julietta I drove through looking for a Woody that might have served as a kidnap driver's car.

I live in Santa Maria, seventy miles north of Santa Julietta, up Highway 101. Santa Maria is a working man's town that owes its initial existence to the fact that it was one day's horseback ride from Santa Julietta for the Franciscan missionaries who, beginning with the friar Father Junipero Serra, established the string of missions from Southern California to San Francisco, following a path just east of the low Coastal Range.

Santa Maria remained a quiet little burg until the army base at Vandenberg was transformed into a missile base in 1953. Prior to that it was called Camp Cooke. When it became a missile test site, the town's population exploded and with it came a corresponding increase in crime. When I left the Burbank police force under a cloud of misplaced suspicion, I chose to move to Santa Maria, in part because it was the only town where I thought I could get an affordable mortgage.

However, no self-respecting bank would loan me money, even though I begged on bended knee. Income on my tax returns for the first two years as a PI was not all that shabby. But a steady, respectable income wasn't enough. Bankers don't draw to inside straights and the *irregularity* of my gumshoe fees looked to them like I was a longshot to keep my payments up. Luckily, an attorney in Santa Maria, Jacob Wurstheimer, was willing to loan me money. While still on the Burbank police force, I had rescued his daughter from a kidnapper. Part of his eternal gratitude consisted of selling me a small rental house he owned on Pine Street in central Santa Maria at a below-market interest rate.

In addition to selling me a house, Jake put me on to an additional source of frequent detective work. He introduced me to Amanda Reynolds, one of the best known and respected criminal defense attorneys in Santa Julietta. Amanda told me she would give me a chance to help her out on a case and, if I proved myself, she would deliver additional work my way. When I quickly found evidence that would help set her client free, I found I was thrown a steady diet of "meaty bones", as she called her cases.

She had handed me one such "bone" the day before I visited the convent for my four minutes, twenty-two-seconds conversation with Mother Agnes. I found myself sparring with yet another member of the Catholic clergy when I finally found time to visit Miss Reynolds' latest jailbird punter – a priest.

My father used to joke that he would have made a piss-poor Catholic because, he said, "My knees are the weakest part of my anatomy. So I couldn't take all the kneeling that the pope requires. Plus, as you already know, I won't eat fish." Two good reasons, although I had my own set of objections, but none of them made for much humor.

But anyway --

At my initial meeting with the padre, I found Father Reed Mackenzie reading from the Book of Leviticus, chapter twenty, verse two, as he perched on a squeaky cot in a Santa Julietta county prison cell.

Anyone who giveth any of his children to Molech
will be put to death. The people of the country must
stone him.

He was charged with molesting two teenage boys at a summer camp near Yosemite back in July.

"Do you think the people of California will want to stone me to death if I am convicted, Mr. Fletcher?" he asked in the most casual way, as though he might be asking if members of the Academy of Arts & Sciences might be going to award him an Oscar.

"Not a chance, Father Mackenzie. Instead, the people of the state of California will prefer to give you a whiff of cyanide gas." Only I was sure the penalty in California for buggering choir boys was not death, though maybe it should be.

According to the file Amanda Reynolds had provided me ahead of time, Father Mackenzie had been transferred out of Ireland by the Catholic hierarchy there, presumably when they ran out of parishes to transfer him to. Then, following his arrival in Southern California, the office of the Archbishop of Los Angeles had been kept busy trying to spare the priest from a local stoning.

Finally, however, accusations by two Santa Julietta teenagers could not be swept under the rug by the Archbishop and his legal minions. The boys' parents insisted on pressing charges against the priest and neither persuasion nor *sub rosa* threats to the parents would dissuade them. So, now here he sat, in a draughty jail cell, awaiting arraignment.

"Quite a journey you've had from Dublin to Santa Julietta," I said, to get his mind off his having given children to Molech. "Did your leaving Ireland break your mother's heart?"

"My sainted mother was long since dead when Mother Church decided to give me opportunities here," he said, with only a slight Barry Fitzgerald movie brogue. I passed on what he might mean by *opportunities here* and focused on his lie.

"Your mother is still alive, Father."

"Oh, is she now? Well, for all practical purposes she's dead to me."

"She disowns you?" I said.

He shook his head. "'Tis I who disown her."

"And why might that be?"

"She failed to back me when they showered me with lies."

"What lies?"

"You know the ones. I'm sure you've read my file by now," he said.

His file was thin. Very thin, consisting of Amanda's notes and a scant background report, heavily redacted, provided by the Church in LA. He was born in Dublin in 1927, making him forty-one years old. His father, Brendan, was a Canadian sales rep for Jameson whiskeys, who won a company-paid trip to Dublin in 1929 as a reward for his sales acumen. While in Dublin the father met Stacy O'Day, the owner of a pub called Fiddler's Tune. The two were married seven months later, months before McKenzie was born.

"What can you tell me that might help prove you innocent of the current charges against you?" I said, pulling up the wooden chair a deputy provided me when I asked for one.

"Those boys, both of them, are lying. They made up the charges against me, then convinced their parents that I …well, you've read their accusations."

"Why would they have done that?" I said.

The priest ran a forefinger back and forth along his mattress seam several times before finally saying, "Somehow they found out about the reasons for my previous transfers. They thought to amuse themselves by making life miserable for me again."

"How did they find out?"

He threw up his hands. "I don't know. What does it matter?"

"It might. Perhaps, I can prove someone put them up to it, planted the idea in their heads."

"You believe me innocent then." An assertion, not a question.

"I didn't say that. But if you are innocent, it will surely be useful to expose who whispered your past to these young men and what his or her motive was in doing so," I said.

His shoulders sagged. "I barely remember seeing those two scoundrels at the summer camp. Yes, they attend church where I am priest, but people their age are supported by a youth minister. In my church's case, Father Spannard. Why didn't they pick on him instead of me?"

"Does this Father Spannard have a dark past?"

Father Mackenzie shook his head. "None that I know of. Father Frank cares for his charges, and tries to get close to them, but, from what I've observed of his behavior so far, not *that* close."

"Well then…."

"I don't see why that would have stopped them," he said.

The two accusers were Tyson and Bryson Ledbetter. Both had just graduated from Santa Julietta Catholic High and were attending a basketball camp at Bass Lake, south of Yosemite National Park, a camp run by the Central California Catholic Youth Sports Association. Father Mackenzie was there with a group from his church because one of his added duties in Santa Julietta, besides being head priest at Our Lady of Perpetual Help Catholic Church, was to serve as head basketball coach at SJ Catholic High.

I was going to have to wait until Thanksgiving to interview the two young men. Both had gone off to college, each attending the University of San Diego on a basketball scholarship. In the meantime, I would look into who they might have spoken with, besides their parents, before going to the police about their alleged locker room experiences with Father Mackenzie.

3

When I returned home to Santa Maria I found a note from one of my neighbors, Fowler Payette, stuck in my screen door. It read: *Call me. Urgent.* So, I phoned him but got no answer. When I walked over to see if he might be puttering in his back yard, he wasn't there either. Nor was his car in his garage when I peeked in through a smudgy window. I knocked on his back door, but again no one answered. So I returned home.

I was halfway finished with my beer-and-bologna-sandwich supper when Fowler appeared at my back door. He explained that he had been at the Santa Maria branch of the Santa Julietta County sheriff's office when I came looking for him.

"I might as well have told the stupid bastards that a hamster had gone missing for all the interest they showed, Fletcher," Fowler said when he came huffing and puffing into my kitchen.

I offered him a beer and he nodded. I then pointed toward my other kitchen chair and he sat while I fetched a beer from my fridge. "Who or what has gone missing?"

"Germaine." His daughter.

"When?"

"Day before yesterday. At least that is the last time anyone saw her," Fowler said.

"Where? What time was she last seen?" I asked.

He inhaled half his beer in one gulp, then swallowed hard. "Interlaken Country Club. Five o'clock. She and her teammates had just finished playing against the girls from Las Serpientes. Everyone changed clothes in the women's locker room then headed home. Germaine had driven her own car and hadn't been with anyone else. That's the last time anyone saw her. In the locker room. Her car is still in the country club's parking lot."

Interlaken and Las Serpientes were two of the flossiest country clubs in Santa Julietta County. Interlaken lay at the edge of Lompoc and Las Serpientes was tucked into a narrow valley just east of Solvang. I had been in both parking lots recently while looking for a Woody.

I said, "Are her golf clubs in her car?"

"Yes. All except her putter. Sarah and I drove down to meet my brother to look for her and that's when we found her car. You've seen it. Mustang convertible. Bright red. Germaine almost never locks her car. The clubs were in the back seat. I'm the one who noticed her putter was missing. One of those new-fangled ones called a Ping. It, in fact, makes a pinging sound when it strikes the ball. The thing is made by some little gnome

11

working out of his garage in Phoenix. My brother bought it for her one time when he was over there. Heard about the putter from a guy he plays golf with occasionally in Scottsdale."

I said, "I assume you've asked people at the country club."

"Everybody from the club president to the kids who clean the carts at night. No one has seen her."

"Tell me about these teams."

"UC-Santa Julietta doesn't have golf teams. So, college-age kids, guys and gals, from the two country clubs formed their own teams to compete against each other. Given that my brother has a family membership at Interlaken, Germaine plays for them."

"What has been her routine following past competitions?" I said.

"I have no idea. As you know, she's a sophomore at UCSJ. She belongs to a sorority there, Alpha Chi Omega. Her sorority sisters are all fretting. She's always at the house by dinner time, but not for the past couple nights. It was her roommate, Sissy Tomlinson, who phoned us to ask if she had driven home after the golf competition."

I said to Fowler, "Let me approach the county sheriff and the Santa Julietta police department. I am on a first-name basis with both the sheriff and the SJ chief of police." I didn't add that my past relationship with both men was checkered.

"Sarah and I would be ever so grateful if you would, Stu."

"First thing in the morning I'll drive into Santa Julietta and see both men." Assuming they were in their offices, of course.

Despite the claim that *good fences make good neighbors,* my backyard fence kept me from knowing whether most of my neighbors were good or bad. Sarah and Fowler Payette were living in their house when I moved into mine. I first met Fowler while mowing my front lawn shortly after I moved in. The blades of the ancient mower than Jacob Wurstheimer had left in his garage for me had been in serious need of sharpening. Fowler recognized what a shabby job the push mower was doing and offered to lend me his power mower. I had felt indebted to him ever since that day.

Mary Ann Chase lived between Fowler and me. She had retired from the Santa Maria Public Library two years earlier. Five-foot two, with an impish smile, she had worked there as a reference librarian for forty-two years and had lived in the house next to mine for thirty-six of those years. She was the only person I knew, besides a handful of experts in Central American archeology *and me*, who knew that the name of the Aztec god Huitzilopochtli meant *left-handed hummingbird.*

The only other neighbor I know by name lives on the other side of me. Hella Blauvogel. Hella knew a lot about looking for missing persons. She is sixty-one, plump with rosy cheeks, and speaks with a heavy Bavarian accent. Hella arrived in Santa Maria in 1947, a DP, displaced person, as European immigrants were disparagingly called back then. Her parents were killed when Allied bombs wiped out the city of Würzburg. Hella had been out foraging for firewood and hid in a neighbor's cellar when the bombing began.

In broken English she once told me, without any sense of shame, "We so desperate that me and other women in my building go out to find victims of the bombs so we can strip off their clothes to use ourselves, bundle up their broken furniture to take home for firewood. How else we survive?"

The story of Würzburg, a city on the Main River, is a shameful one. Not only was Hella's house demolished by Allied bombing, the entire city of Würzburg, including forty hospitals, was flattened on March 16, 1945, during the roughly the twenty minutes it took for 225 Lancaster bombers to fly over. Why shameful? After all, it was wartime. But the war would be over in less than six weeks. Germany was already defeated and destroyed.

However, one of the strategic principles of Allied bombing, formulated early in the war, was that every single German city with a population over 100,000 was to be bombed mercilessly, bombed until it was flat. Until spring of 1945, no one at Allied headquarters in London realized Würzburg's population was just a couple of thousand over the 100,000 mark. So, ze rules being ze rules being ze rules, Kaboom! Würzburg had to be destroyed. Post-war historians labeled Würzburg *Der Grab am Main*, the graveyard on the Main.

Hella had been lucky, but her dear husband, *"mein lieber Johann"*, was declared missing in action on the Russian front in the summer of 1944. By then the German army was putting up hopeless defenses, as it retreated slowly but steadily. In addition to those German soldiers killed facing the Russian onslaught, more than 100,000 became POWs that summer on the Eastern Front.

She once told me, "Hope my Johann not captured by Red Army. Better he dead than prisoner of war. Better to die quick of bullet than die slow of *die Erfrierung* and much little to eat," she said. *Die Erfrierung*. Hella didn't know the English word *frostbite*.

Despite her broken English, Hella was fun to talk to across our common backyard fence. On those occasions when she invited me over for dinner, her dumplings were incredibly delicious and the dish she called *Jagerschnitzel*, breaded veal, fried and served in a butter-based mushroom sauce, was to die for.

Hella's cooking was heavy on the butter, as her cheeks and waistline confirmed. She said that, when the tide of war began to turn against Germany in 1942, food rationing was instituted by the German Reich. Soon, she said, the butter ration in Würzburg was reduced to zero.

"Night after night for three years so many of my dreams were about butter. Every day we ate only cabbage soup and butter-less bread. Then, every night I dreamed of spreading great gobs of butter on my bread. Now, even here in California, the land of plenty, I still have such dreams!" she said.

California may be a land with plenty of butter, but it was also a land with plenty of crime. How could I say no to the Payettes? The trick was going to be keeping three cases in the air at the same time. I had tried to learn to be a juggler as a kid but failed hopelessly in my efforts to keep three tennis balls from bouncing onto my driveway. After a week's efforts, I realized that P.T. Barnum was never going to offer me a spotlight in the center ring.

At least all three cases – finding two girls missing from the convent school yard, proving Father McKenzie Mackenzie hadn't tried to bugger two of his basketball pupils, and finding Germaine Payette – were centered in Santa Julietta. Because one of the cases was at the behest of Amanda Reynolds, I packed a suitcase with the intention of camping out in Amanda's guest apartment in Santa Julietta, on High Street, a block from the yacht club, where Amanda parked her fifty-foot sloop, *Shanghai*.

I had called ahead to receive her permission to use the apartment. At worst, if she'd booked it for use by an out-of-town witness in one of her criminal trials, I would ask her to let me sleep on her boat. But the apartment was available, so I would not have to listen to the slosh, slosh, slosh of the Pacific Ocean against *Shanghai*'s hull throughout the night.

4

Triage on my three cases told me that looking for Germaine Payette was the most critical. Reed Mackenzie wasn't going anywhere, and I could interview the mother of the two young men at my convenience. As for the missing youngsters, they were likely dead by now, their youthful bones moldering in shallow graves. As a former cop, I knew the statistics.

Because Interlaken Country Club is outside the city limits of Santa Julietta I had no need to consult the usually cooperative SJ Chief of Police, Wallace Fry. But I did need to check in with the touchy sheriff of SJ County, Sam Huddleston. He and I got along only marginally well. Also, I felt the need to get permission from the chief of UCSJ police, Ernest Calipatria, whom I had only met a couple of times, both instances involving an alleged rape on his campus. In each case the accuser lied to cover up her own misbehavior.

"Look who's come to ruin my day," Sam Cuddleston said when I entered his office. "What has Murky done this time?" He gestured for me to pull up a chair.

Murky Murtrans is a friend of mine who owns a ranch in the eastern part of the county, along the Sisquoc River. A year earlier Sam had arrested Murky for the murder of Murky's fourth wife, Cynthia. Near the end of Murky's small retirement party at his ranch house Cynthia was found dead is the darkened billiard room, beaten to death with a pool stick. Eventually I gathered almost enough evidence to get Murky's son, Clyde, to confess to the murder.

Sam continued to hold a bit of a grudge that I had showed him up.

"Nothing to do with Murky this time," I said as I sat down. "I'm here to find out why you haven't taken the disappearance of Germaine Payette seriously."

"Who?"

"Are you serious?"

"I am. Who is this person?"

I explained, he shrugged.

He said, "She's hardly had time yet to drop her panties for her boyfriend at whatever secret rendezvous they settled on. Jesus, Fletcher. If I went chasing after every coed who didn't return to her dorm room for a night or two, I'd need a hundred more deputies."

I should have known better than to waste my time with Sheriff Cuddleston. Chief Calipatria was more understanding and accommodating.

15

"Her sorority sisters are worried. They say she is quiet and reliable."

"Any ideas? I gather you've already questioned the women at Chi Alpha," I said.

The campus police chief said, "Yes. And when asked if Germaine has a boyfriend, they all turned cagy."

"So she may have eloped?" I said.

"I haven't ruled it out, but I'm leaning toward abduction. Her sorority sisters may be cagy about a boyfriend, but they are also genuinely worried. *Worry* and *boyfriend* don't exactly mesh."

I would think that might depend on the character of the boyfriend.

I then said, "You're leaning toward abduction?"

"Yes, but that raises two questions her sisters can't answer," the chief said. "Why an abduction? And why her?"

Chief Calipatria's mind was sharper than Sheriff Sam Cuddleston's. But then his position was not an elected one. Cuddleston was entirely a political animal, and, as such, was chosen not for his intellect but for his boorish charm.

I said, "I assume you've questioned all the players on both teams."

"All but one." He shook his head. "None of the ones we questioned were aware she was meeting anyone after their match and the players on the Las Serpientes say they barely knew her. Only as a golfer on the Interlaken team. The one player we failed to question is out of town."

My heart was already aching for Fowler and Sarah Payette. Back in February they had lost their other offspring, a son, Andy, who was three years older than Germaine. *Was.* Andy had graduated from the United States Naval Academy in 1966. Afterwards, he served his compulsory post-graduate year at sea. Eager to become a navy jet pilot flying aircraft-carrier-based bombing missions over North Vietnam, Andy had been learning to fly trainer jets in Texas when he crashed. The Navy ruled the crash had been due to pilot error. Everyone but the Navy thought otherwise.

After chatting with Chief Calipatria, I drove back to Santa Maria to meet Fowler and Sarah Payette at the city library, where I had asked them to show up armed with pens and notepads. To help them burn off nervous energy I had asked them to bring their address books and had them sit at a carrell beside phonebooks of cities from LA to San Francisco. I wanted names and addresses of everyone Germaine knew in Southern California. I had asked Sarah also to bring a roster of the sorority sisters of Alpha Chi Omega. Chief Calipatria had refused to share those names on grounds of protecting privacy. I hadn't argued.

Sarah hit me with a new development the instant I found them, dutifully scribbling down names and addresses.

"One of Germaine's small duffle bags is missing from her closet. She has used it in the past, instead of a suitcase, for overnight trips. Her travel toothbrush is gone as well," Sarah whispered as I took a seat beside her.

"She obviously made no mention of taking a short trip anywhere? With anybody?" I asked.

Fowler and Sarah both shook their heads, looking guilty at suddenly realizing they knew too little about their daughter. I sympathized, thinking the psychology of college-aged students fell into the same textbook as the psychology of space aliens. I'd be rich if I had a nickel for every mother and father who solidly believed they knew their children's every thought, then doubled over with shock when they learned their Susie or Johnny possessed a deep and totally secret mine filled with unwelcome notions.

I had changed my mind about what information I wanted them to find in the phone books. I asked them to assemble a list of friends and acquaintances Germaine might have run off with. I told them to leave their lists inside the rear screen door of my house.

While they thumbed through the phone books I headed to the Alpha Chi Omega house to find someone there who could cobble together a list of sorority sisters she might have run off with. Above the sorority house door a pair of well-crafted, paper-mâché cats – one black, one orange – arched their backs, with their mouths open, issuing hissing threats playing on a hidden tape deck. I hoped I wasn't in for the same sounds from the women inside.

The sorority's president turned out to be mellow enough. Too mellow, maybe. She began by telling me her name was Shelton Brown. "Never Shelley, please." she insisted.

I asked about Germaine.

"It's the middle of the quarter. Why would she skip classes and take off on a hoot?" Shelton said.

"You know her better than I do. You tell me," I said.

"Whoa! I hardly know her at all," Shelton said, taking a step back literally to distance herself.

"How about a list of those among your sisters who do know her well, okay?"

"Yeah. Sure. But I hope you're not in any hurry. I'll have to chase down our house secretary, Molly Olson. She knows all the sisters really well, including Germaine." Pause. "Oh, dear. God knows where Molly is. I'll have to check her class schedule." She departed up a set of ornate winding stairs.

While waiting, I looked about. I had never been inside a sorority house before. Even Long Beach State sorority girls had considered themselves far too grand for the likes of me. Off to the side of a central waiting area, where I sat, was a door over which read: *Main Dining Room.* On the door itself, at roughly face height for an average woman was a plastic-molded male penis – erect. Just above that was a mat of wool, which I assumed represented pubic hair. Finally, above the wool was a small, neatly lettered sign: *Suck for Luck.*

Much of the rest of the downstairs interior's Halloween décor consisted of the usual crepe paper ghosts, witches, and goblins. However, because this was California and because 1968 was the Chinese zodiac's Year of the Monkey, several paper dragons blew fire toward the large stone fireplace, and elsewhere long-tailed, organ-grinder monkeys, sitting in pots of gold, doffed leprechauns' hats and wore signs urging the ladies to "Make a Naughty Wish".

Shelton returned quickly, giving me no time to look for other signs urging suggestive performances. The best Shelton could offer me was a shrug. She had no idea where I might find Molly or Germaine. I left, telling Shelton I'd contact her later to pick up the list I had asked for.

One gift from Sam Cuddleston was a list of the golfers on both teams. I had names and addresses, but no phone numbers. Ma Bell is a major security-gate guardian for the rich. She agrees not to publish the names and numbers of anybody not wanting to grant phone access to the public. So, I drove.

The fourth name on my list was Stephanie Crowder, whose home lay behind a security gate. The booth was manned by a pair of uniformed guards, both elderly-looking and not quite a danger to any healthy invader, I thought. Their uniforms were ill-fitting, full of wrinkles to match those on their faces. Retirees, I judged, members of the growing rent-a-cop clan seen walking the corridors of upscale shopping malls. That each man carried a holstered sidearm was a sign of the times. I was well-practiced at talking my way past such men. Telling them I was a former cop always worked, although too often I found myself obliged to listen to their life stories.

After the guards gained permission from someone in the mansion, they waved me through. When I pulled up in front of the Crowder home six toothy pumpkins sat grinning at me from one side of the Crowder's front porch. The house itself struck me as Cecil B. DeMille's notion of Spanish Mission style. An architectural Edsel. Hollywood kitsch that Spanish grandees of old wouldn't begin to recognize. However, in California wheelbarrows full of money all too often buy nothing but embarrassment. I was looking up at one such instance. In spades.

Stephanie Crowder, I had learned, was a freshman at UC-Santa Julietta. Her mother answered when I rang the doorbell. Evelyn Crowder was a tall, thin-boned woman. She wore a black dress. Perhaps, she was in mourning and I was interrupting her grieving. To be safe, I asked.

"What? Oh, no. Black is one of my favorite colors. I own several black dresses. I guess you could say I'm in permanent mourning," she said by way of greeting.

She gave me a nervous giggle and I decided not to pursue what she meant. Instead, I merely introduced myself and explained why I was there.

"Please come in, Mr. Fletcher. My husband is at work, but I hope you'll not try to take advantage of me because of that, eh?" Another nervous giggle.

"No, ma'am. I promise to behave myself."

Her shoulders sagged and she gave me a pouty lip.

"I'm pretty sure I can tell you where Germaine Payette has disappeared to, but I'll disclose what I know on one condition."

"And your condition is?"

"That you do not divulge that I am the source of your knowledge."

"Because you're afraid Germaine will chase after you with a golf club?" I said.

"No, rather, because my husband might."

A.C. Crowder, Evelyn's husband, was the owner and CEO of ACC Oil, Ltd., the man responsible for planting oil derricks offshore along the Santa Julietta coast. That made the man popular among many, despised by many others. Hence the iron gates at the beginning of the long driveway leading up to the Crowder mansion.

Months earlier I had read Mr. Crowder's remarks on the topic of *well-deserving* versus *undeserving* in Santa Julietta's newspaper, *The Globe Examiner.* He viewed his work as a battle of world-saving progressives struggling against destroyers of worlds, against anti-capitalist anarchists. In fact, many of Mr. Crowder's spoken words amounted to plagiarism from Ayn Rand's novels, in which The Deserving were always under siege by the Un-Deserving.

The presidential election was coming up and code words embedded in one particular candidate's speeches reflected Crowder's world view – and worse. Deep racial fears barely lay hidden between the lines of that candidate's whistle-stop warnings. That man was Richard Nixon, a former U.S. Senator from our state. Vote for me, Nixon always warned, or else blacks, Hispanics, and other *underserving types* would take over the country. As one of his female supporters had once assured me, "Give the niggers an inch and they'll take a mile."

Mrs. Crowder struck me as a woman who would not give an inch to anyone. However, I accepted her offer of tea and cookies. Not because I was thirsty or hungry, but because putting a frightened woman at ease was the only way to get her to talk. Her coffee was strong, and her cookies were fresh. She said that baking was her way to pass otherwise empty mornings at home alone. When I suggested she might like to have a dog, she flinched, a gesture I took to mean that a dog might also end up too often on the wrong end of her husband's wrath.

"Germaine went with my son and daughter to San Francisco," she said as she sat down across from me on a sprawling, genuine-leather sofa. When the hem of her black dress crept up, I made a healthy effort to maintain eye contact.

I repeated, "San Francisco."

"Yes. A music group from Los Angeles that my son, Randall, favors is playing at the Avalon Ballroom Saturday night. Stephanie likes them, too. Just not as much as Randall. Teddy also wanted to go, but I assured her she is too young to go that far without adult supervision."

She picked up a sheet of paper from the coffee table and handed it to me.

"Teddy is another daughter?"

She nodded. "Theodora."

I tried not to roll my eyes. Another reason I was glad I didn't have children. No given names to rule out. No calculating what a daughter's given name that sounded cute at age fourteen might sound like when she turned sixty-five.

"Stephanie plays on the young women's Las Serpientes golf team," she told me as I studied the handout.

That much I had learned from the sheriff's list.

The Byrds, November 2nd, 1968. Avalon Ballroom, 8 p.m., with a grainy photo of five long-haired young men wearing sport coats. The Beatles look-alikes. I was familiar with two of The Byrds hit tunes, "Mr. Tambourine Man", and "Turn, Turn, Turn". I understood why they were popular with college-aged students. Men who had initially made those songs popular, Bob Dylan and Pete Seeger, were now idols to war protesters on colleges campuses everywhere.

Everywhere. Berkeley, the East Coast, Chicago. The Democratic National Convention, held in Chicago in August, had proved a disaster for the party establishment because of hundreds, maybe thousands, of young protesters. Events such as those made the Law & Order platform of Richard Nixon resonate. He was now heavily favored to win the election on November 5th.

Additionally, in Southeast Asia a war was raging that many portrayed as yet another battle of Good versus Evil. I remained doubtful. Young war protesters across the country had no such doubts. And, in their minds, who represented good and who represented evil was the reverse of what the millions of "Silent Majority" supporters of Nixon believed.

The war was high-tech versus low-tech and there was scant evidence the former was winning. Here in the States many, if not most, major college campuses outside the Old Confederacy had been erupting with protests against American involvement.

In my days as a naive youth, prior to attending college myself, I had served in Korea and was familiar with all the Western draw-the-line arguments, only I had stood on that line, M-1 in hand, and knew it looked entirely different from that perspective. I knew I had not been protecting American freedoms from assault by hordes of little yellow men – and women. I had been fighting off Asians who were fighting to overwhelm other Asians. Our battle in Southeast Asia looked no different to me. No junk boats or sampans would ever be sailing into San Francisco Bay.

I finally said, "Have you heard from your children since they left?"

"No, but I hadn't expected to hear from them. They're young adults now. They don't have curfews or reporting-home rules any longer, Mr. Fletcher."

Young adults? She had just told me Teddy had been forbidden to tag along because there would be no adult supervision of her.

"Do you know any reason why Germaine would not have told her parents that she was going with your son and daughter?" I said.

"I do not. Why don't you ask them?"

"I have."

"I have never met Germaine's parents. I know nothing about the rules they set, or try to set, for her. I understand she lives on campus. By living there she is now, *de facto,* no longer under their thumbs," she said.

De Facto. I suspected there was an attorney in the family somewhere. That was more likely than a professor of Latin or philosophy. I thanked Mrs. Crowder for her time and insights, next turning myself back toward Santa Maria to pass along my news to Fowler and Sarah Payette. Whether they would take my information as good news or bad news, I wasn't sure. Perhaps, equal measures of both.

5

"She's where?"

I thought I was going to have to scrape Sarah Payette off her kitchen ceiling. As it was, flour billowed into a small cloud over her mixing bowl as she began waving her arms excitedly, like a bird about to take wing. At the sink she washed her hands and dried them as though they had suddenly been infected with biblical sin. The look on Germaine Payette's mother's face was the look I had once seen several years back on another mother's face, when I was a cop in Burbank. That mother saw her twenty-year-old son lying on his bedroom floor, dead from a drug overdose.

"Somewhere in the Bay Area, on her way to a concert in San Francisco."

Fowler arrived home, his arms filled with brown bags full of groceries. One look at his wife and he nearly dropped them.

"What's going on? What have you found out?"

He set the groceries on a counter and went to put his arm around Sarah.

"Did you find her, Fletcher? Is she okay?"

Sarah broken into tears. "Mr. Fletcher says she's run off with Stephanie Crowder and her older brother. They've gone to San Francisco."

Fowler looked dumbfounded. "Who is the Crowder girl?"

I told Fowler what I had learned from the sheriff and from Mrs. Crowder.

"I didn't even know she knew any of the Crowders. Why didn't she tell us where she was going?"

"I take it neither of you have ever met any of the Crowder family," I said.

Sarah laughed a crazy laugh. "Don't you know? The Crowders are the Rockefellers of Santa Julietta. We're not good enough to shine their shoes."

"Apparently your daughter is good enough to run off with the younger generation of them," I said.

"But why wouldn't she tell us, Stu?" Fowler said, looking betrayed.

"She's old enough not to have to account for her every move any longer."

Sarah said, "But we're her parents."

I wanted to say, "Exactly," but I didn't.

"Maybe she'll call home," Sarah said, the look on her face declaring she didn't believe her own words.

"Then again, maybe she won't," Fowler said, mirroring my own suspicion.

"Will you go after her, Stu?" Fowler said, after a quick, sideways look at his wife.

"No! We can't afford Mr. Fletcher's time, Fowler," Sarah said. "We'll just wait for her to phone us."

"Jesus, Sarah. I'm not going to stand around here waiting for the phone to ring while, in the meantime, I watch you wring your hands until their bloody."

Sarah interlaced her fingers, and her hands began to tremble.

"See what I mean?" Fowler pointed at his wife's hands, but he was looking at me.

Not wishing to take sides, I remained silent. I had found myself in husband-versus-wife squabbles before. Silence was my best defense against either, or both, parties later misremembering what I had said, whose side I had taken – usually neither, but that is seldom how anyone but me remembered such episodes.

Sarah said, "He doesn't even know where to begin to look for her."

"I'm sure the Crowders can draw him a map," Fowler said. "Isn't that right, Stu?"

"Maybe."

"Tell my husband you are too busy, Mr. Fletcher. Now that we know Gemmy hasn't been kidnapped, we can just wait to hear from her. You are right. Our daughter no longer owes us an accounting of her every movement."

"Like hell," Fowler barked. "You tell me who is still paying her tuition, plus room and board, at the university? She damned well does owe us an explanation, if she's skipping classes to run off to San Francisco."

Sarah said, "Maybe her trip has to do with one of her classroom assignments."

"What difference does that make? She still should have told us."

Sarah looked defeated. Certain he had carried the argument, Fowler looked excessively imperious. If I were him, I'd hire a food tester for my next few meals at home.

In any case, this was a side of the Payettes I had not seen before. I had not socialized with them at all, had never been invited to dinner. I had rarely been inside their home. I had encountered Mrs. Payette no more than half a dozen times since moving into my house three years earlier.

During the 1950's a popular television comedy show was called "Father Knows Best", starring Robert Young and Jane Wyatt. Robert Young, as James Anderson, never acted smug. Jane, as Margaret Anderson, never acted disheartened to the extent of appearing desolate. Almost always, she agreed with whatever tidbit of reconciling wisdom her husband dispensed.

Sarah and Fowler had not fallen into line with TV-comedy sagacity. Even when Fowler may know best, he fails to know the best way to convey his epistemic superiority in a way that soothes. In that regard I was of the opinion he differed little from most husbands, which is why, in part, I was still a bachelor. Misogynic violence isn't always physical. In fact, wife-beating surely represents only a small percentage of harm inflicted by men on their spouses.

When I served as a detective in the Burbank Police Department, the only domestic violence calls I showed up for were those where the husband had murdered his wife – with inebriation usually being the trigger – and those where the wife had killed her husband, nearly always in self-defense – against a raging drunk.

I hoped the Fowlers didn't keep a gun in their house. I hoped this even though I had no problem with wives shooting drunken husbands who came after them with a wrench, a lead pipe, or a candlestick, in the library, lounge, or the billiard room. I had become a bit of an expert helping Amanda Reynolds reconstruct, then dramatically reenact, events in front of a jury, for the purpose of proving a wife innocent of murdering her drunken, raging husband.

"Will you find her, Fletcher? Bring her back, safe and sound?" Fowler said.

I looked at Sarah.

"No, Fowler. Let her be," his wife said.

In an angry tone Fowler said, "Do you know something I don't know, Sarah?"

Sarah whimpered. Then emitted a squeaky, scarcely audible, "No."

"Is Germaine knocked up? Has she gone to San Francisco to get herself fixed?"

Fowler had just raised the stakes in this game of psychological poker.

"Oh, Husband. How could you think such a horrible thing?"

It was at that moment I remembered that the Payettes were church-going Catholics. The notion of their daughter's getting an abortion had to be devastating for both of them.

"Well? Did she?" Fowler barked.

"I don't know," came the meek reply.

"What *do* you know?" he said.

"She recently mentioned an interest in a rock-and-roll concert of some kind somewhere up north. I don't remember. She just mentioned it in passing and I didn't take her seriously."

"Why didn't you take her seriously?" Fowler said in a quieter voice, but still filled with full of anger and menace.

"She had other, more important things on her mind," Sarah said.

"Like where to find a back-alley abortionist?"

"She never said that."

"Who's the father?" Fowler yelled, upping his voltage again.

"She never mentioned being pregnant."

"Is she or isn't she?"

"I don't know," Sarah sobbed.

"Jesus, Stu. Will you please find my daughter before…."

I didn't have to ask, *"Before what?"*

In California abortion-performing doctors had gone from back-alley to front-door, from using coat hangers in filthy back rooms to using medical instruments in more sterile conditions. Who knew how many practitioners practiced their skills between Santa Julietta and San Francisco. I didn't.

What I did know was that Germaine Payette would not have had to travel far from home to find a licensed physician willing to abort her fetus – if she was pregnant. Sarah Payette was acting so coy with her husband, she was not making clear whether she knew if her daughter was pregnant or not.

Finally, I said, "Sarah, what things were on Germaine's mind when last you spoke to her?"

"She was worried about her mid-term exams. She allowed that she had not really been studying as much as she should."

Fowler jumped on that. "Too busy humping some randy jock, no doubt. She should have known better. My God, Sarah. Didn't you ever take her aside and explain to her how to keep from getting knocked up?"

This harsh assault by Fowler on his wife was getting too sordid for me. I felt like a coward for wanting to extract myself, but even the most unflappable angels inside my conscience had heard enough. "Get out! Get out!" they whispered.

"I'm going to revisit the Crowders to see what details I can find out about where Germane and the Crowder children are heading exactly," I lied. I already knew. Or thought I did.

At the door Fowler said, "Let me know the minute you know where she's heading. We can take my car to go retrieve her."

I walked away without making any comment. I had no urge to ride shotgun with a wild man.

6

Before returning to the Crowder estate in Santa Julietta, I stopped by my Santa Maria Public Library, where my next-door neighbor, Mary-Ann Chase, had served as a reference librarian for thirty-eight years. Now, her replacement – a lovely young woman named Harriet Oakley – helped me sort through volumes of *Who's Who in America* to find information on A.C. Crowder. What I learned was most insightful and I took copious notes.

In 1945 President Harry Truman issued an Executive Order that expanded American territory beyond the previous three-mile limit to the edge of the continental shelf. His motive was a concern for American control of its offshore oil reserves. Shortly afterwards, A.C.'s father, Warren Crowder, developed an oil-rig platform he unabashedly named the Crowder Platform. It was a variation on what is known as a jack-up rig, a self-elevating platform on which to mount deep-water oil drills.

Warren Crowder was an industrial engineer with a Ph.D. from Georgia Tech, following an undergraduate degree from Santa Clara University in San Jose. He had spent a gap year studying at the Technical University of Munich, where he met the woman he was to marry, Irmengard Zellfurt, the daughter of an industrialist, Klement Otto Zellfurt, who was contemporary with the age of American robber barons. An A-type personality and non-stop worker, Warren died in 1956 of a cerebral hemorrhage at the age of 51. Irmengard was still alive and living in Scottsdale, Arizona.

A.C., born in 1926, was the eldest of five children born to Warren and Irmengard. A devout Bavarian Catholic, Irmengard had insisted her children all be named after saints, in both their given and middle names. Hence: the three sons Alyosius Cyril, Jude Ignatius, and Francis Jerome; one daughter, Mary-Margaret Louise. Only A.C. went by his initials.

Following his graduation from high school, A.C. resisted his parents' strong urging that he attend Santa Clara University. Instead, A.C. went to Cal Poly San Luis Obispo before doing graduate work at Purdue. Afterwards, he returned to California to build the company that used his father's customized oil-derrick creation. Now his oil-sucking machinery lined the Santa Barbara Channel from Ventura to Point Conception.

Neither A.C. nor his wife, Evelyn, whom I had talked to previously, was at home. Theodora answered the door and introduced herself after I explained who I was. She was a cute kid. Curly brown hair, wearing blue jeans and a red shirt with Fred and Wilma Flintstone on the front. She stood barefoot with nail polish only on each of her big toenails. Purple.

"My parents aren't home. They went to some kind of political meeting for Mister Rafferty."

Max Rafferty, California's current Superintendent of Public Instruction, was running for the United States Senate seat held by Senator Thomas Kuchel. Raffery had defeated Kuchel in the Republican primary in what some historians were claiming to be the greatest upset in the annals of Senate primary races. Rafferty's views on education, in my opinion, were as enlightened as nuns' notions of improving penmanship by hammering students' knuckles with rulers. His views on national and international issues were not much better.

"Maybe you can help me, Theodora."

"You may address me as Teddy."

"Thank you, Teddy. Now let me explain why I am here. I'm looking for my neighbor's daughter, Germaine, and earlier your mother told me she had gone away to San Francisco with you brother and older sister."

"That's right."

"Do you know where they might be staying while they are in the Bay Area?"

"No, but I heard Randall say that they were going to visit Aunt Mary-Margaret on their way home. She lives in Cupertino."

"That's a great help to me, Teddy. Anything else you might know that could help me locate them sooner?"

I guessed Teddy to be ten or twelve years old.

"Well…."

"Go on," I said.

"Uncle Francis died two weeks ago in a small plane crash out in the Mohave Desert. And last week Randall was going through some of Francis Jerome's things in Francis's attic and found an old diary he kept. Uncle Francis lives – well, lived – in Montecito. That's…."

"Yes, Teddy. I know where Montecito is." Just outside Santa Julietta.

"In the diary Randall read where Francis and some other boys from Francis's fraternity at Santa Clara College buried one of their friends who died at a campus party. Francis wrote that he and his other friends didn't know what else to do to keep from getting in trouble. They lied to police that their friend just disappeared from the party, telling authorities they didn't know where he went."

How was I to react to that?

"What did Randall think or say after reading the diary?"

"My brother said that Francis gave directions in his diary for where the body is buried and that he, Stephanie, and Germaine were going to go look for the grave before they went on to San Francisco. What an adventure, eh? I begged Randall to take me along, but he was too chickenshit to ask Mom for permission to let me go too."

No wonder Germaine didn't want to tell her parents where she was going, not that she would have had to add that little tidbit when she explained her itinerary to her parents.

"Did your brother happen to tell you where this gravesite was?"

Teddy shook her head. "No, but…."

"But?"

"When Randall wasn't looking I sneaked a peak at Francis's diary, the diary volume where he wrote about the dead guy, whose name was Morgan Crowder, a cousin of my dad and uncles from New York. On another page in the diary Uncle Francis wrote that Morgan Crowder went to school at Stanford, which is near where Aunt Mary-Margaret lives."

"Do your parents know about Cousin Morgan's death? About his being buried by Francis and his mates?"

Teddy gave me a sideways smirk before saying, 'Nope!"

"Are you going to tell them?" I said.

"I kinda want to…as payback to Randall for not begging Mom to let me accompany him and Sis."

Accompany? From the mouth of a twelve-year-old. What a private-school education will get kids these days. At least I assumed the Crowders were sufficiently snooty not to send their kids off to public schools. In *Who's Who* I had read that, for their primary and secondary educations, A.C. and his siblings had all attended private Catholic schools.

"Where do you go to school, Teddy?"

"Sacred Heart Junior High. I'm in the seventh grade. I got put ahead a year for being so bright."

I didn't doubt her.

"Where is your uncle's diary now?" I said.

"Randall took it with him."

"Do you remember anything about the map?"

"Sure, I do." Another smirk.

"Would you care to tell me?"

"Not unless you promise to take me along," she said, twisting to give me an aren't-I-clever pose.

"Did the diary say anything about when this disappearance and burial occurred?" I said.

"Just whenever Francis was in college at Santa Clara. Hundreds of years ago, I suppose."

I tried to remember when I was Teddy's age and imagined that I thought anyone over twenty-five struck me as older than they really were. Not yet ancient, but stale, crusty, and soon to be moldy. Telling myself another trip to the library would allow me to work backwards from A.C.'s time at Cal Poly to calculate the four-year period when Francis was a student at Santa Clara College. Then from the archives I could bring up San Jose and Palo Alto newspapers from that era to scan for any stories about a missing Stanford undergraduate from New York.

7

I left Teddy to pout and drove to the Santa Julietta County jail, which makes no pretensions about wanting to correct anyone. Not even local do-gooders who wrap themselves in euphemisms refer to that edifice as a *correctional facility*. It is what it appears to be: a grim holding tank for drunks and for low-life felons marking time until they are escorted to San Quentin.

Years earlier I had done research to find out about Saint Quentin. It turns out he was a third-century Roman evangelist whose Christian proselytizing in France earned him the enmity of local authorities. Judged to be a sorcerer, he was tortured and beheaded. Afterwards his body was secretly buried but rediscovered in the fourth and seventh centuries. Sainthood followed.

Canonization for himself as a saint was not on Father Reed Mackenzie's mind when I visited him in jail, although I was sure he would be envious of Saint Quentin's alleged talent for escaping from locked rooms.

"Why can't I get out on bail?"

I sat down on the cold metal chair a deputy provided me.

"Amanda's working on it."

Bail had been set at ten thousand dollars, meaning someone had to pony up a grand to a local bail-bond company. Mackenzie claimed to have no assets. He had no relatives and, given his current reputation, he had no friends. And that included Amanda Reynolds, who sometimes goes soft on a client and covers his or her bond. She was softer on women in that regard. I also knew, but didn't say, that his attorney was convinced he was guilty again of molestation and was just as happy to make him suffer the confines of a jail cell for as long as it took to bring him to trial.

"Paul Drake! That's who I was trying to connect you with last time," he said and straightened himself, sitting on the edge of his bunkbed.

I winced, knowing I wasn't nearly as handsome as actor William Hopper, the man who played the role of Paul Drake, Perry Mason's private investigator, on the *Perry Mason* television series.

"Tell me your version of what happened at basketball camp," I said, scooting my chair closer to the bunk.

"Those boys lied."

"Lied about what specifically?"

"Lied when they claimed I groped them. Lied when they claimed I asked to perform oral sex on each of them."

"Set the scene for me, Padre. When, where. I know it was at the summer basketball camp up near Yosemite. But did the alleged events take place in the locker room? Morning, noon, night? Sorry. I've just been assigned to look into your case. I've been busy with other things and I haven't read any of Amanda's notes."

"Very well." He sat up.

"When I arrived at Thomas Aquinas High I was made the new basketball coach. The man who had been coach moved to LA to be closer to his ailing mother. Anyway, I knew these two young men. Tyson and Bryson. The Ledbetter twins. Seniors. They graduated last May. They both played in my starting lineup for Aquinas High all last year. They were both eager to attend the summer camp because both had been granted basketball scholarships to San Diego University. It's a Catholic school, you may know."

"Yes. I do know," I said. I had been there. Lovely campus. "Go on."

"The camp lasted two weeks. I was invited to participate by the camp's organizer, Lindsay Horner. He played collegiate ball at Notre Dame and then for one or two seasons with the Fort Wayne Pistons. A benchwarmer mostly. Didn't last long. But then he came West and played up his reputation as an NBA player working for the Levy clothing company in Santa Clara. Later-- a couple of years ago – he started this summer camp. He called it an opportunity for high school-aged men to further develop their skills, which was true. But mostly Lindsay just wanted to show off, have an audience for his own skills, meager as they were, as it turned out."

"I hadn't heard of him," I said. "I had to look him up."

Mackenzie laughed. "Yeah. Everybody does."

"Anyway, the last day of camp, as we were showering, before packing up our things are heading home, the twins approach me in the shower. Naked. Tyson has an erection. Bryson points to it and asks me if I would like to suck it. When I brushed them off and continued to dress, Tyson said, 'Oh, come on, Father. We've heard about how much you like to go down on choir boys, like to bugger acolytes.' Somehow they'd found out about…well, about the rumors from when I was in LA schools."

"I suppose it's beside the point how they found out," I said.

"Everett Ledbetter chairs the high school's governing board. He knew and, in fact, argued against allowing me to coach."

"So how did you gain permission?"

"The rest of the board argued in favor of forgiveness and second chances," he said.

I thought to myself: According to Amanda, this was his seventh chance. Surely, the twins' father had a point.

"Was that it? The incident in the locker room?" I said.

"No. For sleeping arrangements the camp has bunkhouses. Eight bunks to a house; the houses are simple screen affairs with roll-down canvas flaps in case of inclement weather. Each bunkhouse houses seven players and a counselor. I was the counselor in the twins' bunkhouse. The same night following the afternoon locker room confrontation they cornered me again in the bunkhouse after dinner. This time Dyson was the one who exposed himself to me and Tyson demanded I perform fellatio on his brother."

"Demanded?" I said.

He nodded, "Ordered me. Threatened me.'

"Threatened you in what way?"

"Tyson told me they'd go to the camp's director, Mr. Holland, if I didn't do as they wanted. Tell Holland I had threatened to blackmail them."

"Blackmail?"

"Yes," he said glumly. "Dyson said they'd tell Mr. Holland that I'd see to it their scholarships to SDU got cancelled unless…."

"Did you go to see Holland about either or both incidents?" I said.

"No. And, from hindsight, I realize I should have. But I wasn't sure whether Dan Holland knew anything about my history. If he didn't, I sure as hell didn't want it to come out by my telling him what had happened."

"Damned if you did and damned if you didn't?"

"Something like that," he said.

"What next?"

"Nothing immediately. Camp was over the next day. Everybody packed up their stuff and went home. But then when I arrived home here in Santa Julietta, the sheriff's department showed up and arrested me, telling me the twins' parents had filed charges against me for molesting their sons."

After making copious notes, I left the priest and stopped at Hugo's for a burger while I waited to meet with Wendy Ellen Sheldon at her house. Hoping for get a feel for Father Mackenzie's veracity, I failed to do so. He was a clever man, but so, too, are all priests. There is even an adjective for their kind of cleverness: Jesuitical. It roughly means *sly dissembling.* The efforts by priests to make black appear to be white. A case that sticks in my mind is one told to me by one of my professors at Long Beach State. Catholics believe that infants who die before they are baptized cannot go to Heaven. Instead, they are stuck in Limbo forever. Now this may seem like an awful fate for such tiny children to suffer. But Jesuits argue that such infants are actually dwell in a state of eternal bliss. Now *that* is a piece of Jesuitical reasoning.

Despite my general dislike of priests of any nature, I shared Catholic padres dismay at being thought of as being queer simply because they were unable to marry. In my case, of course, I had a choice. Still, I had endured my share of whispered snickering due to my resistance to marriage. Much as I tried to ignore such remarks and be charitable toward those who whispered them, I often worked up a strong anger and had to fight my temptation to unleash on such jerks. If I had had a drink or three by the time I overheard such slander, I had to fight myself even more to resist throwing a verbal or a physical punch.

Father Mackenzie was going to be an interesting man to work with, a man whose true character he kept well masked. And Amanda Reynolds was paying me good money to rip that mask off. Was I up to the challenge? I told myself that I always am.

8

Wendy Ellen Sheldon was folding laundry in her rundown two-bedroom house in a cul-de- sac off Cathedral Oaks Road in the lower middle-class neighborhood of northwest Santa Julietta. She was barefoot and wearing a faded, floral-patterned muumuu. She had pinned up her hair, I assumed to help cool her neck. Steam coming off the iron brought beads of sweat to her temples. The house smelled of boiled cabbage and fried onions as I took a seat on her worn sofa covered with cat hair. Wendy Ellen's ironing board resided where most people's coffee table would be. I couldn't help but notice how dingy her neatly folded undergarments were, looking as though they had endured a thousand trips through *cold wash* and *tumble-dry hot* cycles.

During my first visit to Wendy Ellen's house, when she engaged me to find her former foster children, I had asked her for photos of Melissa Hargrove and Eileen Sanchez. She told me she didn't have any, which didn't come as a shock to me. On Wendy Ellen's household budget owning a camera and film was not an affordable expense. She told me then that, last time she was at the mall – just to window shop and fantasize -- she had inquired at Sears's photo studio how much she would have to pay to have pictures taken of the two girls. *More than she could afford* turned out to be the answer. She said she ended up cramming the two girls into an instant-photo booth at the mall's arcade. But the resulting snapshots were unsuitable for framing, unsuitable even for keeping in her purse. In a fit of pique she trashed the entire photo strip and rued the coins she had fed into the photo machine.

At the end of *that* visit she recalled that one of her friends, Rita Schreckler, has taken a couple of snapshots of Melissa and Eileen, with Wendy Ellen posed between them, once when they all had a picnic at El Capitan State Beach. Before I drove away, Wendy Ellen promised to contact Rita, who now lived in Oxnard, to try to get a copy of Rita's photo. I had given her money to have a copy made at any photo shop in Oxnard, Ventura, or Santa Julietta.

When she finished with her laundry, she walked to a side cupboard and returned with the photos she had promised me. Ignoring Wendy Ellen for a couple of minutes, I stared at the girls' faces. Children's faces are always unfinished. Eyes are not set in their sockets, cheeks filled with the remnants of baby fat. Hair fine, noses pinched.

But like adults', their eyes are giveaways. Both Melissa's and Eileen's sparkled, unimpeachable evidence that both were content, if not happy, under Wendy Ellen's care.

Given the girls' pillar-to-post life before Wendy Ellen, there could well have been a dullness in those eyes, a leadenness reflective of mistreatment and indifference toward them that washed away any hint of sparkle, any suggestion of joy.

However, Child Protective Service apparatchiks are not allowed to judge the wellness of any child by such intuitive signs. Instead, they measure a caregiver's competence by arcane rules devised, one can only assume, by that broomstick-riding hag from the land of Oz, a figure representing equal parts mean-spiritedness and folly.

I once had a math teacher in high school, Mr. Stephenson, who never had time to teach us any math. During every instance when he raised his chalk to the blackboard to write an equation he would suddenly swirl to try to catch some student or students committing this or that negligible infraction – whispering, chewing gum, tweaking Sally's pigtail.

Misconduct spied, he would whip out a little black notebook and enter so many demerits beside the miscreant's name. The entire length of every class consisted of Mr. Stephenson's penning in demerits. The only math we learned consisted of guessing the sum of our demerits at the end of each week and deducting that total from the points we garnered from taking weekly quizzes, the knowledge of how to succeed on such tests coming solely from reading the textbook.

So far as I could discern, Wendy Ellen Sheldon had no CPS textbook from which to learn the State of California's expectations in raising Melissa and Eileen.

"I want them back, Mr. Fletcher. I love them dearly. Find them, please. Find them, find them, find them."

"Finding them won't gain you custody," I said.

"I know. But it's a start." She grabbed the photos from me. "Right now I just want to see their smiling faces again."

"I understand. So please sit down. I have a few questions to ask you. Questions the police may have asked before. Should have asked. But they are not sharing the answers you gave them with me. Please be patient."

She sat, lacing her fingers and twisting them nervously.

"Okay. Good. Now for this line of questioning I want to assume the girls were not kidnapped at all. Got that?"

She nodded, but her doubt was evident.

"Who might they willingly run away with?"

"Leo Hutchens, my cousin. The girls like him, although I don't know why. He's a jerk – except to them."

"Explain that."

Well… Hutch – that's what everybody but me calls him – is a blowhard, a know-it-all loudmouth who has all these grand ideas and is forever trying to borrow money from members of the family in order to try to get his stupid projects off the ground."

"What kind of projects?"

"Oh, his latest idea is to build one-man helicopters that everyone can fly to work instead to driving cars. For a while he was hustling magic bracelets made of copper. Guaranteed to make you lose weight, become stronger, and improve your memory. What a scam that was."

"Okay. I get the idea. I take it, these silly notions charmed your girls?"

Wendy Ellen nodded. "Plus, he was always giving them money, buying them tee-shirts and tennis shoes, taking them to movies and promising to take them to Disneyland sometime soon."

With Father Reed Mackenzie in mind I asked, "Do you suspect that he ever tried to molest either of the girls?"

She gave me a nervous look. "Not that I know of."

"Any suspicions on that count?"

She hesitated before saying, "No. Leo would never do that! I'd kill him."

"If in fact he was the one the girls rode off with, why do you think he lured them away?" I quickly realized lured wasn't the word I wanted, but there it was, out of my mouth, out in the open."

"Who knows? To take them to the beach? To a movie? To…. I don't know."

"Why take them away from school? Does Leo have a day job?"

"No. Last I knew he was working graveyard as a cook at the Denny's in Goleta."

"What kind of car does he drive?"

"A dumpy black Cadillac. An old thing in need of new paint job."

"You know, don't you, that's not the car the nun's described to the police."

"Yeah. I know."

"So, chances are Leo is not the man the girls left the schoolyard with. Unless…."

She grimaced. "Unless he's turned into a car thief for his latest windup."

"Would that be like him?"

A shrug. "Can't rule out anything when it comes to Leo Hutchens."

Rule out anything. Including child molestation.

"Is Leo married?" I said.

"Not anymore."

"What happened?"

"Carole Lee couldn't take his shit anymore."

"And by *shit* you mean?"

"Leo drinks and gets mean. And he's such a control freak. Especially with women. He even tried to tell me I was raising the girls all wrong. I was making them too lady-like, too prissy, too sissy. Too weak. He even tried to turn them into lady wrestlers. Whenever he was here he turned the TV channel to the wrestling shows. Told Eileen he could turn her into Gorgeous Geogianna. She could grow up to work the women's wrestling circuit and make millions."

"What did Eileen think of that?" I said.

"She ate it up. She'd toss a bath towel over her back and parade around, holding an arm up, showing off her bicep."

"And Melissa?"

"Leo told Melissa she could be Eileen's manager. Or, sometimes Leo would tell both girls they could join the circus, become flying acrobats, jugglers, or even lion tamers."

"I see what you mean by Leo's having a suggestive imagination that would excite the girls."

"Hell, maybe all three of them did run off to join the circus," Wendy Ellen said, in a voice that was half joking, half shock at the possibility it might even be true.

I wrote down Leo's address.

I said, "I assume you've seen and spoken to your cousin since the girls vanished. What did he say?"

"He mocked me," she said. "He invited me to search his house, after reminding me the police had already been there, thanks to me. 'Where else would I hide them, Annie?' he said. I had no good answer to that. 'Maybe I sold them to a passing band of gypsies,' he said, laughing. When I screamed at him, 'Aren't you even concerned that they're missing, Leo?' he replied, 'They're just toys to me. Two-legged animals I could take off your shelf to play with once in a while. Now they're gone. No longer on your shelf. What a pity! Now I'll have to find other little toys to play with.' That's how uncaring he is, Mr. Fletcher."

From those remarks I didn't expect to get much from interviewing Leo. Still, I felt I had to do it. For all I knew, Leo had actually taken the girls against their wills, maybe even killed them. He sounded like the kind of creature who might pull the arms and legs off toys for a bit of amusement. Perhaps, something provoked him to do just that. The world was full of Crazy Leo types. Nasty, narcissistic, soulless.

9

Wendy Ellen became a foster mother for the money. She was neither shy nor ashamed about admitting that. She worked as a waitress at a high-end restaurant called Strawberry Sands, between the beach and Highway 101, near the only stoplight on 101 between LA and San Francisco. Tips were good but rent for even a low-end house in Santa Julietta ate up much of her pay. I knew she didn't file tax returns and supposed that, even if she did, she wouldn't claim her tips. That didn't distinguish her from any other worker in the service industry.

I had no problem with her screwing Uncle Sam and Sacramento. Tax laws were written by and for the rich. And my being a private detective did not include detecting tax fraud. Child Protective Services, I knew, did not demand to see tax returns before certifying someone to be financially, as well as morally, capable of overseeing otherwise unwanted youths. CPS also was desperate enough that they were willing to overlook the fact that Melissa and Eileen would be home alone after dark, until Wendy Ellen returned home from waiting tables, sometimes coming home on weekend nights close to midnight.

Wendy Ellen finished folding her laundry, collapsed her ironing board, and carried both into her bedroom, making two trips. When she returned the second time she had shed the muumuu. Wearing only a bra and panties, she revealed how shapely she was. She wore no makeup. For the first time I noticed the light red fingernail and toenail polish she wore. Most of it had peeled away. She had let down her shoulder-length hair.

"I'm lonely, Mr. Fletcher. Very lonely. I am ever so thankful you agreed to hunt for the girls for free, but I feel bad asking you to work for nothing. I'm not much, but I'm yours, if you'll have me."

Did I have any reason to turn her down?

"Are you sure, Anna? You're very lovely. I'd be honored."

"It's been so long since I've had sex. I crave it. Yet, every man since what seems like forever that I've invited into my bed has broken my heart. I've pretty much given up on men. They use me like an ashtray, think nothing of what might please me. I've told myself that you might be different. But…even if not…. I feel I owe you."

She unhitched her bra and let it drop.

I stood, walked to her, and clasped her by her upper arms.

"You are not obliged to do this. Do you understand that?" I said.

She stepped forward, pressing against me.

"Yes. I know," she said, then kissed me.

Funny as it might seem, we took time to put freshly ironed sheets on her bed before we made love. Doing so was part of her sense of tidiness. I had already taken note of how orderly the rest of her house appeared. No magazines lying about, no dirty dishes in her kitchen sink. Furniture squared away. Even the clothes I watched her fold had a military preciseness to the corners when she finished.

I knew a bit of her background. For a brief time she had been married to a motor-pool sergeant and had lived on the base at nearby Vandenberg Air Force Base. She said he was a handsome brute, with the emphasis on *brute*. He liked his sex rough and didn't care what she liked. So why had she married him?

"He was a ticket out of Sisquoc. And he had a sense of humor."

Sisquoc was barely a pinpoint on the map. Situated along the Sisquoc River, fifteen miles southeast of Santa Maria, the town consisted of a small church, a fire station, a grocery store, and an elementary school. The area around the town consisted of vineyards and strawberry fields. I knew of the place because I occasionally stopped at the grocery for a candy bar and soda when on my way to visit my friend Murky Murtrans, who owned a ranch in the Sisquoc Valley. A year earlier I had saved Murky's miserable old ass from murder charges by finding out who really had killed the two male students found buried next to a shed in the middle of his vineyard.

"You left your husband because of bad sex?" I had asked Wendy Ellen in my previous interview with her.

"No. I'm not even sure I'd know what good sex is. I could kinda tolerate getting raped in the bedroom, but around our friends he talked about me and treated me like I was his whore, not his wife," she had told me. She also had said, "I found out that, in that regard, I wasn't all that much different from the other enlisted men's wives on the base. But I finally decided I wasn't going to put up with it forever. So I left him before I got knocked up and had to have a gorilla for my children's father."

After an hour in bed together, Anna smiled and said, "I've never been treated like that before, Mr. Fletcher."

She refused to call me Stu, which made me think I was her father. But my insisting on being called by my given name seemed like a small point. No need to interrupt her momentary contentment. More than once I had watched parents, thinking themselves helpful and instructive, intrude on their child's moment of joy by being demanding over some minor point of etiquette. It was heartbreaking to watching the child's bubble pop, see the sudden sense of miscommunication. A young person's joy shrunk to bewilderment, confusion in the child's eyes segueing into a blank stare toward the Middle

Distance. And the parents? Clueless. I didn't want to spoil Wendy Ellen's bliss. She rolled toward me, kissed my arm, then hugged me. It was a moment to remember.

Still, there was work to do.

Dressed, she made a pot of coffee, after I turned down a glass of wine. She gave me Cousin Leo's work and home addresses. Though not looking forward to meeting him, I judged it obviously necessary. He would hardly be the first self-absorbed sociopath I had had to deal with. LA crawls with such creatures, two-legged cockroaches, only with less charm that the sewer bugs.

Wendy Ellen kissed my cheek when she served me coffee.

"Could we do that again sometime soon, Mr…um…Stu?"

"I'd like that, if you would," I said.

Another kiss. She gave me her lips and tongue this time.

"Work, please," I said after letting her tongue linger for a moment.

She smiled and sat across from me.

"Other people, besides Leo, who might have shown up at Santa Franchesca to coax the girls into a car, right?"

"You'd make a good detective, Wendy."

Her eyes brightened.

"The nuns are sure it was a male who drove off with the girls?" she said.

"Yes. They're sure they saw a man. A young man, they think."

"Try Lonnie Foster."

"Who's he?"

"A bum fuck." She laughed when she said it.

I gave her a look.

"Okay. He was going to be my boyfriend. Or so I thought. I let him move in with me here. Well, saying he moved in is a joke. He barely owned a change of underwear. He lasted a week before I threw him out."

I waited.

"Like I said. He was a bum fuck. Talk about getting fucked without getting kissed. He was on and off of me before I could count to ten."

"Why is he a possibility?"

"The girls both liked him. And he liked them. He kissed them more than he kissed me."

I frowned.

"No, no. Kissed them on top of their heads before he surprised them with candy."

"So you think he might have played 'Want some candy, little girls?' with them?"

"He might have. He wasn't happy when I showed him the door."

"How soon between….?"

"A couple weeks from the time he left until the girls were taken," she said.

"And you told the police this?"

A firm nod.

"I assume the police interviewed him."

A shrug.

As a former detective with Burbank PD, I knew there were good cops who conscientiously pursued all leads, and lazy cops who didn't. The latter gave criminal defense attorneys occasions to buy expensive rounds of drinks at post-acquittal celebrations in upscale bars after juries found their thug clients not guilty. Many a day I found myself following up suspicions that one of my police partners had been a lazy cop. Luckily, doing so didn't make me cynical. I left the force for another reason. And, I still owned my good-cop attitude.

10

The waitress working the till at the Denny's in Goleta could punch cash register keys and chew bubble gum at the same time. Her name tag told me her name was Wanda Mae and that she had been working at Denny's for two years plus. Either the tips were good or she suffered from misplaced dedication.

"Leo? Naw. He stopped showing up last week. Too bad. He was kinda cute."

So even Leo Hutchens had a little something going for him.

"Know where I can find him?" I said.

She gestured for me to step aside to allow a paying customer to pay his bill. When the customer walked away, pocketing his change, she said, "I might know where he is."

I knew *coy* when I saw it. I bought a breath mint with a five -dollar bill. "Keep the change."

"Try the blue apartment building next to Walgreen's Drugs at Hawthorne and El Moreno Place, two miles that way." She pointed south.

"Upstairs? Downstairs?"

"In my lady's chamber," she replied smartly. "The chick's name is Marla. Long black hair. Big boobs. No brains."

"None?"

She laughed. "Leo may be cute, but that's all he's got going for him. Well, except for…. Eh, you can figure that out. You're a guy."

I appreciated her affirmation and left before she rescinded the compliment.

I had literally flipped a coin to decide whether to follow up interviewing Leo Hutchens or Lonnie Foster. Leo won the toss.

"Yeah?"

Wanda Mae's description was accurate.

"Marla?" Long black hair and busty.

"Mister, if you're lookin' for a blowjob, I don't do that anymore. My gynecologist told me givin' head too often was gonna give me buck teeth."

Whatever happened to "Take two aspirin?"

"I'm looking for Leo Hutchens."

"Who isn't? You a cop or a bill collector?"

"Private detective."

"Really? I thought you kinda guys only happened in dime novels."

She definitely rated higher than "No brains."

"No. A few of us actually make a living at it," I said.

"Not a very good living, I bet. Peeping through windows, catchin' wives cheatin' on their scum-bag husbands. Usually with another creepy scum-bag." She threw up her hands. "All men are scum-bags, you know." Pause. "Well, maybe present company excepted. Are you a scum-bag? Oh, never mind. Scum-bags never confess to bein' what they are."

"I've been told Leo is a scum-bag."

"He's a man, isn't he?"

"I've yet to meet him."

"Whadda you want him for? Stealin' meat outta Denny's walk-in?"

"Maybe giving candy to little girls," I said.

"Oh, Jesus! I don't think so. I mean, Leo's...."

"Leo's what?"

"Leo likes his women with…"

"Long black hair."

"Yeah. Among other things."

And busty, I supposed she meant.

"Anyway, Leo hangs out here. Even sleeps here some nights. And I mean sleeps. Snores like an elephant. Ha, ha! You ever hear an elephant snore?"

An experience I had missed.

"How irregular is his…uh…presence here?" I said.

"Irregular? I thought that means being constipated."

Her graph was dipping toward the *no-brains* axis again.

"Do you expect him back soon?"

"I dunno. But you're welcome to stay. I might even change my mind about the blowjob. Are you really a private dick? If so, why don't you wear one of those…those kind of hats private eyes in the movies wear? Humphrey Bogart and Robert Mitchum, you know."

"Men wearing hats went out when Eisenhower came in. When Harry the Haberdasher retired."

"Harry who?"

"Truman."

"Oh, yeah. That guy Dewey beat."

"Exactly."

"You're welcome to wait for Leo. My place is kind of a mess, but I ain't got mice or fleas or cobwebs."

"No, thanks. Maybe I'll come back later."

"Sure. Later. My blowjob offer still stands. I swallow, too. Or did I mention that already."

Peeking over Marla's shoulder, I saw no evidence that children had ever been present in her apartment. As for fleas, mice, or cobwebs? I didn't get that good a look.

I could have popped into the nearby Safeway, bought myself a bottle of milk and a jar of peanut butter, then camped out in my car across from Marla's place. But I decided I wasn't all that keen to find Leo Hutchens just yet. Maybe I was turning into a lazy detective, but more likely, I preferred to collar Leo in a more civilized setting. One more certain to be free of cobwebs, mice, and fleas. Such places existed in Santa Julietta, but rarely on this side of town. It was too close to Isla Vista, UCSJ's next-to-campus, student-apartments village.

I put in a call to the Payettes. Sarah answered. Germaine had no made contact with her and Fowler yet.

"Please, please, Stu. Go to San Francisco to look for Germaine. I don't care what you charge. I want my baby back."

I wondered what had altered her attitude, but I didn't ask.

"Okay. I'll leave tonight. I'm in Santa Julietta and I have a little task to finish up here. But I'll swing by my house, pack a suitcase, and be on the road by midnight."

"Thank you, thank you."

After I hung up, I dialed Amanda Reynolds. I explained to her I was headed toward the Bay Area later, then lied to her. "I'm spending the next couple hours looking into Father Mackenzie's story. I'm headed toward the boys' parents' house," I lied. I figured I could always tell Amanda they weren't home.

"Both boys will be home from San Diego this weekend. They've agreed to meet with you." She gave me the time and place. I wrote it down and promised I would be there.

Lonnie Foster proved to be the kind of guy who stood as a compelling argument in favor of abortion. What he lacked in physical deformities, he made up for with character failings. As my grandmother used to say of such people: "What a waste of space!"

On Hollister Way Lester Kane's Garage & Tire Sales had five repair bays. Wendy Ellen had told me Lonnie worked there as an auto mechanic. Lester Kane told me otherwise.

"I had to fire Lonnie on Tuesday. He attacked a customer with a crescent wrench. Dumb sumbitch."

In a slow drawl Lester explained that he employed five mechanics, each of whom had to supply his own set of tools. He pointed to four chest-high steel boxes on casters, one at the rear of each the bays.

"Them tools is expensive and my guys take pride of ownership in their sets. Protective of 'em they are, too."

A large sign on the rear wall of the garage read: *Customers are not permitted to borrow tools.* I began to picture what led to Lonnie's getting fired.

"I promised Mr. Hydler we'd have his car fixed by close on Monday, but Lonnie didn't finish. So Tuesday morning Hydler was waiting when we opened. Lonnie was late so Hydler opened the hood of his car, then tried to unlock Lonnie's toolbox. Just then Lonnie showed up, saw Hylder messin' with his box, grabbed a wrench from Elmer's box, and gave Sam Hydler a hard whop on his shoulder blade. It took Elmer and me all we could manage to hold Lonnie back from hitting my customer again."

I could see why Lester had to fire Lonnie, even though he was only defending his property.

Lester went on, "Sam threatened to sue me, as well as sue Lonnie. I talked him outta callin' the cops. But to settle him down I had to have Elmer finish up work on his car and then give him all that work for free. Over three hundred dollars."

I nodded sympathetically.

"Then, on top of it all, when I told Lonnie he was canned, he demanded his wages right there on the spot. When I refused, he threatened to call Sacramento. He's a damned barstool lawyer on top of bein' a hothead."

I already knew that the State of California's labor laws required a terminated employee to be paid off immediately, if said employee insists.

When Lester finally ceased with is indignation and slowed from pouring out his grievances to me long enough to take a breath, I asked what I really wanted to know.

"Where do you suppose I can find Lonnie now?"

"Drinkin' his wages away, I imagine. Down at the pool hall bad-mouthin' me."

The pool hall was called Femme Fatal. Dim lighting provided more shade than any self-respecting lady would need. The short redheaded woman with a kangaroo tattoo on the back of her left hand pointed with that hand toward a group of four young men playing pool at a rear table. Not knowing what Lonnie looked like, I stood at some distance for a while trying to guess which of the four ratty-looking thugs he might be.

Then one of them saw me watching and took exception to my presence.

"Somethin' you need, Mister? This here is a closed game."

"I'm looking for Lonnie Foster."

"Well now, by damn you found me."

I had guessed right.

"What can I do for you, Mister? You a lawyer for Sam Hydler? If so, you'll know by now I was just defendin' what was mine. Same as if a man broke into my house and tried to steal my television."

Lester was right. Lonnie was a barstool lawyer. And not a bad one – maybe. Sam had tried to take Lonnie's wrench, although Sam and others may think of it as *borrowing*. Borrowing without permission. I could picture a burglar who heisted Lonnie's TV arguing in court that he was merely borrowing the television set. Whether a jury would scoff at such a claim depended on the jury. As a cop in Burbank I'd sat in court and listened to "not guilty" verdicts handed down by juries that were based on more bizarre claims.

"Wendy Ellen Sheldon has asked me to look into the disappearance of the two young girls she had been caring for. She suggested you might be able to shed some light on what happened to them."

Lonnie was holding a pool cue. So I kept my distance. The wife of my friend Murky Murtrans had been murdered with a pool cue, in the billiards room at Murky's ranch. But Lonnie handed his cue to another player and gestured for me to follow him toward the bar.

I figured Lonnie's age to be on the low side of thirty. He was short in stature, but not short enough to suffer from short-man syndrome. His fingernails bore the ineradicable oil stains of an auto mechanic, but his face was clean-shaven, and his hair was combed neatly, what there was of it. Lonnie was going to be bald by the time he reached forty. With a baby face and a bald head he was going to look like Al Capone. God indeed works in mysterious ways.

"You good for buyin' me a beer?" he said as he sidled up onto a barstool.

I gestured for the redhead to draw two beers. The woman nodded and clearly knew Lonnie's choice of barley water. Coors.

He scooped a handful of beer nuts from a bowl on the bar and said, "Only Wendy Ellen could play Pied Piper to them kids. If anyone suckered them two away from the penguins, it had to be her."

I assumed by *penguins* he meant nuns.

"Go on. Why only her?"

"'Cause she had them girls believin' she cared about them. Melissa and Eileen knew nobody else gave a shit whether they lived or died. Not even the phonies who ran that school."

"Why do you call them phonies?"

He cocked his head and smirked. "You gotta be kiddin'. Them Catholics cry rivers about abortion, breed like fruit flies, but don't give a shit whether parents have two nickels to rub together to raise the little turds after they're born."

"Why do you think Wendy Ellen was conning the girls?"

"Why? 'Cause at bottom she's a heartless bitch. You haven't found that out yet? Why not? Too busy fuckin' her brains out?"

I tried to give him a blank look.

In a falsetto voice he mocked Wendy Ellen. "'None of you wicked men ever care about what I need or want. You're all such selfish fucks.' Did she give you that line – just before she dropped her drawers and sashayed slowly toward you, lookin' shy as can be?"

I continued to stare.

He continued. "Yeah, she fed them girls, gave 'em a soft bed to sleep in. But she was only doin' it for the money. If the State of California hadn't been sendin' her a regular check, she'd have let them kids sleep in the street and starve. She said as much to me."

"So who took them?"

Lonnie's turn to give me a stare.

"Did Wendy say I wiggled a lollipop under them girls' noses?"

"What kind of car do you drive?" I said.

"Now?"

"At the time the girls were kidnapped, assuming they were."

"White '57 Ford."

"What model?"

Pause. "Custom Ranchero."

Ford Custom Ranchero. Neither fish nor fowl. A car with a pickup truck rear, perfect for allowing two young girls to hop into easily as it slowed for them.

"You don't have it now?" I said.

"Sold it."

"When?"

"Right after…. A while ago."

"Did the sheriff examine it?"

"Yeah."

"And?"

"Of course, the girls' fingerprints were all over it. I used to take 'em out for ice cream and stuff. That don't mean nuthin'."

"What happened next?"

"Not much. The car the nuns saw wasn't white. That's all I know. Except for knowin' it wasn't me that took them. I'm tellin' ya, Wendy Ellen knows more that she's let on."

The tattooed redhead appeared and pointed to our empty schooners. I nodded and she filled another pair, failing to hold the glasses at an angle, paying too little attention to how much foamy head each glass sported. She was either new to the job or old to it and indifferent. I figured new. An experienced bartender wouldn't have thought twice about how to draw a beer correctly.

Lonnie downed his second beer in one long swill.

"We done here, Mr. Private Detective? I gotta pool game waiting for me and my cue is hot."

"One last question. What do you think has happened to the girls?"

I took a deep breath.

"I'd say they're dead and buried, only…."

"Only what?"

"Only I'm hopin' otherwise. I really, truly liked them kids. Both of them. I don't like to imagine either one of them is eatin' dirt and feedin' worms somewhere."

For not wanting to imagine the girls' fate, he had a vivid imagination.

11

My watch read six minutes before midnight when I parked my Biscayne in front of my house in Santa Maria. A light was still on at the Payette's. I quickly turned my car's headlights out, hoping whoever was up -- Fowler, Sarah, or both – wouldn't notice my return. I wanted to pack a bag, brush my teeth, and hit the road again before either or both of them could accost me. And I sure as hell didn't want to have to drive away with Fowler hanging by his fingernails from my rear bumper.

Santa Clara lies just over 200 miles north of Santa Maria up Highway 101. Knowing I'd find slim pickings on the long stretch between Paso Robles and Soledad, I remembered an all-night diner just past Soledad. My thermos held three cups of coffee. I drank all three , one after another and figured I'd worry about where to stop to pee when the time came.

That time arrived when I reached the town of Soledad.

Soledad means *solitude* in Spanish. So, maybe that is why John Steinbeck chose the town as the backdrop of his 1937 novel, *Of Mice and Men,* where the characters in his story all suffer from barrels full of loneliness. Steinbeck hailed from the Monterrey Peninsula. For sure, a lonely place.

A well-known state prison with an eponymous name lies three miles north of Soledad. Nearby I found a 24-hour diner called Prison Coffee Blues. *Blues* stood out in flashing neon. The parking lot was full of vintage cars. In some I saw the driver slumped over the steering wheel – asleep, not dead, I presumed.

On the diner's door was a *Nixon for President* sticker. Nixon was the guy running on a law and order platform. In a town with a prison-based economy that made sense. Give a boost to the guy who was promising to boost the prison's inventory.

The exterior of the diner was decorated with uninspired Halloween trappings. The usual ghoulies and ghosties and things that go bump in the night. The one piece of décor that made me smile featured a pair of young ladies wearing pink bikinis and witches' hats atop their flowing blonde hair and, in place of a broomstick, they were riding in tandem on a Harley-Davidson motorbike with custom handlebars. Varoom! Varoom!

Inside the diner the opposite of solitude prevailed. Every table was taken, every counter stool filled. On the jukebox I recognized a song an old girlfriend had played for me, "I Won't Come in While He's There" by Jim Reeves. She was a C&W fan and had showed me the LP album cover proudly. It had read: *Blue Side of Lonesome.* I remembered that Reeves was very popular when, four years back, he had crashed his airplane while trying to land in a thunderstorm at Nashville.

Blue Side of Lonesome. I wasn't aware there was any other side. Maybe that's why I had only a tenuous grasp on C&W music. That girlfriend and I didn't last together very long. Marty Robbins, on the other hand, was a man I thought I understood.

Most of the folks hanging around the entrance to the prison were waiting for the sunrise opening of the prison's gates so that they could visit with a friend or relative serving time inside. For a lucky few said friend or relative might even be getting released in the morning.

After peeing in a smelly restroom, I returned to the lunch counter to order a coffee to go. I caught a couple lines of lyrics from a twangy voice coming out of the jukebox.

Just listen to your children while they play,
It's not really very funny, what the children say.

I learned later the song title was "Skip a Rope" by somebody I'd never heard of. Nelson Cargill. But then my widest experience with County & Western music came via my mother. Her favorite crooner was Red Foley; her favorite songs of his: "Chattanooga Shoe Shine Boy" and Peace in the Valley".

As I headed toward my car I looked for the usual panhandler or two that hung around the parking lot of such diners, but not here. Maybe hobos feared asking a handout from a man who might turn out to be the dangerous cousin of some infamous thug.

Eager to press on, I cranked the engine and headed north. Passing the prison, I reminded myself that, on more than one occasion, I had been inside, each time interviewing this or that grim, nasty hoodlum being defended by Amanda Reynolds. In every case but one she had not only later won the lout a retrial, but had managed to get him released entirely, based on some technicality. Twice I had been the one who dug up the facts that provided the technicality. Talk about getting paid to do a dirty, degrading job.

The city of Santa Clara sits on the north edge of San Jose and is home to Santa Clara University, the oldest university in the state of California. Counted among the university's alumni and alumna was A.C. Crowder's father, Warren, along with three out of four of Warren's children. The exception, as I've already noted, was A.C., who went to Cal Poly SLO.

From the town of Santa Clara I drove a few miles west, to Cupertino, where I had been told A.C.'s sister, Mary-Margaret, owned a home. Finding it took a while and, when I did pull into the driveway, I was disappointed. "Virgin Mary", as Teddy Crowder precociously referred to her aunt, owned a home in need of paint and a new roof. Asphalt cracks in her driveway looked like WWI trenches.

I parked on the street and walked to the front door. No one answered.

The lot on which the house sat was large and lined with tall hedges, not neatly trimmed. The garage was a large, stand-alone affair, in need of even more paint, though the roof had newer shingles than the house. Yard grass was patchy, front and back. In the middle of the back yard stood a white gazebo with a Madonna and child statue in the middle. When I took a closer look, Baby Jesus was grinning from ear to ear, but Mary looked less than beatific. Pained even. No wonder. On a rear corner post hung a crucifix. Adult Jesus was bleeding profusely. Unlike Protestants, Catholics want everyone to feel His pain.

I returned to the front of the house before I began peering into windows. There I was less likely to be taken for a burglar casing the joint, in case one of Mary-Margaret's neighbors was a curtain-twitcher, although, from her front porch, I couldn't see any of her neighbor's houses. The untrimmed hedge rows were too tall.

It crossed my mind to go to the back door and let myself in, to see if I could detect any signs that Germaine Payette had been there. But I heard a neighbor's dog bark. A loud, deep bark, indicative of a large, unfriendly critter.

So I left.

Driving away, I felt lost -- but only in the sense of what to do next. I should have given more thought sooner regarding what to do if I found no one home at Mary-Margaret's. Heading north, up the peninsula toward San Francisco, was out of the question. I had been inside the Avalon Ballroom once before, three years earlier. My experience there had been part of a baby-sitting adventure, accompanying the late Frank Mortimer, a fellow PI and a resident of The City, an appellation San Francisco denizens proudly use to refer to their fairy-tale metropolis.

The purpose for which Frank and I had been hired was to watch over the daughter of one of California's biggest investment bankers, Howard Dixon, who lived in a mansion in Sausalito, a flossy little burg just over the Golden Gate Bridge, in Marin County.

Mr. Dixon was off to Hong Kong to check up on some of his wheelbarrows full of silver, gold, and cash. He was accompanied by another prominent investment guru, Simon Song. Frank had been hired by the pair of them to…to do what? Safeguard, baby-sit, accompany, watch over, hang out with their daughters.

Howard's college-age daughter, Della Daisy Dixon, was better known as Dee-Dee. Apparently, Dee-Dee-Dee sounded too much like the beginning of a Morse Code signal. Dee-Dee was a freshman at Berkeley, and Simon Song's daughter, Samantha, was Dee-Dee's roommate. Sammy. Jesus. What a pair of names. Sammy Song and Dee-Dee Dixon. With names like that they could have been characters out of a Broadway musical.

Why don't parents think about what their kids' names will sound like when the kids are a hundred years old? I tried to imagine a photo in the society section of the *San Francisco Examiner*. The caption reads: *Sammy and Dee-Dee turn one hundred*. I could hear the article's author snickering up her sleeve – or cackling.

I tried to imagine Sandra Dee, the bikini-clad star of Columbia Pictures' *Gidget series*, as a ninety year old. Ouch! My stomach churned with revulsion at the thought. So, too, with Sammy and Dee-Dee. But…the money was good and Frank had pleaded with me. He wanted the job – needed it, I supposed – to make his office rent, and he was sure he wasn't up to riding herd on a pair of eighteen-year-olds alone.

So there I was. In the city, playing escort to two women half my age. And one of the places where Frank and I found ourselves holding hands with the two girls was the Avalon Ballroom. The ballroom occupied the upper two floors of a building on Sutter Street, in an area of the city called Polk Gulch, named after America's least laudable president, James Polk. The Gulch was also home to San Francisco's hippie population, as well as where most of the West Coast's queers hung out, male and female. The occasion that put us in the ballroom was a concert by a group I had never heard of, a skanky-looking bunch calling themselves The Grateful Dead.

The lead guitar was a young fellow with thick black hair that wound around his neck and over his shoulders. His name was Jerry Garcia, but he didn't look Hispanic. Jerry's face looked sickly white, like he was riding a roller-coaster and about to lose his lunch. Sammy and Dee-Dee were enchanted by the music. My regret was that I hadn't brought ear plugs.

Afterwards, the four of us went to a coffeehouse called The Bean Grinder, where, at last, we could hear one another speak.

The coffee was great. The conversation? Not so much.

"Do you like sex, Mr. Fletcher?" is how it began. Sammy, gave me an exaggerated, slant-eyed smirk, pulling at the corner of each eye with an index finger.

"Yes. I do."

"Would you like to have sex with Dee-Dee and me?"

"No."

"Why not?"

"You obviously didn't get the cookie with the fortune that reads: No fuckee the hired help."

Dee-Dee spilled her coffee, laughing.

"How about suckee the hired help?" Sammy said.

"There's probably a fortune cookie for that, too," I said.

More spilled coffee.

Frank was blushing and staring off into the Middle Distance.

I told the girls, "Give Frank a break, won't you?"

Dee-Dee poked Frank. "Is Sammy embarrassing you, Mr. Mortimer?"

Frank glared at her.

"I'll take that to mean 'Yes'," she said.

Sammy poked me. "Mr. Fletcher here isn't embarrassed, are you Stu?"

"I'm embarrassed for you two ladies."

"Do you really think we're ladies? How kind of you to possess such a thought. I'll have to tell my daddy. Maybe he'll give you a bonus," Sammy said. "Or would you rather that I get down on my knees to give you your bonus?"

I said nothing.

Dee-Dee laughed. "He's thinking. He's thinking, Sammy."

"But what exactly is he thinking, Dee?"

"He thinking…um…um…he thinking: 'This hot chick is about to give me a boner. Oops, I mean bonus. I already have a boner.'"

I decided to change the subject.

"Tell me, girls. Who is Baby Blue?" As one of their pieces, The Grateful Dead had done a cover of Bob Dylan's song "It's All Over Now, Baby Blue".

"Great question!" Dee-Dee said and clapped her hands.

"Nobody knows for sure," Sammy said. "Some people think it refers to Joan Baez, Dylan's one-time girlfriend. Some think it refers to his ex-wife. After that there are a dozen other guesses."

"But Dylan remains silent on the question, I take it," I said.

Dee-Dee said, "Yup!"

"Hey, you're a detective. Why don't you solve the mystery for us," Sammy said.

I shook my head. "Nobody's hired me to solve it."

"Oh, shame! Such a mercenary attitude." Sammy jabbed an index finger at me.

Dee-Dee added, "I could write a term paper on the matter and my father would pay you to be my research assistant."

"Why don't you simply ask Dylan?" I said.

Dee-Dee grinned and said, 'Maybe I could offer to give Dylan a blowjob in exchange for the answer."

Sammy said, "Maybe he'd insist on two blowjobs, in which case…."

I made a stop-it gesture. "This is getting out of hand. Drink your coffees and let's get out of here."

Sammy giggled. "As in 'Let's blow this joint'?"

Frank scooped up the check and stood.

Sammy pointed to Frank and whispered loudly to Dee-Dee, "Can he spell s-t-i-c-k-i-n-t-h-e-m-u-d?"

Dee-Dee responded, "No, but I bet ol' Frank here knows how to stick it in a pud. Eh, Frankie?"

Frank turned and went to pay the check.

As she slid her purse strap from the back of her chair, Sammy said to me, "Good thing Frank brought you along, Tonto. He's no fun at all."

I'd never thought of myself as Mister Fun. I still don't.

12

That had been my one and only experience of seeing the inside of the Avalon Ballroom. It was enough. As I drove away from Mary-Margaret Crowder's home I switched on my car radio in hopes of finding something to flush the refrains of *Baby Blue* that were looping through my head. Fiddling with the dial, I finally backed into the Mamas and the Papas' *California Dreamin'*, followed by a pair from the Beach Boys: *Good Vibrations* and *California Girls*. Just in time to watch late morning fog roll in.

I drove a short while with my headlights on. Visibility ranged from ten yards to a hundred yards and back to ten. *Patchy fog*, meteorologists call it. By any name it was stressful and hazardous. So, I pulled into yet another diner, this time in Los Altos. I was tempted by a patty melt with a side of onion rings. But my stomach overruled my taste buds. I ordered a toad-in-the-hole instead, with dry toast and a glass of milk.

Not really sure where to look for Germaine Payette, I sat nursing a second glass of milk as I tried to remember more of what Teddy Crowder had to told me about her dad's brother's diary. Uncle Francis, who had just died in an airplane crash, had been in on the coverup of the death of Cousin Morgan from New York. Morgan was attending Stanford but got drunk at a fraternity party on Santa Clara's campus and choked to death on his own vomit. Afterwards, Francis and his brothers – except for A.C. – buried cousin Morgan and his roommate Lennie, while agreeing on a fib that the two men had vanished.

Morgan supposedly left the party and disappeared into one of San Francisco Bay's notorious fogs, identical to the one I was now experiencing. As I sat in my car, staring out into a blanket of white, I barely saw the pair of women who passed by my car close enough for me to reach out and touch them. They disappeared as quickly as they had materialized.

Teddy's brother Randall apparently had figured out where Morgan had been buried. I should have pressed Teddy to tell me more of what she had seen in the diary. She had been playing cagy with me, and I felt lucky she had mentioned the story to me at all. And my point of being in the Bay Area was to find a live body, not a dead one. I told myself I should be able to find Germaine Payette without having to search for long dead Morgan Crowder, Stanford student from New York state.

At a pay phone outside the diner I thumbed through a well-worn phone book, its pages curled by frequent immersions into soupy-thick fog. When I found the listing for an M.

Crowder, I dialed the number. No answer. When I hung up I was startled by the sound of the phone returning my change. Knowing I lacked enough change to sustain a call to the Payettes, I dialed for an operator and asked that my call to Fowler and Sarah be charged to my home phone number. In my wallet I kept a little card with my AT&T account number to prove I wasn't some scam artist trying to dump long-distance charges on an unsuspecting stranger. Even then I had to answer questions up to, but not including, my mother's shoe size.

Fowler answered.

"Stu Fletcher here. I'm calling to let you know I'm in the Bay Area, doing what I can to locate Germaine. So far no luck, but I'll keep trying."

"Jeez, Stu, you should have let me come with you."

Rather than explain to him how dumb an idea I thought that was, I said, "I didn't get back to Santa Maria from Santa Julietta until after midnight. I didn't want to wake you or Sarah." Lame, but serviceable.

"Sarah and I were both up. How can we sleep when our daughter's gone AWOL?"

"I understand, Fowler, but I really do better when I'm on my own."

"Have you checked out any abortion shops yet?" he said.

"No, and I won't until I have more reason to believe that is the issue."

I heard him turn away from the phone and yell at his wife. When he returned he said, "Sarah's not really sure."

"What would it take to make her more certain? Is there a boyfriend?"

"No. No boyfriend."

How does one go about asking for a list of suspects without implying their daughter is a whore? Or, at minimum, utterly stupid. Obviously, if pregnant, Germaine provided herself with no adequate means of contraception. But why not? When I was in college not only did every guy I knew keep a condom tucked into a slot in his wallet, when a moment of passion was building, our dates were not loath to interrupt the heated proceedings and ask to be shown the sealed packet containing a prophylactic. Even Catholic girls asked. Those poor schlemiels who were unable to display the magic packet had to settle for a blowjob.

And yet, it was otherwise-bright college girls who kept back-alley abortion clinics humming. Only, in many cases, such venues had moved from back alleys to parlors with lace curtains. Prices soared accordingly. Abortionists' expenses explained part of the increase. Besides having to pay rent, the practitioners had traded coat hangers for more costly medical devices. Some of them even sterilized their instruments.

"How much is your trip going to cost us, Stu?"

"I'll have to think about that, Fowler. Tell Sarah not to worry. I promise not to bankrupt you.". Misplaced humor. I knew it the second it came out of my mouth.

"We've been good neighbors, you know," Fowler said.

Had he and Sarah been good neighbors? Not especially. On the other hand, they had never behaved liked neighbors from hell. That would count for a lot when the time came for us to settle accounts. Unable to provide Fowler with any encouraging news, I wondered why I had bothered to call him. How righteous was it for me to deflate their expectations?

Frank Mortimer might have known where to guide me towards Bay Area abortion houses, but Frank was dead and I doubted if he would be able to provide me with any insights from his grave. I didn't know who else to ask. In the two years since Frank's death I had failed to cultivate another reliable contact in the San Francisco area. In fact, I hadn't even tried very hard. I'm not sure why. In California all crime eventually leads either to LA or San Fran. LA I was comfortable with. I had plenty of contacts from my previous years as a homicide detective in Burbank. In the Bay Area my worst enemies were San Francisco PD detectives. A cabal of them had killed Frank Mortimer.

In any case, I decided to return to Mary-Margaret's house to wedge my business card into her front door screen. Having done that I intended to return to Santa Maria, though a corner of my conscience started urging me to head north to buy a ticket to The Byrd's concert. Their "Turn, Turn, Turn" began playing in my head.

"A time for every purpose under Heaven." Maybe so, but I wasn't so sure this was my time to revisit the Avalon Ballroom. I vaguely remembered what Germaine looked like, but present at The Byrds' concert would be a thousand near-look-alikes to her, the nuanced differences apt to be indistinguishable amid klieg lights, marijuana smoke, and orgasmic screams from hysterical young women.

13

I returned to Mary-Margaret's house but again no one answered the door. So I inserted my business card between the screen door and the door frame. The fog had lifted and a stiff breeze had come up. I imagined the smiles on local sailors' faces. Lyrics from The Kingston Trio's "Sloop John B" popped into my head.

> *Hoist up the John B's sails,*
> *See how the mainsail sets,*
> *Send for the captain ashore,*
> *Let me go home.*

There would be no sailing home for me, I had decided. After my conscience had wrestled with my more sensible instincts, I decided I would make the drive to San Francisco. I knew doing so would be a waste of time, but at least my conscience would shut up.

To be one-hundred-percent certain nobody was home – maybe Mary-Margaret had become hard of hearing as she aged -- I took another stroll around to the back of her house. No one answered when I knocked on her back door. No one became visible when I peered in her rear windows.

As I was about to leave, the wind whipped up and a door to her storage garage began swinging widely and banging against the door to which it was supposed to be latched. Good Samaritan that I imagine myself to be, I decided to close the door and latch it, lest it break loose from its hinges. The wind off the bay continued to pick up.

Closing the door, I peeked inside the garage. Up on blocks perched a silver Studebaker Commander. I could tell because the car announced its brand and style right in front of me, where the hood met the grill. I guessed it was a 1947 model, because shortly thereafter Studebaker began calling that model a Starlight. Lots of dust all over the body meant lots of recent neglect. Was Mary-Margaret an auto mechanic? Though rare, female mechanics were not unheard of. In fact, if I recalled correctly, England's Queen Elizabeth II was an auto mechanic in the British Army during WWII.

I found a small block of wood and jammed it under the door that had been swinging, jammed the door in an open position, letting light into the whole of the interior. Stepping further into the garage, I saw that the walls were covered with photos of light airplanes, each photographed with a pair of women wearing aviation caps, smiling widely as they sat atop the plane's cowling. Each photo was pinned with a carpet tack. I stopped counting when I reached tallying sixty-three photos, because the sixty-fourth photo stood out as slightly different. Instead of the women sitting on the cowling, they sat on the hood of a car that was parked beneath the plane's starboard wing. The car in the photo was a green Chrysler Town & Country Woody with a New York license plate, black numbers and letters on a yellow background. The number on the plate was 884 RFZ.

"Excuse me. Who are you and what are you doing here?"

Startled, I turned to see a middle-aged man with snow-white hair standing at the entrance to the garage. He wore a black suit and a priest's collar.

"I'm sorry. I was looking for Miss Crowder when I heard this door banging wildly in the wind. When I came to shut it I couldn't help notice the Studebaker and then the Powder Puff Derby photos. I take it Miss Crowder is an accomplished pilot."

"Why are you looking for Miss Crowder?" the man said.

"My name is Stu Fletcher. I'm a detective in search of a young woman named Germaine Payette. She's my neighbor's daughter in Santa Maria. I was told she had come north with Randall and Stephanie Crowder and that the three of them might be stopping off here before continuing on to San Francisco."

A woman appeared behind the man.

"What's going on, John?" Then she saw me. "Oh! Who are you?"

The man she called John repeated to her what I had just said.

"Steph and Randy were here, but no one was with them. Who told you this Germaine girl would be with them? By the way, I'm Mary-Margaret Crowder, in case you hadn't guessed."

"No Germaine, eh? Your niece Teddy was the one who told me about Germaine's being with Randall and Stephanie. She said she saw the three of them get into Randall's car together."

"Theodora lives in a world of fantasy. Like Alice, Teddy spends most of her time down a rabbit hole, living in a land of make-believe. She's not to be trusted when it comes to providing eye-witness accounts. I'm afraid she's wasted your time, Mr. Fletcher."

"It appears that she has. Sorry to have come trespassing, Miss Crowder."

"That's quite all right. I'm sure your neighbors are very concerned about their daughter," Mary-Margaret said.

"By the way, are you the airplane pilot?" I asked her.

"I am."

"My dad took me to the start of the 1955 Powder Puff Derby in Long Beach. My folks lived in Torrance and my dad had been a flight instructor stationed in Seattle and then San Diego during WWII."

"So you know a bit about light aircraft?" she said.

"I believe the plane in most of the photos is a Cessna 180."

"Correct. The other woman in the photos is Jordan Douglas, my co-pilot for most of our cross-county races. We made quite a team, although we never won any of the races. Engine problems usually. But at least we never crashed."

"Very impressive. My father would be proud of you, as am I."

The man she called John cleared his throat.

"Oh, dear. How rude of me. Mr. Fletcher, this is my…uh, my companion, Father John Ackerman. John is a professor at St. Patrick's Seminary in Menlo Park. He teaches classes in the seminary's pre-theology program."

Not knowing whether I was expected to bow or kneel, I extended my hand. He took it, giving me a cold, tepid handshake.

"Maggie's right. Young Theodora is a compulsive liar, possessed by the devil is that one. I don't know what's to become of her," John said.

Maggie said, "Such a contrast with her sister. Stephanie, bless her heart, is obsessed with the notion of staying free of sin. She prays daily for her little sister's soul, asking God to make Satan loosen his grip on her."

I never thought of myself as fluent in Catholic-speak, but I realized I was learning fast. I understood that they judged their God to work in mysterious ways and right now the mystery confronting me was: What connection is there between Mary-Margaret Crowder and the Sisters of the Convent of Santa Franchesca Ornella? At least two of the sisters, the two who provided authorities with a description of a kidnap car and its license plate.

In my mind there could be nothing coincidental between the descriptions provided the convent sisters and the car in the photo on the wall in Miss Crowder's garage. That the plate had been issued by the state of New York explained why California authorities had been unable to pinpoint the vehicle's identity among their records. I also knew that California did not routinely exchange vehicle-registration information with other states and it was rare for one state to ask another for such information.

My only contact in New York was a large detective agency in Albany, one I had only used once before, four years earlier, when I was trying to track down the maiden name of a woman who had scammed my client out of several thousand dollars, then fled from California. My own research pegged her having grown up in the Ithaca area, but she had changed her name several times, my client not being her first effort at defrauding a gullible male.

I told Mary-Margaret and Father John, "Sorry to have made a nuisance of myself. Shame on me for being so credulous. Cute children can be so disarming."

Miss Crowder said, "You're not the first, Mr. Fletcher. Theodora can be quite convincing when she turns on her charm, gives you that adorable smile."

I nodded and said, "More fool me," while thinking: Who's the more cunning? Precocious Teddy? Or this pair? Standing here wasn't going to provide the answer. So, I added, "Again, I apologize." I pulled out another business card and handed it to Father John. "If, or when, Mary-Margaret's niece and nephew return after the concert in The City, I'd appreciate a call. The number on the card is my answering service. You may leave a message. I'm now at a loss as to where to look next for my neighbor's daughter and I'd like to ask them if they know anything at all about her. Germaine Payette is her name. Stephanie plays golf with her. Perhaps she overheard Germaine mention where she was off to."

Father John stared at my card as though it might bite him on the thumb. However, priest and professor that he is, when he looked up at me he forced a smile and reminded me, "As we told you, Mr. Fletcher, your Miss Payette was not with Maggie's niece and nephew. Not did either of them mention the young woman."

I said, "I understand. Germaine was surely no more on their minds than the man in the moon. I've been told that the band they are going to see is quite a phenomenon."

Mary-Margaret said, "Their music is not to our taste, I'm sure."

"Oh, really?" I said. "Are you aware that one of their most identifiable songs is based on Scripture? Ecclesiastes, Book 3, verses 1-8, if I recall correctly. You can look it up."

Father John returned my card. "I'm sure we have no need for this."

I accepted the card with a forced smile. "*Turn', Turn, Turn* is the name of the tune. Before I turned to leave, I sang softly, "*A time to plant, a time to reap; a time to laugh, a time to weep.*"

In downtown Cupertino I stopped at a phone booth and dialed the operator.

14

Scarolli & Robbins is a large detective agency in Buffalo, New York that specializes in helping New York City and New Jersey prosecutors track down money being laundered by sundry Mafia families. I had used them once when trying to track down a pair of newlyweds who had been reported headed toward nearby Niagara Falls. The couple had stolen a quarter of a million dollars from the bride's father's safe, treating themselves to a sweet, juicy wedding present.

S&R found them for me, but – per the request of the bride's parents – did not notify authorities. Daddy just wanted some of his money back. He settled for having them return $100,000 in exchange for not going to jail. Of the hundred grand, I split twenty thousand evenly with Scarolli & Robbins as our joint fee.

We had had no contact since then – three years ago. The man I had worked with then was Sam Scarolli. I'd never met him, but I knew the sound of his voice. New Jersey Italian, from West Orange.

"You want an address for an old license plate? Sure. No problem." When I told him there would be no fat fee this time, he said, "Hey. I'm still eating off the last head of cabbage you sent me. When do you want this piece of vital information? Yesterday? Last week? Last month?"

"At your earliest convenience, Sam."

"Tomorrow? You'll hear from me then. Your answering service, right?"

"Thanks. I hope your winter's mild."

"Sitting here at the ass end of Lake Erie? Not a chance. But thanks for the good wish."

While still in the phone booth, I picked up the local phone book as it hung forlornly on a lengthy chain. The white pages encompassed all of greater San Jose, so I was hoping to get lucky. Shannon Diane Postlewaite had shared a couple of humanities classes with me at Cal State Long Beach. We even went out on a couple of dates together, before I realized that her amorous preferences didn't include men. I was just a free meal to her.

She had majored in accounting and, despite no mutual love interest, we had stayed in touch. Last I heard she had accepted a job with a firm in San Jose called Dietrich, Semmich, and Brown. When I dialed the company I was told she no longer worked there, that she had left for reasons the woman talking to me said she was unable to disclose. Because Shannon was bright, diligent, and personable, I immediately assumed she got fired for being queer.

The phone book showed nine listings for Postlewaite, including an S.D. Postlewaite. I dialed the number and got lucky.

"Stu Fletcher? Of course, I remember you. I dearly wanted to give you a dynamite blowjob, only --."

"Only you're not a blowjob-giving kind of gal."

"Exactly. Now, did you dial me up to offer me a free lunch? Of another sort, that is."

"I did."

"Wow! I'm available. What's in it for you?"

"Information."

"I'll do my best."

"I'm sure you will."

We met a place in San Jose called Clementine's All-Day Breakfast, off Monterey Road and Curtner. Shannon had aged more than I expected, her short, natural blonde hair in college now an uncomplimentary red. Long and stringy. She wore too much black eyeliner and had a tattoo of a donkey on the back of her neck. Maybe that was the point on which she had parted ways with Dietrich, Semmich, and Brown. Her voice was scratchy, too. From smoking, I guessed, when I saw when he pulled a pack of Camels from her purse.

"Last I heard you were a hot-shit vice detective in Burbank."

"Homicide, but yeah."

"Too many bad guys to deal with?" she asked.

I nodded. "Too many bad guys inside the defensive perimeter."

"Sounds like Vietnam. I've got a girlfriend who's brother is up on charges for fraggin' his flaming-asshole lieutenant. The dumb sonofabitch looey was trying to get the men in his platoon killed, for chrissakes. The platoon's motto was 'Everybody goes home alive'. The lieutenant refused to sign on."

I'd been there – in Korea—but didn't want to talk about it. I gestured toward our menus and Shannon knew enough to change the subject. I could tell she wanted to know why, out of the blue, I had looked her up, but she figured she'd better make sure she had first downed a plate of eggs, bacon, and hash browns.

"Where are you living these days, Fletcher? Somewhere in greater LA, I assume."

"Santa Maria."

"Why that pissant little burg?"

I shrugged. "It suits me."

"Cheaper rent, eh?"

"I bought a house."

"Holy shit! You've gone bourgeoise. I suppose you've got a wife and kids, too. No wait. I don't see a wedding ring."

"No wife, no kids, no cuddly dog."

The waitress came to take our orders. When she left Shannon leaned back in her chair and stared at me.

"You're looking damned good, Stu. Well, for a middle-aged guy, that is."

I lied by responding, "You, too, Shannon. Is life treating you well?"

She made a fluttering motion with her right hand. "I'm not getting rich or famous, like I'd hoped, but I'm doing okay. Work is…well, it's a paycheck. It didn't take long for me to get tired of lying, cheating, and stealing for my obscenely rich clients, making them even more obscenely rich. But that's what I'm good at. So here I am."

"Tell me about your love life," I said, knowing that would get her going.

"You know, Stu, it's really, really hard to find a gay chick who doesn't want to tie me up and slap the shit out of me. I'm still trying to figure out what vibe I give off that makes bull dykes think that turns me on."

"Sorry. I can't help you there."

"I know. I'm just whining. And I'm learning to be content with self-love. Only you can't begin to guess how many batteries my vibrator used up last month."

"A thousand?" I said, grinning.

"Give that man a kewpie doll."

"Really?"

"Oh, come on. A girl has to sleep once in a while, right? And I'm not allowed to give myself a buzz while I'm on the clock, lying to the IRS. My machine takes four double-A batteries and, if I change them out every two days, that adds up to how many?"

"You're the accountant," I said.

"Fifteen change-outs times four is sixty. And sixty times a quarter for ever battery makes fifteen dollars. A decent glass of Chablis costs a buck and a quarter. That's twelve glasses. Sitting at a lesbian bar, I usually assume it will take two, maybe three, glasses of wine to get the chick next to me spinning. So that's four to six drunk women a month I can drag home and rape. Hell, I'd rather invest in batteries than spend my money on wine and seduction talk. Maybe I should write book. Call it *How Duracell Helps Me Endure.* What do think, Stu?"

Before I could answer, the waitress brought our food.

I doubted if the battery company would be flattered by Shannon's tome, were she to write it. But maybe there would be enough of a voyeuristic audience to lift her book onto the *New York Times* best seller list. With royalties from the sales she might even be able to quit her day job, give up having to fudge counting leisure yachts under business expenses.

Eggs and bacon gone, and with only a few hash browns left on her plate, Shannon finally dared ask me why I wanted to see her.

"I'm sure you don't need your taxes done, Stu. Any more than you make as a detective, I bet you file your taxes on a single sheet of toilet paper. So what do you need from me? No taxes, no blowjob. What then?"

I waited until I had cleaned my plate before I answered.

15

"If you were desperate to get an abortion in this town, where would you go?"

Shannon dropped her fork. It fell to the floor. After she retrieved it she sat staring at me, her head cocked, a quizzical smile on her face.

"Are you serious?"

"I am."

"What makes you think I would know the answer to that question?"

"Would you help me find out?" I said.

She shook her head, not to reject my request, but to express astonishment. When she finally looked me in the eye, she said, "You're not talking about some back-alley butcher, are you?"

"I don't think so. More likely some kind, fatherly gynecologist who also carries on a dark side-practice."

"I'll nose around."

"Don't get it cut off," I said.

She grinned. "At least, in my case, it would only be my nose."

I said nothing.

"Come on, Stu. In your business you put more than your nose at risk.

"Sorry I can't prove to you I still retain my manhood."

Shannon let out a little sigh. "I'm sorry about that, too."

She reached across the table and rested a hand on mine. "Maybe in our next lives."

I said, "Maybe so." Even though I didn't believe in *next lives*, I didn't want to let her down.

The waitress cleared away our plates and left the bill on the table.

"Thanks for the free breakfast. I'll start looking into where I can get a quiet, upscale abortion. You got a phone booth number where I can reach you, Superman?"

I gave her a card with my answering service number on it.

"I check in a couple times a day," I said.

Mary-Margaret and her boyfriend priest knew what my car looked like, meaning I had to settle for making drive-bys every five minutes, rather than park and watch. The disadvantage to that was I might miss seeing them leave. Or worse, I would assume they were gone when they weren't. I was lucky they hadn't called the police on me the first time I was there to charge me with trespassing. As it turned out, I got luckier. Just as I was coming around a curve where her house came into my view, I saw Mary-Margaret and Father John back out of the garage attached to their house. The car was a Cadillac La Sabre.

I had stopped at a 7-Eleven to buy fresh film for my used 35mm Leica M3 camera. It was rated the best in every way, especially great for catching spouses humping non-spouses from long-distance. But Leica stopped making that model a year ago and their new model cost $1,000, well beyond my affordability.

I waited ten more minutes, in case Father John or Mary-Margaret forgot to leave the cat out, or something else, and came back to correct the issue. They didn't. So I headed straight for the free-standing garage at the rear of the property. This time the door had been padlocked, but that only slowed me down for four minutes.

Camera and flashlight at the ready, in I went. And immediately I faced a shock. All of the photos of Mary-Margaret, her co-pilot, and her Cessna 180 were gone. The wall was bare. No photo of a Woody with its New York license plate. The Studebaker was still up on blocks. So, Father John and Mary-Margaret Crowder are afraid of something. Somehow, they had a connection with Sisters Melda and Carmen for those nuns both to describe the car they saw as having California plates, So, why were all the photos missing? Because they expected me to return to the garage.

I drove to the 7-11 and used the outside telephone to call my answering service. Shannon Postlewaite had not phoned in the names of any abortion clinics, but my next-door neighbor, Mary Ann Chase, had left a message for me to phone her, adding that it was urgent. So I called.

"Sorry to bother you, Stu, but I thought you'd want to know. Fowler and Sarah are going to be driving your way. Sarah finally broke down and told Fowler that Germaine was going to have an abortion. The site is in Los Gatos. Sarah even gave me the name and address of the abortionist." She read off the information after I told her I was ready to copy it down.

"Why was Sarah telling you all of this, Mary?"

"She said she couldn't keep it in any longer. She says she broke down and told Fowler. He went into a rage and she needed to get out of her house, needed to talk to someone who would be civil to her, who would listen without ranting."

"Anything else?" I said.

"Sarah said they are going to take turns driving and drive all night. I doubt if either one of them will fall asleep at the wheel. They'll be too busy screaming at one another."

"Thanks, Mary Ann. As always, you are a saint."

"No, Stu. I'm a Protestant. I don't believe in saints."

"Nor do I. *Gracias* again and *adios*!"

I tried not to picture Fowler and Sarah driving north on the 101. I called my answering service again and this time Shannon had left a message. The name and address Mary Ann had provided me was the third abortion clinic on Shannon's list.

It was late afternoon and I figured Fowler and Sarah couldn't get to San Jose until early morning. I decided to drive by the clinic to see if they listed an opening hour on their front door. For all I knew such clinics didn't keep regular hours. But I had to check.

The clinic turned out to be in a residential area south of Blossom Hill Road in the tony suburb of Los Gatos. It was a white stucco house with a blue tile roof. Street parking only, no doctors' names or business hours listed. For all anyone could tell, it was just a family home in a family neighborhood.

After finding another pay phone, I called Shannon to thank her and told her I would be visiting the clinic in the morning.

"Where are you staying tonight?" she asked, coyly.

"I'm starting to look for a hotel already. There ought to be some near where SR 17 crosses the 85 loop."

"There's Best Western on SR17, a couple miles south of the 85."

"Great. Thanks." I was even more thankful she hadn't suggested I spend the night with her. Twenty minutes later I found the Best Western and booked a room.

A long, hot shower and a close shave scrubbed away more than dirt and whiskers. I lay down on the queen bed and realized how sleep-deprived I was. Next thing I knew I was dreaming about watching an abortion and awoke with a start. I wasn't particularly in favor of the procedure, more for the physical and psychological damage it did to a woman than to the not-yet-a-person thing growing inside of her.

I didn't quite buy the female argument that it's their bodies, therefore they can do whatever they want to themselves. As a cop in Burbank, I once confronted a self-destructive young woman who held me at bay with a hatchet and went so far as to threaten to chop off her hand if I tried to disarm her. It never crossed my mind to say to her, 'Go ahead, if that's your preference. After all, it's your body. You can do whatever you want to it."

How did that end? Even worse. She turned the blade around and swung hard, driving the blade deep into her forehead. She died in my arms, her eyes staring back at me, devoid of any shock or pain, but, rather, telling me, "It's okay, Mr. Policeman. It's okay. This is what I choose."

I sat on the edge of the bed, images of the hatchet blade intermingling with a man in a white coat, wearing a white mask, holding a coat hanger. I reached for the pint bottle of cheap whiskey I had picked up before checking into the motel.

16

Being alone in a motel room, drinking whiskey from a plastic cup, made me feel one cut above a homeless dumpster-diver. But, what the hell. That is how most people I've met view a private detective – resilient as an alley rat, but with less charm. I preferred Ross Macdonald's psycho-drama, murder-buried-in-family-history detective, Lew Archer, to Mickey Spillane's misanthropic, tough guy, Mike Hammer, but best seller lists assured me I was in the minority. I had even brought along one of Macdonald's latest, *Black Money*, and had started it while staking out Mary-Margaret Crowder's place. So far, it was proving to be one of his best.

Just as I leaned back onto a pillow and reopened the paperback novel, I heard a soft knock on my door. I doubted if it was a maid asking if I needed fresh towels. Of course, it never crossed my mind to bring my .38 special with me into the room. I always keep it under my car's dashboard.

"Who is it?" I called out.

More tapping.

I walked to the door and tried to peer through the peep hole. All I could see was three fingers, each of them wearing red nail polish. I unhooked the latch and opened the door.

"Hi, there. I'm Angie. Shannon sent me. I hope I have the right room. Are you Stu Fletcher?"

Angie was a freckled redhead, slim, busty, wearing pink-framed glasses, pinker lipstick, a décolleté yellow dress with matching stiletto heels. Large-hooped earrings. Right out of central casting for a Phillip Marlow damsel-in-need-of-a-detective movie.

"Come on in, Angie. Tell me your plight."

She crossed the threshold, sat down on the end of my bed, looked up, and said, "I don't have a plight. I think that's one of the things I lost just about the same time I was growing boobs and giving up braces on my teeth."

I tried not to laugh and wondered if that was a mistake. She was a natural comedian with an understated style. In better light I recognized that her red hair wasn't natural. But her ample boobs seemed to be real, and she was offering me a good look at the upper third of them.

"How did you know my room number?" I said.

She giggled. "I bent waaaay forward when I asked the desk clerk. I was ready to slip him a fiver, but that proved not to be necessary."

"Tell me. Why did Shannon send you?" I asked, trying not to sound rhetorical.

"She was sure you could use some company. Well, my company, that is. In addition to…." From a paper sack she pulled out a fifth of Old Overholt rye. How could I not have noticed the paper bag before now, I asked myself.

She stood and whispered into my ear, "Hadn't you better kiss me? In a minute I'll be all whiskey breath, but surely you'll want to know what the real me tastes like, won't you?"

I was right. A comedian. But I kissed her anyway and found myself struggling to keep my tongue from being swallowed.

"I thought all of Shannon's girlfriends were swishy," I said when our mouths finally untangled.

"You thought wrong."

Proving that being wrong can sometimes feel just right.

"I give a pretty good blowjob, too, if you're ready to find that out. Or would you rather we take a shower together first?"

I found myself mentally counting towels and wondering if maybe it wasn't too late to phone down to have a maid bring more. Unfortunately, I never got to rate Angie's blowjob talents. A bomb exploded in the motel parking lot just as I began to unzip Angie's yellow dress. The explosion commanded more of my attention that the lady's freckled backside.

My ego attributed the blast to someone wanting to reduce my car to cinders. With me in it perhaps. After a quick look out the window, I ordered Angie to stay put and I hustled downstairs, taking the steps three at a time. With flames rising high from the area near where I had parked, a crowd had already formed, oblivious to the possibility that another blast or blasts might occur. At least the night clerk had sense enough to remain standing inside the door, craning his neck to see what could be seen.

"Is this how guests are welcomed every night?" I asked him.

"Not hardly. We haven't had a mob-incident in months."

I took his "not hardly" as one explanation for why he was a desk clerk. "In months" was not very reassuring.

Two fire trucks and three police squad cars arrived within a few minutes. The cops shooed gawkers back while the firemen doused the flames. By then I had treated myself to a slightly closer look. The blast hadn't centered on my car, but might as well have. The driver's side of my Biscayne was scorched to the point that, had I been sitting at the wheel, I would have been as toasted as a marshmallow.

The car at ground zero was a Cadillac Coupe de Ville. Emphasis on *was.* Far too upscale for a Best Western motel, but then slumming, in itself, was not a crime. Instead, the crime everyone present was witness to a murder. Double homicide. When the fire was out and the smoke had cleared, the sight of two charred bodies in the Caddy's front seat was unmistakable.

"Jeezus, Stu. I've never seen anything like that before." Angie was standing beside me, shivering in the cold night air, though I doubted the cause of her shaking had anything to do with the temperature of the air.

I explained to the cops that the car to the right of the Caddy belonged to me and that the Coupe deVille had been parked there when I checked in.

"Ignition bomb," the police lieutenant said. "Don't suppose you set it?"

He snickered at his own graveyard humor, but, had I replied in kind, I doubt if he would have appreciated my effort. I knew cops, having been one for a few years. They're not very good at taking what they dish out.

I whispered to Angie to go back to my room before she shivered herself right out of her dress. She didn't argue as I handed her my room key. The lieutenant, whose nametag read L. Castrell, watched her walk away, then gave me a look that assured me he thought I was underserving of such a delicacy.

"Why would I park next to a car I intended to blow up?" I said.

"To throw us off the scent," he said. That made some sense, but only some.

"How then would I make my getaway? My car is no longer drivable."

"Maybe your girlfriend has a car stashed nearby."

I nodded. "Maybe she does."

"You know these people?" he said, waving his notepad toward the pair of corpses in the Cadillac.

"No. And I didn't know them before this happened either."

"Stop trying to be funny."

"I wasn't aware I was trying."

"Do I know you from somewhere?" he said, looking me over.

"Not unless you guzzle free coffee and eat your donuts in Santa Maria."

"What brings you up this way?"

"Dia de los Muertos fireworks."

That baffled him. He decided focusing on his information-gathering was suddenly more important, I imagine because he saw his captain walking toward him.

"That yours?" the captain said, pointing to my car.

I nodded glumly.

"Don't try to move it. We need to take photos."

"The only thing that's going to move my car is a tow truck."

"Hope you've got good insurance. Maybe you can file for a claim under natural disaster. Better yet, send your repair bill to Manny Salazar."

I gave the lieutenant a puzzled look.

He said, "Local big-dick honcho. Rents women by the hour, sells marijuana by the bale."

"His work?" I pointed to the Caddy.

"Most likely. Don't piss him off." Pause. "Or elbow in on one of his ladies." He jerked his head toward the motel doorway. "No free pussy, even if she agrees to give it away."

I looked again at the pair of burnt bodies in the Cadillac.

Nearby lay two others, innocent passersby who were in the wrong place at the wrong time. Only the victims' feet were visible, sticking out from the police tarpaulins. Two women wearing high heels.

Even if the cops didn't impound my car, there was little I could do at the moment. And maybe not even the next day. I knew my bare-bones insurance coverage was not going to cover my lining up a rental car. So I hoped my credit was good enough to pay for one on my own.

Returning to my room, I found Angie snuggled under the covers, half-asleep and humming a Dylan tune: "I'll be Your Baby Tonight", from his album released last year. The smell of marijuana smoke hung thick in the air. The bedside ashtray held the tiny butt of a self-rolled joint.

Neither my mind nor my body was in the mood for a sexual performance, but Angie was nude and clingy. So I did my best, while keeping one ear cocked for more threatening noises. By 3 a.m. I found myself sitting up in the dark in the room's one poorly upholstered wingback chair, wishing I had my handgun. Angie's bottle of Old Overholt was now only half full. I decided to keep it that way.

Angie finally slept soundly, waking just after seven.

"You up for another round?" she said when she returned from brushing her teeth.

"No, but please tell Shannon *'C'est un maquereau primier'*." I repeated myself and wrote it down for her.

"What's that mean?" she said, scowling as she began dressing.

"I'm telling her she's a five-star pimp." I had learned the phrase in the Army, when I was undergoing swamp training in Louisiana, in preparation for facing down the Red Chinese Army in frozen Korea.

Angie and I had just finished breakfast at the Sambo's down the street from the motel and were on our way to Angie's car, a 'beat up '65 Plymouth, when Lieutenant Castell drove up and waved for us to join him.

"We had your car towed to a junkyard, courtesy of the county. Our mechanic who looked at it declared it unfixable, short of replacing half its parts. I left a receipt at your motel desk." His gaze turned to Angie, next back to me. When he looked me in the eye he shook his head, meaning: How could you stoop so low?

Angie caught his look and gave him a middle finger.

I asked him, "Who does the Caddy belong to?"

"The pair in the car were Tina Salazar, a niece of the infamous Manny Salazar the captain told you about. In the driver's seat sat Curtis Chung, a young attorney from The City, son of big-shot lawyer Wendell Chung. The fact that we found a gook lawyer sitting next to a greaseball princess says it all. The slanty-eyed dope peddlers are trying to cut in on the spics' marijuana trade. Pretty little Tina sold out her Uncle Manny to the slopes."

A public servant full of equal-opportunity slurs. Not surprising. When I worked on the Burbank PD, white officers routinely called their fellow black and Asian officers *niggers* and *gooks* respectively. In turn, those officers referred to white cops as *honkies* and *round-eyed devils*. When whites and minorities were assigned to work together, internecine backstabbing was a daily circumstance.

"What about the Italians?" I said.

"What about 'em? The smart ones stick to peddling flesh and drugs in Reno and Las Vegas, so they don't get caught in the middle of these Spic-versus-Chink turf squabbles. Same for us. Cops from here to Sausalito try to sidestep this kind of shit. Unfortunately, when Manny decides to off a gook in a place where his dynamite brings harm to others, here we are."

"So, it's a two-way war?" I said.

The lieutenant nodded. "At least as far as importing goes. Peddling? For a while there was peaceful chopping up of territories. Even the coons were granted some action – still are -- but only up around Oakland, in the neighborhoods that make up Niggertown. Their peddlers buy from three different spic gangs, but now – as you see – the gooks are coming south, cuttin' in on the spics."

After the lieutenant gave me the address of the junkyard now in possession of my Biscayne, I asked Angie if she was willing to drive me to the abortion clinic.

"Sure. Just promise not to let anybody start waving a coat hanger at me."

I promised and wondered what I would have done, had she not been willing to chauffeur me. Asked her to drive me to a car-rental agency, I suppose. Maybe my credit rating would be good enough for me to rent a bicycle for a day or two. My Santa Maria bank had been reluctant to give me a credit card when I had applied, and when they finally did choose greed over caution, they set my maximum charge limit at their minimum. As a last resort, I could phone Amanda Reynolds and ask for an advance on the money I would be due for dealing with Father Mackenzie.

Before getting into her car, Angie leaned on the roof, looked across at me, and said, "Are all cops racist shits like that guy is?"

I said, "Yeah. Most of them. If you're not white, they'll just as soon shoot you as look at you."

"You, too?"

"No."

She nodded and slid in behind the steering wheel. Looking me in the eye, she said, "Even so, I feel safer with you knowing I'm made out of white bread."

When we arrived at the clinic, parked at the curb was Fowler and Sarah's blue '61 Dodge Dart.

17

As I walked toward them, I motioned for the Payettes to remain in their car. I was nervous because I really wasn't quite sure what to say to them. What could I tell them or ask them? Begging them to turn around and go home wasn't going to get me anywhere. And I was certain their frames of mind were as explosive as the bomb that killed two people at the Best Western motel just hours earlier.

Fowler rolled down his window.

I said, "Mary Ann told me you were headed here. Please allow me to go in to see what they're willing to tell me about Germaine."

Fowler pounded a fist on the steering wheel. "Willing to tell you? Jesus Christ, Fletcher, they'd damn well better tell you everything. If you don't walk out that door…" he pointed to the clinic's front door, "…I'll go in there and start ripping people limb from limb."

"Now, Dear," Sarah whined. "That is exactly the reason Mr. Fletcher should go in and why we should wait here until he finds out where our Germaine is."

All I could do is nod in agreement.

"All right, but make it quick, Fletcher. We didn't drive all this way to get put off," Fowler said, giving me a fierce look.

"Nor did I, Fowler."

I looked at my watch. Someone was opening the shades on the long, narrow window next to the front door. I said to the Payettes, "I'll be back as quickly as I can."

Walking toward the clinic, I gestured to Angie to sit tight, then gave her a thumbs up, meaning I had momentarily stifled Fowler Payette's urge to play the role of a charging bull seeing red. That a doctor's office was open on Saturday came as a surprise to me. I was under the impression that doctors of every kind, save those working ER, kept their weekends free. The phrase *bankers' hours* could now apply to physicians' work time as well.

I was closing the door behind me when a middle-aged woman wearing a nurses' uniform, including a traditional white nursing cap, emerged from a door marked *Private.* She stopped, sized me up in one stern look, then disappeared through a door over which read: *No Admittance.* To my left, sitting behind a sliding glass window, was a younger woman wearing casual street clothes.

She opened the window, smiled and said, "Are you with Miss Ralston?"

76

When I shook my head, she blanched, realizing she had erred in giving away a patient's name to a stranger.

"No. I am looking for Miss Payette."

The woman straightened shoulders, sat up taller, and became officious.

"Sorry, sir. Privacy laws prohibit us from discussing patients or divulging any information about them."

Another mistake on her part. Maybe she was new.

"So, Miss Payette is a patient here, right? A patient about whom you may not reveal anything, eh?"

Following a panicked blush, she stuttered, "I'm afraid I can't…can't help you, sir."

"You already have. What I want to know next is: When was Germaine Payette here? And: Where did she go after being…being treated here?"

From behind Miss Prohibited a door opened and in came the nurse I had seen moments earlier.

"Is there a problem, Sandy?" she said, looking at me.

"This man was asking about someone," Wendy said to the nurse. To me she said, "What did you say her name was again, sir?"

"Germaine Payette."

I saw a flash of recognition appear in the nurse's eyes.

However, her response to me was, "Sorry, sir. I'm not familiar with that name. And, even if I were, I would be unable to discuss any matters regarding her."

"You're not familiar with Germaine? But Sandy here just told me Germaine has been here for…. Well, you know why she was here."

The look on the nurse's face I can only describe as horrorstruck.

But Sandy spoke first. "I told him no such thing, Loretta. I swear I didn't."

Loretta couldn't decide who to eviscerate first. Me or Sandy. Likely both of us. I was glad she wasn't holding a scalpel.

Glowering at me, Nurse Loretta said, "Sir, I must ask you to leave. Otherwise, I will call the police."

"To tell them what?" I said. "That a man is here asking impertinent questions?"

She nodded, her scowl not fading.

I said, "Germaine's parents are outside. Will you speak to them? Tell them what you've done to their daughter? Tell them where she went when she left here?"

Nurse Loretta looked stunned and stood speechless, her mouth open.

I looked at Sandy and said, "Yes. Please, do phone the police. I'm sure they will side with the Payettes." If the local police force was anything like the ones in LA, there were plenty of Catholic cops, all of whom opposed the idea of abortion They especially despised the clinics that provided abortion services. So Sandy and Loretta would almost certainly be facing a hostile gendarmery.

I could almost see the gears whirling inside Nurse Loretta's head as she calculated the advantages versus disadvantages she would face, were she to allow Sandy to summon police. Finally, she said, "We have nothing more to tell you or your young woman's parents. So again, please leave us."

It was then that I noticed two sets of golf clubs leaning against the wall near where I had come in. Ignoring the two women, I walked over to the clubs. One set was a set of Wilson Staff clubs, but the other was a set made by Powerbilt. Classy and rather expensive. Something doctors could afford, but not any ordinary hacker. As I stared at the two sets of clubs the putter in the bag with the Powerbilt sticks caught my eye. I pulled the putter from the bag to get a closer look at it. The bottom of the brass-colored blade read: *Karsten, Phoenix, #7.*

No doubts after seeing that. Germaine Payette had been here. This was her putter.

Turning back to the two women, I held up the putter and shook it. "This belongs to Germaine Payette."

Loretta spoke, her voice loud and angry. "That belongs to Dr. Greenwood. Put it back."

The door marked *Private* opened. A tall man with white hair, a pencil mustache and wire-framed glasses, and wearing a red golf shirt, looked at me. "Who are you?"

After I explained who I was, I held up the putter. "I was just admiring your putter. Brand new, it looks like."

His eyes wary, the man's brain was spinning faster than Loretta's had. I could tell he was searching for just the right lie to dish up to me.

"Yes. The pro shop at my club just got a batch of new putters in and, when I tried several of them out, that one suited me best."

I replied, "What does this Karsten, Phoenix, #7 mean?"

"I assume it was made in Phoenix," he said glibly.

"What is a Karsten?" I said, feigning ignorance.

"You're not much of a golfer, are you?"

I allowed that I wasn't.

"A man named Karsten Solheim makes that kind of putter in his garage. It makes a little pinging sound when it strikes a golf ball. In fact, he calls them Ping putters."

"And the #7? What does that refer to?"

The man finally smiled. "It means that is only the seventh putter of that kind that Mr. Solheim made."

I said, "That must make it very valuable, eh?"

"Indeed!"

"Valuable enough to pay for an abortion, I suspect. Am I right?"

His smile faded.

I said, "This is Germaine Payette's putter. Her heart must have shattered when she gave it up."

Muscles in the man's face began to twitch. "I…I don't know what you are talking about."

"Of course, you know. Obviously, Germaine paid for her abortion by surrendering her beloved Ping putter to you. Tell me what kind of horrid creature would do such a thing?"

"I must ask you to leave, sir. Leave immediately, before…."

"Before you call the police? Your nurse already tried that threat. I shoved it back down her throat."

The man looked at Nurse Loretta, who dropped her gaze. Sandy, too, looked away.

"Where did Germaine go when…when you finished with her?" I said.

"I have no idea," he said.

"When did she leave?"

Silence.

"Tell me or you can tell her parents. They are waiting outside. I'm asking politely. Fowler Payette may be more inclined to bust your fancy Powerbilt driver over your head in order to get answers about his daughter."

"I don't know where she went. There was a young woman with her." He described her: Stephanie Crowder. Though I had never met Stephanie, I had seen photos of her at the Crowder home when I spoke with her mother.

I pulled out my wallet, retrieved a hundred dollars, and handed it to the doctor. "Let's just say Germaine lost her putter, you found it, and I'm graciously giving you a reward for finding it for her. Use the money to buy yourself a new putter at your pro shop."

The doctor's eyes narrowed, but he decided not to argue.

Outside, I walked to Sarah's side of their car. She rolled her window down and I waved the putter at her.

"Yes, she was here, but she's gone now." Through the window I handed Sarah the putter. "Go back home. When Germaine returns home, give that to her as a love token. Meanwhile, I promise to carry on looking for her. No charge."

Neither of the Payettes said anything. Sarah rolled her window up and I returned to Angie's car, not looking back. By the time I slid into the car seat Fowler Payette had driven away.

"So what happened?" Angie said, starting the engine.

I was in no mood to talk about it, yet Angie, given all of her help, deserved an explanation. So I told her everything that had happened.

"Jee-suz, you got *cojones*, Fletcher."

I laughed hard and thanked her. An inartistic compliment is better than none at all.

18

As we drove away from the clinic I said to Angie, "How would you like to go to a Byrds concert with me?"

"I dig The Byrds. When and where?" she said.

"Tonight in The City." *To dig.* Of beatnik origin, I assumed. Verb transitive. *To like.*

"How much are tickets? I'm just a poor girl."

"They're on me," I said.

"We have a date, Fletcher."

"I'm afraid we'll have to use your car."

"I figured that much. By the way, do you want to swing by the junkyard to retrieve anything from your car?"

"Good idea," I said. I kept a .38 special hidden under the dashboard. I hoped it was still there and still serviceable. Also, my .35mm Leica was in the glovebox, the camera I had hoped to use to photograph the photo of the 1946 Woody that had been in Mary-Margaret Crowder's garage. If the camera was gone, dare I ask Amanda to underwrite the cost of a new one? Why not? I could justify charging her, given that I had intended to photograph the Woody. If my handgun was missing, I'd stop at a pawnshop to pick up a temporary piece.

My main reason now for our going to San Francisco to The Byrds concert was not to try to find Germaine Payette, but to find Randall and Stephanie Crowder. I believed they could help me make a connection between the license plate number on the Woody in the photo and the license plate number on a Woody that Sister Melda claimed to have seen on the abduction vehicle.

When we arrived at the junk yard I recognized immediately that my poor Biscayne would never turn another mile on its odometer. It was *ganz kaput*, as my Great Uncle Heinrich would say. Totally fucked. I examined the interior of my scotched vehicle. No camera, no Smith & Wesson.

"Don't look at me," the automobile graveyard's owner told me, giving me his fiercest look of innocence when I told him some of my valuables were missing from the Chevy's interior.

"Then who should I be looking at?"

"Whatever's missing, the cops must have filched. Coppers can empty a car trunk faster than a school of piranhas can strip a man's flesh off."

Policemen competing with piranhas. What a picture that made.

The old man had a furrowed face of thick, tanned leather and his hands were as big as catcher's mitts. He shook a bat-sized forefinger at me. "My son's my tow truck driver and he ain't no thief," he said.

Ah, so many opportunities, all resisted. What a paragon of virtue his son must be. In any case, whether cops or junkyard rats stole my revolver and camera, neither was going to reappear. So I left.

"No luck?" Angie said as she drove us away.

"The owner assured me the police took them before his son towed my car away."

"A thieving cop? Come on," she joked.

"In Burbank, squad car patrolmen had their very own thriving black market in goods lifted from cars they stopped and examined. They even had a central drop-off site. So they never brought items they confiscated back to the police properties check-in. They used the back room of a small furniture store owned by the brother of one of the lieutenants."

Angie said, "*Confiscated.* I like that. Sounds official. Even legal."

"Sometimes it was, but most often the men in uniforms might just as well have been thugs in police costumes, masquerading as rogue cops. Holdup men. Cops as robbers. And not just occasionally but regularly."

"To serve, protect, and confiscate," Angie mocked.

Near the salvage yard I spotted a pay phone. I called my car insurance company and explained what had happened. They promised to send an adjuster to examine the Biscayne on Monday. No offer came for me to rent a car to return to Santa Maria and to carry on until they could cut a check for me to find and purchase a replacement for my beloved Biscayne.

I then called Amanda to fill her in on the highlights and lowlights of my trip so far.

"Did you take a photograph of the license plate on the Woody?"

"No. The priest and Mary-Margaret had cleaned out the garage by the time I fetched my camera and returned. The entire wall of photos was gone. At least that will be harder to explain than if they had only removed the Woody photo."

Through the telephone line I could almost hear her brain whirring. Finally, she said, "I'm glad you're safe, Stu. Stay that way," was her terse reply after I had finished my monologue. I translated her succinctness to mean she was unhappy, although I wasn't. I had found a connection between the Crowders and the missing girls.

An hour later Angie and I got caught in football traffic on El Camino Real in Palo Alto. I should have checked a newspaper, but I didn't. The Stanford Indians had just finished playing Oregon State. I turned on Angie's car radio briefly to learn the game's score. OSU 29, Stanford 7. The traffic was relentless, so I asked Angie to pull off and look for a site for lunch. Eventually Angie spotted a Sambo's. The wait for a booth was 20 minutes, but two side-by-seats at the counter were vacant. So we hustled to take them before the hostess could object.

Afterwards, as we drove through Atherton, a few miles closer to The City, I saw a policemen-only gun dealer called The Copper Bullet. Angie waited in the car while I went in to see if I could pull a bluff. In my wallet I still carried an ID showing me to be a member of the Burbank California PD. I didn't turn it in when I left the force and no one asked for it back.

The man behind the counter was dusting off the rack of rifles lined up behind the counter. A bell had jingled when I entered the store but he paid it no mind, his feather duster continuing to whisk away. I had to clear my throat loudly to get his attention.

"Oh, sorry. I missed hearing the bell. I'm a tad hard of hearing. We didn't used to have to wear safety plugs in our ears, you know."

His nametag read: Buster. I estimated the man to be on the high side of fifty years old. Thin black hair, giving way to gray. He had a chaw in his mouth. The wrinkles in his blue shirt told me he was single. No self-respecting wife would allow him out of the house wearing such a tatty garment.

I told him, "I'm looking for a S&W 640."

"Got one right over here. Have you used one before?"

A test question. Was I a cop?

"Homicide detective. Burbank."

"Whatcha doing up in these parts?"

I grinned. "I'm looking to buy a revolver."

"Lose yours?"

"Left it at home. My weekend off. I came up for the Stanford game. My son's a student at Stanford."

"So whadda you need a new gun for? Gonna shoot one of them know-it-all Commie professors?"

"I wish I had the time," I said, playing along with his redneck attitude. "But no. I got a call from my department wanting me to check out a guy who slipped through our fingers a few months back. Robbed and killed an elderly couple who ran a mom-and-pop grocery. Burbank got a tip that he might be hiding out in San Mateo. Asked me to see if there's anything to it."

"Sounds legit. Show me some ID."

I handed over my fake identification.

"I got a cousin who works vice in Santa Ana. Ed Grissup. Know him?"

"Santa Ana's too far south. I never get close to it."

"Ed says Santa Ana's got more spic whores that you could fuck in a lifetime. How 'bout Burbank?"

"I'm not sure. I've never worked vice."

Out of the blue he asked me, "Who's that woman behind the wheel of your car out front?"

So. A curtain-twitcher. He wasn't an enthusiastic shotgun duster after all.

"My younger sister. She lives in Santa Clara. I flew up from Burbank. How much for the revolver?"

"Sixty bucks."

"Sold. And a box of ammunition."

"Ammo's extra."

"Yes. I assumed it was. I'll want a kit to clean it, too. Do you take cash?"

A huge red sign on a far wall read: Cash only. Buster pointed toward the sign.

"I know. I saw it when I came in. I'm a detective. I get paid to be observant." I said all of that in a jesting tone of voice, hoping Buster possessed more of a sense of humor than most rednecks.

As he wrapped up my purchases he said, "Your sister goin' with you to San Mateo?"

I said, "She has a friend in Foster City. She'll stay with the friend while I take her car and check out the suspect."

"Too bad your son's gettin' brainwashed by them Commie professors. Expensive brain-washin' at that."

"Well, he hopes to go to med school after he graduates."

"What kinda doctor is he gonna be?"

"He hopes to become a podiatrist," I said, just to humor the man.

"What the hell is a pod? And how do you fix one?"

"A podiatrist is a foot doctor."

He laughed. "Hell's bells. After he graduates tell him to come look at Buster Holcamp's feet. I got bunions growing on top of bunions. Pretty soon I'll be hobbling on a goddamn cane."

"Thanks, Buster. I'll tell my son to drop by and check your feet out."

"Hope you find that grocery store killer and put a bullet up his ass. Better yet, put five. Empty the damned cylinder."

A S&W 640 is a snub-nosed five-shot pistol. Compact, weighing less than a pound and a half, I can tuck one into the small of my back. The downside to the model is that it has no manual safety. So, there's always a chance I'd end up shooting myself in the ass.

19

Finding an open parking space anywhere in San Francisco is always a challenge. Then, after finding a space, out-of-towners must always try to remember: Does one, for safety's sake, turn one's front wheels in or out? Facing downhill, if the car slips into neutral and begins to roll, by turning the wheels in it will roll onto the sidewalk. Out? The car would roll out into the street. So turn them in. Do the opposite when facing uphill. Angie knew without my explaining it to her.

The place we found to park was next to the Sergeant John Macaulay Park, six blocks from Avalon ballroom. The ballroom is on the second floor of a two-story building at the corner of Sutter and Van Ness. From Macaulay Park we walked up Larkin, crossed Geary, Cedar, Post, then Hemlock before coming to Sutter. Turning left of Sutter we could see what we supposed was the line forming for the concert. An icy wind off the ocean whistled at us.

"How am I going to get a ticket to this event? I heard it was sold out," Angie said.

"There'll be scalpers. Some hippie willing to forgo live music in favor of dope money will offer us a deal," I said.

"How can you be sure?" she said.

"Love may be free among this crowd, but marijuana isn't. Long-haired dope dealers are as greedy as any Wall Street banker. They need money to buy drugs. Supply and demand rules the market here, too."

"Except for pussy," Angie said, poking me in my ribs. She thought for a moment as we continued walking toward the queue, then asked, "If these women are giving it away, how do they decide who gets the prize?"

I poked her in her ribs before asking, "How did you decide on me?"

After further thought she told me, "I lined six guys up and decided you looked to be the neediest," she said, followed by a cheesy grin.

As we neared the line, I was right. Two scalpers approached us, waving tickets.

The first one to reach us gestured with his pair of tickets at the scalper behind him, "That guy's tickets are counterfeit. Don't trust him."

I said, "Give me a reason to trust that yours aren't phony."

He ignored me. "Ten bucks apiece."

He reeked of marijuana and his reddish beard needed to be combed to rake away the crumbs from whatever he had nibbled on recently. His granny glasses had fingerprint smudges on both lenses. His woven snow cap needed mending and the hair that hung down over his ears was as greasy as a ten-cent burger. And this guy wanted me to trust him. The face value of the tickets he waved at me was three dollars.

"I'll give you five. And I only want one."

"They're a wedded pair," he said. "No divorce."

The fellow behind him pushed him aside. "I'll sell you one for six dollars."

The second young man was just a scruffy, but his winning smile made the sale. I pulled out my wallet and handed him a five and a one.

"You'll be sorry," warned scalper number one.

I gave him a shrug.

"Is the ticket for your chick?" he said. "You're kind of old to be a tambourine man."

I sang to him, *On to my own parade cast your dancin' spell my way.*"

He gave me a look of astonishment before saying, "Cool, man. You qualify after all. Peace be with you."

As we walked away, Angie said to me, "What was that all about?"

Feeling full of myself, I sang her "Mister Tambourine Man" in its entirety.

When I finished, she grinned and said, "Cool, man. Peace be with you."

My plan was for Angie and me to be the last ones to enter the ballroom. The last ones with tickets, that is. First, I wanted to camp out near the stairway entrance in order to try to spot Germaine Payette.

"Give me a better idea what this chick looks like."

I described Germaine as best as I could, having seen her so seldom.

"Thanks, but does she have big tits? A fat ass?"

"Neither."

"I'm bettin' she died her hair before she went into that coat-hanger clinic. Maybe even cut it. What color was it? And how long?"

"Brunette. Shoulder-length."

"So, we're lookin' for short hair. A blonde or a redhead. My money's on blonde."

I jokingly said, "How can you bet? You told me you didn't have any money."

"Gas money. I can't spend that on a concert ticket and expect to get back home."

Apparently, Angie had forgotten that I paid for her to fill her car's gas tank before leaving Santa Clara.

"Just kiddin'. Still, you look for blondes, I'll look for redheads. Okay?"

I nodded and we both scanned the crowd that milled as loosely as cattle, rather than form an orderly line.

We passed several minutes silently watching before Angie tapped me and pointed across the street. "Isn't that the couple I saw sittin' in the car at the abortion clinic? The parents?"

Sure enough. Fowler and Sarah Payette stood together, scouting the crowd. How was it they knew their daughter planned to come here? I hadn't told them. And certainly Germaine hadn't told them. Had they contacted the Crowders? Had they been handed deific insight? If so, why hadn't their God whispered to them sooner? In time for them to stop Germaine from aborting her fetus? All part of the *God works in mysterious ways* tenet, I supposed.

Less mysteriously, as I stared at the Payettes, another pair I recognized walked past Fowler and Sarah, oblivious to who the Payettes were. I was looking at Mary-Margaret Crowder and the man she called Father John. Just then the doors leading to the Avalon ballroom opened, and I lost sight of both pairs, neither of whom had tickets to the concert, unless, like me, they made deals with the scalpers.

While speculating whether Fowler or Father John dared to buy tickets from street vendors, I caught sight of Germaine, walking hand-in-hand with the pair I assumed to be the younger Crowders. And, indeed, I recognized Germaine only barely, by her spindly shoulders, red eyeglasses, and high forehead, above which hung a mop of straw-blonde hair, cut pixie length. Hail Angie's divination! Hail Fletcher's keen detecting skills!

<h1 style="text-align:center">20</h1>

Except for the red eyeglass frames, Germaine's appearance was unlikely to draw her parents' attention. But, lucky for Germaine, red frames were "in", to use a hippie term. Within minutes I counted eleven women wearing them. Soon enough Germaine and her companions joined the ballroom queue and the lad I guessed to be Randall Crowder put an arm around Germaine. She reciprocated his gesture of affection by patting his arm. The sister, Stephanie, snuggled up to Randall on his other side. Taking Angie by a hand, I pulled her to where we cut in line just in front of Germain and her friends.

"Why, Mr. Fletcher," Germaine said, above the cries of several people objecting to my crashing the line.

"Germaine. Good to see you."

"What brings you here?" she said, though her look suggested she had an inkling why I now stood in front of her.

"Your parents sent me."

She shook her head. "How did they know I was here?"

"They didn't. I was the one who figured it out." I gestured and said, "This is Angie. She brought me here. My car…uh…had some difficulties."

Germaine gave Angie a little wave and said "Hi." Angie reciprocated.

"These are my friends, Randall and Stephanie."

"Yes, I know," I said. "Crowders."

I shook Randall's hand. Stephanie simply gave me a wan smile by way of acknowledgement.

"Angie and I have concert tickets. I don't intend to disrupt your reason for being here, but, Germaine, I would like to talk to all three of you afterwards, say over coffee in Palo Alto."

"Talk about what?" Stephanie said.

"You father's cousin Morgan from New York."

Stephanie and Randall both tensed.

"Teddy showed me Uncle Francis's diary," I said, which wasn't precisely true, but close enough.

Randall said, "Have you told anyone else?"

89

I didn't want to be cagy and lose their willingness to commit to talking afterwards but saying no might suggest to them their knowledge was still safe and give them risky ideas. My merely hesitating in answering, however, was enough to make Randall uncertain in his calculating how to deal with me.

"Okay. We'll talk," he said, and gave his sister a nod meant to coax her into acceding.

The ballroom was raucous by the time a warm-up band came onstage and began to play. I missed hearing the name of the group and, thankfully, they kept their set brief. The Byrds opened with "Old Blue", followed by "Mr. Spaceman". Randall, Stephanie, and Germaine quickly got into the mood of the rest of the youthful audience and began clapping, swaying, and singing along. Angie bobbed gently and clapped softly. I contented myself with a bit of clapping, trying but failing to recall the lyrics.

Most rock-band guitarists are skinny creatures. If there is an overweight player it is almost always the drummer. But David Crosby was a guitarist for The Byrds and was so overweight I feared he would have a heart attack before the night was over.

An hour passed, though to me it seemed like a day and a half, before the band finished their concert by playing "Nashville West", although neither San Francisco nor the band's songs struck me as anything resembling the Nashville I had visited several years back. Maybe the band had some other place in mind, some other tunes.

"There's a back door," I repeated to Angie, Germaine, and the Crowder siblings. I pointed in that direction. They followed. As other patrons pushed and shoved their ways toward the same exit, I motioned for the four to wait inside while I looked around outside, checking for Germaine's parents and the Crowders' aunt and her companion. When I saw neither pair, I motioned for Germaine and the young Crowders to follow me.

Dozens of other attendees also knew of the rear exit, so we were all a block and a half from the Avalon before we had separated ourselves from the last sing-along group loudly serving up an off-key rendition of "Mr. Tambourine Man", which, oddly I thought, The Byrds had not included in their concert.

After waking another half block we stopped to allow Germaine to catch her breath. Getting an abortion and attending a rock concert on the same day? Insane to me, but the three of them had planned it all long before they left Santa Julietta. Not my business to tell them it was poor planning. My job was to return Germaine safely home.

Randall Crowder politely asked, "Who are you anyway? I mean, Germaine said you are her parents' neighbor, but why are you here?"

I patiently explained the Payettes' having asked me to seek out their daughter. Randall and Stephanie nodded understandingly. Next I repeated my conversation with Teddy Crowder regarding the murder and burial of Morgan Crowder.

"What? Why is my little sister telling a stranger a family secret?"

On her knees, taking deep breathes, Germaine finally paused and said, "He's a detective, Randall."

Randall said, "Well, so? What business does he have sticking his nose into my family's affairs?"

Germaine spelled *m-u-r-d-e-r* for him. She then began to cry.

"It's just a brief recollection in a diary," Stephanie said.

"A story you and your brother are excited either to confirm or disconfirm. Right?" I said.

"You are a real detective?"

I dug out my wallet and showed them my state license.

"No police," Randall said. "At least not until we know for sure."

I reluctantly agreed, but said, "If there is a body, you can't wait too long. Waiting won't look good for you."

Randall looked to Stephanie, who gave him a nod. "Okay. It's a deal."

Germaine at last stood and nodded that she was ready to carry on. After a long walk we found our cars. All the while I had continued to scan the crowded sidewalks for both the Payettes and for Mary-Margaret and her creepy, collared friend. Germaine refused to separate herself from the young Crowders and I wanted to ride with Randall in order to question him further and to make sure he didn't try to get away from me. Angie ended up driving alone. She said she didn't mind and allowed that, that if Randall drove slowly I rode shotgun while Randall drove and kept a sharp eye in his rearview mirror so as not to lose Angie. Germaine enough, she could follow him with no difficulty.

Germaine slept in the backseat with her head resting in Stephanie's lap. During the drive Randall and Stephanie both opened up more about their Uncle Morgan. Just over an hour later we stopped at a Denny's in Redwood City.

Listening to them reminded me of how much I was glad to be out of The City, glad to breath air not filled with language I barely understood. Not Bob Dylan's music, which was fuzzy enough, but with the lingo that now made up the everyday babble on the campuses of Berkeley, Stanford and other less chic Bay Area towers of ivory and ivy.

I, for certain, was not a *hip cat*. I wasn't *far out,* let alone *rad.* I wasn't exactly *The Man.* Nor was I a member of the *fuzz* any longer. I didn't *hang loose, smoke grass,* or *burn rubber.* Nor did I have an *old lady,* let alone one who was *choice* or *foxy,* or had a *classy chassis*, or was built like *brick shithouse*. That in itself was a *bummer,* making me at best a *wet rag* and probably qualifying me as a *spaz.*

21

By the time we reached Redwood City I had listened to Randall and Stephanie repeat what they remembered from reading Uncle Francis's diary. I took notes while Randall proved he could drive, remember, and talk, all at the same time. Stephanie sat behind her brother and Germaine slept. Angie seemed to have no difficulty following us.

Randall and Stephanie had been unwilling to rip the relevant pages from their dead uncle's diary, but between the two of them they had made copious notes, padded by excellent memories.

According to them Morgan Crowder had driven down from Palo Alto in his Woody with roommate Lennie Camden to attend a party hosted by Uncle Jude's fraternity on the campus of Santa Clara University. Jude, and Mary-Margaret were present, along with Francis, of course. Nearly everyone drank to excess. Bowls of vodka-laced punch required refilling frequently. Morgan Crowder, according to what Mary-Margaret told Francis later, had downed at least seven 12-oz. cupsful. Lennie's consumption wasn't far behind.

One of Jude's fraternity brothers found Morgan slumped over an upstairs toilet and, unable to get a response from him, fetched Francis to check out Morgan's condition. Francis quickly determined that his condition was *dead.* So he quickly summoned Mary-Margaret and Jude to make a three-person decision about what to do next.

They decided to carry his body down a back stairway and stuff him into his car. Lennie Camden, who had passed out at the sight of Morgan's state, was also dragged to the Woody. This only after Jude warned that, if left behind, Lennie would portray events to authorities that might well differ from the collective accounts of Jude and Mary-Margaret. Francis's diary, Randall said, reported that there was a lengthy discussion regarding what to do with Morgan's body and with Lennie.

According to Stephanie, Francis wrote that there was a serious disagreement among the siblings. First, they argued about what to do with Morgan's body. Jude argued for not calling authorities. He then insisted to use the phrase Francis penned in his diary.

As to what to do with Lennie, Jude insisted Lennie must not be allowed to speak to authorities. When Francis asked how they were going to prevent that, Jude drew a finger across his throat. No one argued against that, because, per Francis, no one wanted to cross Jude.

93

Immediately Jude strangled Lennie, which made Mary-Margaret gag and leave the room. Once he determined Lennie was dead, Jude asked, "Where?" To answer that they needed   Mary-Margaret. Francis retrieved her and she suggested sinking both men's bodies, along with the Woody, in the North Crystal Springs Reservoir, which lay in a vast wildlife refuge, between Redwood City and Half Moon Bay.

Jude dismissed that notion, saying the reservoir was surely fenced in, it's gates locked. Also, Jude had said, the reservoir might be dragged or drained as part of the search for the missing men.

Mary-Margaret then recommended burying the two men somewhere on the newly created Stevens Canyon Country Club. Development of the club's golf course was barely underway. There were excavations and soft dirt spread out over many acres. When Francis asked what to do with the Woody, Jude said he could drive it to LA, where he could make it disappear.

As for burial in the country club, Jude said the site of the country club excavations was much closer to where they were and no one was likely ever to go digging up parts of a country club.

Jude added that he would put phony California plates on Morgan's car before driving it to LA. Once there, he said he could hide it temporarily until he could dispose of it via a Mexican chop shop. The car would disappear, piece by piece, into Mexico before Santa Clara police got around to notifying border authorities.

The fake story they all agreed on to tell authorities was that Morgan and Lennie had left the party early. Morgan, the false story went, was eager to work on an essay analyzing one of Shakespeare's sonnets for his English literature seminar at Stanford. Lennie had agreed to help him. No one had seen them since they drove away.

The country club burial site Mary-Margaret had suggested was on a piece of land west of the town of Cupertino, at the foot of Monte Bello Ridge, part of the low, coastal Santa Cruz mountain range. The land was being developed into what was being called Stevens Canyon Country Club. Bulldozers were at work daily, moving dirt, reshaping the open end of the canyon into eighteen championship holes that was intended to become one of the finest new courses in the Bay Area.

Randall added that Francis claimed Jude, Mary-Margaret, and himself went to the course the next evening at sundown, after all the workers had left. Jude decided the best site on the course was at the back of the third tee, back where low-handicap players teed off. That are had been freshly bulldozed.

"So they killed Lennie Camden, right?"

"Not *they*. Jude strangled him." Stephanie said quietly.

"But Mary-Margaret and Francis were all witnesses to the murder, right?"

Randall and Stephanie both nodded solemnly.

<h1 style="text-align:center">22</h1>

At Denny's Stephanie drew me a map on the back of her napkin. From El Camino Real, we could go west on Edgewood Road, then right on Canada Road and be at the Stevens Canyon golf club in no more than fifteen minutes.

The food we ordered seemed to reflect the moods we were in. Stephanie, Randall, and I ordered full breakfasts. Angie ordered coffee and a muffin. Germaine ordered toast and tea. I thought Germaine belonged in a hospital and said so. Germaine was adamantly opposed.

"I want to go home."

Stephanie patted her hand and said, "I know you do, Gemmy. I wish we could all be home, snug in our beds."

Germaine's eyes were more yellow than my over easy eggs when they arrived. At minimum she needed sound sleep. Next door to Denny's was a motel that looked like it rated several cuts above *fleabag* and its pink vacancy sign was still flashing. I laid three hundred dollars in front of Angie.

"Get three rooms next door, then tell me if what's left over will pay for your driving Germaine to Santa Maria and Stephanie to Santa Julietta tomorrow."

"Jesus, Fletcher, with this much, I can drive them both to Tijuana."

I gave Angie a dirty look.

"Oops. Sorry."

We both knew that Tijuana was the leading site for California girls to get abortions. Germaine knew it, too.

"Yes, Stu. I'll drive them both home."

"Good. Let's all get some sleep. In the morning Randall and I will go in search of the missing Morgan Crowder. Stephanie, call your parents and assure them you're fine, but please tell them as few details as possible."

Stephanie said, "I'll tell them Randall had car troubles. He'll be along when he'll be along."

"Good."

Randall said to Angie, "Two rooms will do. I want to be close to Gem. I'll sleep on a chair."

I said to Angie, "Order him a fold-out cot."

After that, small talk didn't seem in order to any of us. So when our food arrived we ate in silence.

Randall insisted on paying for everyone. I left the tip.

Angie and I snuggled up together and quickly fell asleep. After we checked out in the morning she gave me a goodbye hug. "Good luck finding the ghost and, whatever goes down, don't decide you need to be too big a hero, cowboy. You've done enough for one trip."

"No heroics. I promise."

In the morning Gem, Stephanie, and Randall said their goodbyes quickly, although Randall took an extra moment to hug Germaine and brush lips with her. Angie gave me a look that suggested she had just then figured out who had impregnated Germaine.

After we grabbed coffee and donuts at a donut shop near Denny's, I drove Randall's Caddy while he held his notes in one hand and his sister's napkin map in the other. The big car steered like an aircraft carrier, making me change my mind about wanting to own one. The general election was two days away and the absence of political signs on the backroads was refreshing. A couple of miles down Wexler Road Randall pointed to an opening on the left side in what had been a half-mile of thick scrub oaks. The way was well-trodden, its being the tradesmen's entrance to the country club and now the ruts were even deeper from having golf-course building equipment coming and going day after day.

"Turn in there."

I eased the car onto what amounted to nothing more than a wide grassy pathway leading into a dense forest. I fumbled around looking for the Caddy's headlight switch.

"Three tenths of a mile along this sumptuous highway," Randall joked.

"Half speed or full?"

"Please, be careful with my car, Mr. Fletcher."

"Gentle as she goes, Kemo Sabe."

"Thank you."

I slowed the car when the odometer had turned over three tenths.

"Randall, tell me again what the diary said regarding what happened to the Woody?"

"Uncle Jude put some phony California plates on it and moved it to LA."

"After which…?"

Randall said, "Jude's a criminal defense lawyer. He's always defending guys accused of running chop shops."

Chop shops. Mexicans running disassembly lines. What a waste of a fine-looking automobile. But too risky to take across the border as a complete Woody. It would have, by then, been on the Border Patrol's missing-car list.

So, how was it that Morgan Crowder's Woody reemerged in the telling of the disappearance of two young girls at the Convent of Santa Franchesca Ornella in Santa Julietta? A Woody getaway-abduction car with California license plates bearing the same numbers as the New York numbers on Morgan's Woody. Had Morgan's car not been dismantled in a chop shop, thus allowing it to be used in a double kidnapping? Was the criminal defense attorney Jude Crowder connected to that trail, as Francis's diary claimed? If he took the Woody from Santa Clara to LA, how did it end up back in Santa Julietta? Who took it there? Jude Crowder? Or some connection of his? And why was the Woody used in a kidnapping? And why were those particular girls kidnapped? Is there something Wendy Ellen Sheldon is not telling me? Her relation to Jude Crowder, perhaps?

"Stop a second, Mr. Fletcher. I want to get out so I can look for some tree markings Uncle Francis wrote about."

I stopped in a clearing, ahead of which was a grove of low, scruffy poplars, their trunks only thick enough to carve symbols on vertically. We hadn't reached the excavation for the golf course yet. Morgan Crowder had allegedly been buried somewhere ahead in 1950, nearly two decades ago.

"There! On that big tree straight ahead. Roman numerals for 3. Perhaps referring to the third hole. Uncle Francis wrote of such a tree carving he and the others passed when looking for the third hole on the course. We're headed in the right direction." Randall ran toward the tree and motioned for me to follow. So I dropped the Cadillac into low gear and edged forward.

"Why the third hole?" I said.

Randall said "I don't know. He never mentions it again in his diary."

"Okay."

The path turned and fifty yards further down the track Randall pointed to something on the ground. I rolled my window down and stuck my head out. "What are you pointing at?"

Randall yelled, "A painted rock. Blue. Exactly where Francis said it would be. It's probably a reference point for the course's architect."

I edged the car forward until Randall gestured for me to stop. When he came to me he said, "According to Francis's account, the course's third tee is thirty steps forward from the painted rock. Are you up for digging, or shall I?"

I could see a clearing ahead. So on I drove.

Randall ran ahead. Then held up both hands.

When I pulled up beside him, he said, "This is it. Look out there."

To my right the clearing opened wider and wider. Beyond lay an expanse of bulldozed dirt for several hundred yards.

I turned the engine off and stood beside Randall.

Nailed to a tree on the far side of the clearing was a sign twisted at an angle. In rough letters it read: *Third tee box*.

We walked to the back of the clearing and looked around.

I said, "The dirt is all soft back to here." I pointed to where the course-builders' digging had stopped. Beyond lay hard forest soil.

Excited, Randall began scraping soil. Watching him, I thought again of Germaine. She had nibbled at her food when we were at Denny's. I could see that she was still weak from her ordeal. If a hospital was out of the question, a long restful drive back to Santa Maria was what the poor girl needed. Thankfully, not with her parents. Had she gone home with them, I could picture Fowler and Sarah playing the blame game at the top of their voices all the way home. Sleeping with Stephanie's lap for a pillow, while Angie drove south down Hwy 101 was as restful a day as she was going to get.

"I brought two shovels. You have the keys," Randall called.

I fetched the shovels.

"How deep? Does the diary say?" I asked.

"Not very. Uncle Francis wrote that the dead men were buried one atop the other, and that the grave was shallow."

I began peeling away the grassy layer next to where Randall dug. Beneath the grass roots the ground was a mixture of sand and dirt, easier shoveling than I expected. We were somewhere near the San Andreas Fault, as it worked its way north from LA. I had read that sandy soil made earthquake waves travel faster and more powerfully through sandy soil.

In the late 1950's the Brooklyn Dodgers and the New York Giants moved to California. Baseball humor had it that, given the slow northward movement of one of the fault's tectonic plates, in fifteen million years the LA Dodgers and the San Francisco Giants would once again be crosstown rivals.

23

Twenty minutes of digging left Randall and me with the conclusion that no bodies were buried there. Had Francis misunderstood his siblings? Or had they deliberately lied to him? And if the latter, why?

"Stephanie, Teddy, and I all saw the diary entry. It read: At the very back of the third tee box."

I said, muttering to myself, but loud enough for Randall to hear me, "Might the club have lengthened the tee box since the time when the club first opened? We can't really dig up the whole tee box. This back tee must be fifteen yards long."

He said, "I don't know." Dropping his shovel, he added, "Could be they added this whole back tee box sometime after the course was finished and opened for play. That would mean the middle tee box was the original back tee."

I said, "So, do we start digging at the back of the middle tee, or…."

"Or what?" Randall said, pointing his flashlight at me.

"What we probably should have done in the first place. Go to the Santa Clara police and talk to whoever works cold cases."

"Damn it! I would like to avoid dragging the cops into this."

I said, "Because the result of that will mean Jude and Mary-Margaret might end up getting arrested?"

"Yes. I want to protect them, but…. I know what they did was wrong."

I said, "If they get a good lawyer, they could all plead ignorance. And do you know what *habeus corpus* means?"

"Yeah. Produce the body."

"Exactly."

"They could claim Francis's entire story is a fairy tale. They could claim that they all were convinced of the original story, that Morgan and Lennie disappeared. Eloped maybe."

"Not funny. This is my family we're talking about."

"I apologize."

Randall rammed his shovel into the ground, cursed, then stared off into the middle distance. I could guess what he was thinking: What next?

I offered him my opinion.

"We need to take this story to the Santa Clara police, Randall. Nothing good will come of your trying to protect your aunt and uncles."

"The cops have been flummoxed for over twenty years. Why not let it continue?"

Flummoxed?

"Because, given what you know, your continued silence becomes a crime," I said.

"I don't want to see Jude and Mary-Margaret go to jail," Randall wailed.

"Shhh! I think someone is coming. Let's get out of here."

We retreated into the woods behind the tee box before stopping to listen. Multiple high-pitched voices came from down the third fairway. Looking through the trees we could see flashlights. As the figures came closer I thought I convinced myself the voices belonged to children. Or teenagers maybe. Definitely not police in search of a pair of would-be grave robbers.

Unable to use our flashlights, lest we give ourselves away to whoever was out there, Randall and I bumbled and stumbled our way back to his car. Neither of us spoke until Randall turned on his flashlight to open the trunk.

He whispered, "Are you sure we have to go to the police with this?"

I said, "Yes."

We put the shovels in trunk and, as he slammed the lid shut, he let out a loud, "Shit!"

24

Santa Clara County had two detective divisions, according to the dog-eared phone book that dangled from a chain outside the 7-11 where I placed my call. I was directed to the cop shop in Cupertino.

I gave Randall the directions and he nodded. Then he began to cry.

"If only they hadn't killed Lennie Camden. What they did wouldn't be so bad then, would it? I mean, if they had only buried Morgan, that's not so bad, is it? But what they did to Lennie I can't forgive. Why? Why did they kill him? What was going through their minds?"

"Hard to guess," I said. "Why can you forgive them about Morgan?"

"Because they didn't kill him, according to Francis's diary. They merely got rid of his body."

"Why do you suppose they did that?" I said.

"If the world knew how he died, it might damage the family's reputation. And I know how sensitive Dad and his siblings are about protecting the Crowder name."

I said, "If the world finds out they are murderers, their reputation will start circling the toilet bowl pretty damned fast."

"Do you think by now they feel remorse, Mr. Fletcher? Do you think any of them, all of them, have begged God for forgiveness?"

"Let us hope so."

"Mr. Fletcher, you were once a policeman, right?"

"I was. Yes."

"Did you ever shoot anyone, then sometime afterwards, wonder if you had done the right thing? Or is that too painful a question for me to ask of you?"

"Painful? Yes. Very much so. But, if it will help you to understand, I'm willing to tell you."

We rode in silence for a while and it all came back to me. The first occurrence, I told him, was when I was a cop in Burbank. I had to shoot a man who was trying to kill me. His name was Arturo Mendez and he turned out to be a father with five young children. Additionally, however, he was also a major LA drug distributor for one of the Mexican syndicates. "

I lowered my voice, saying, "I also killed his wife, Bonita, but not intentionally. She jumped into my line of fire when my target was her husband. That I turned her children into orphans might have devastated me, except I knew she had been selling heroin to the cheerleaders of an all-black high school in Compton."

Randall said, "What happened to the children?"

"The Mendez's five children became wards of California's Child Protective Service, which placed the kids a step up from the lives they had been living. Still, I felt conflicted over both of those killings, despite being cleared by a police board of inquiry and by a superior court judge.

I continued.

"My worst case of tortured conscience came when a Hispanic high school kid by the name of Enrico Castro, crazed out on a combo of illicit drugs, walked toward me in a dim alley firing a black-market sub-machine gun. His volleys went over my head, then he stopped to reload. I stepped out and dropped him, centering three shots into his midsection. He was dead by the time I reached him. Afterwards I learned the young man was an honor student and a star fullback on his high school team. Why he traded those glories for white-powder highs, I could not fathom. Unlike many in his school, he had a promising future. He already had received football scholarship offers from Stanford, Berkeley, and UW."

I went on, "Enrico was not a member of any gang, but his older brother, Tomas, was. A sister, Elena, told me, when she came to the morgue to identify Enrico. She added that Enrico was sometimes influenced by Tomas, even though Tomas had spent five of the past six years in prison in Soledad.

"No matter that Enrico was smart and well-liked, he still believed he had to prove his manhood to Tomas. The code of machismo," Elena told me. "Men, they are so stupid," she said, looking me in the eye.

A few women, too, I could have added, but didn't.

"God, I wish I had stayed at home and never have come up here," Randall said.

"I'm sure you do. However, you can't turn the clock back," I reminded him just before Santa Clara detectives took Randall and me into separate interrogation rooms.

My cop's name was Skip Prendergast. A walrus mustache almost made up for his balding pate. He was fiftyish with a belly that suggested a fondness for beer.

"Burbank. Former homicide detective. You left at the height of the corruption-gone-wild scandals. Were you disgusted by it? Or part of it?"

"Disgust."

"You didn't try to sign on somewhere else?" he said.

"No one who walked away felt or looked clean. Other cities treated all of us who ditched as guilty until proven innocent and no one wanted to expend the effort it would take to prove innocent anyone who walked."

"From the beginning, tell me how you are mixed up in the case of the missing Morgan Crowder."

I began with my intent to search for Germaine Payette and my conversation with Teddy Crowder. I was going to omit telling him anything about the photos that had disappeared from the garage wall. Those, I told myself, belonged exclusively to the case of the missing orphans in Santa Julietta. But then I changed my mind. I needed all the help I could get.

When I finished Detective Prendergast said, "Given what you've told me, Fletcher, if it fits what the Crowder boy in the next room tells us, this may end up being a case of failing to report and the mishandling of a corpse, plus wasting authorities time by failing to come forward. We have our own forensic team digging where you and the young man had started. I sure as hell hope they find a couple of skeletons, one of them that of Mr. Crowder. I'm guessing we can begin to look for Miss Mary-Margaret Crowder and her padre boyfriend, not to arrest them, but to ask them what they know and don't know, what they did and didn't do. I gather Miss Mary-Margaret has a brother who is a criminal defense attorney in LA."

By mid-afternoon the detectives decided Randall and I were free to go. We decided to return to Mary-Margaret's house, where I hoped to search for the pictures of the Woody. Next, Randall would drive me to a used car lot, where I would try to find a car that would suit both my temperament and my budget.

Everything went according to plan until I phoned Skip Prendergast six hours later. The forensic team had found nothing at the golf course. Prendergast had also visited Mary-Margaret, who then had telephoned her brother Jude to ask him to speak with the detective.

"Did I ever get an earful. He tells me his brother Francis was a weak link in our species, a storyteller on par with asylum inmates. When he finally hung up on me I told myself I sure as hell would not want to be sitting in a witness box being cross-examined by him, even if I had full confidence in my testimony."

I thanked Detective Prendergast for his patience in what was turning into a circus-clown folly, then I asked him, "Why, if Mary-Margaret knew nothing, or knew the location of Morgan Crowder's body in her brother Francis's diary was not true, was she so eager to take down the photos in her garage, photos that depicted the Woody?"

"Those were old photos, Fletcher. You know that. Pre-WWII photos."

"Then she supposedly had nothing to hide. And yet the panic to hide those photos."

"Maybe she didn't panic. Maybe she just got tired of looking at them."

"Do you believe in coincidences, Detective Prendergast?"

No, but….," Prendergast said. "Look. You ought to know from your Burbank days that half the time on cases like this we have had to deal with crazies who were beyond rational explanation. Stuff right out of an episode of The Twilight Zone."

I had to agree with him on that score.

"Was Father John with her?"

"When I asked where he was, she shrugged. I figured he was hiding in a back room, but I didn't have a warrant."

Skip Prendergast was taking a chance by letting me leave town. That I worked for Amanda Reynolds turned out to be a huge plus for me in the detective's eyes. Though most defense attorneys were viewed by cops as barely above sewer rats in the great chain of being, Amanda was different. Her reputation as a tough-but-fair-minded court opponent was known and respected as far north as the Bay Area.

That I had been a Burbank detective in my former life also helped with gaining Prendergast's trust. I was lucky, because that could have gone either way. Some cops trust former cops, most don't. Cops who have committed punishable crimes, both petty and large, but have never been detained for any of them, fear former cops, because they know how to work the system. I ended up making a leap of faith by assuming Skip Prendergast was a clean cop in a clean shop.

Before heading to Mary-Margaret's house Randall and I stopped to eat at a McDonald's. Twenty minutes later we arrived at Miss Crowder's home. He parked some distance from where his aunt might see me. I waited while Randall banged on her front door. Once she let him in, twenty minutes passed before he emerged.

"My aunt told me she had taken a handful of downers, but she was walking on the ceiling anyhow. Jeez! Non-stop incoherent rage, Mr. Fletcher. If I weren't her nephew, she'd have tried to kill me. She somehow knew we were digging for Morgan's body at the golf course. I had no business looking for Morgan, let alone trying to exhume him, she told me. And on and on and on. She would have tried to kill you for sure if you had come with me. As far as she is concerned, you are the Devil's disciple."

"Lucky me, eh? Did she say anything about where Morgan's body might actually be found?"

"No, and I swear I did ask her."

"Did you get the feeling she knows? No, wait. She has to know. If she was with your Uncle Jude, helping them take Morgan from where they found him to…to where? Think about it. Jude couldn't simply get rid of the corpse by himself and not keep her informed about what he had in mind to do with Morgan's body. It makes no sense that she would be cut out of the disposal plan."

"So we kidnap her and torture her until she talks?" Randall said, grinning.

I said, "Wouldn't that be nice? But no. How about this possibility. They load Morgan and Lennie into the back of his Woody. Francis and Mary-Margaret leave campus in whatever car Francis owned. Mary and Francis go to Mary's house. Jude takes off to who knows where. Two or three hours later Jude returns to Mary's house and gives precise directions to where he claims to have buried the two dead men. Francis writes down what Jude tells him regarding where Morgan's and Lennie's bodies have been deposited. All the while, the corpses are still in the back of the Woody, parked in Mary's driveway. Jude finally leaves to go back to LA and he has Morgan's and Lennie's bodies and the Woody disposed of in LA. To me it makes sense that he would ask whatever chop-shop outfit he uses to get rid of both corpses and the Woody."

"Nice theory, but how can you prove it?" Randall said.

"I don't know yet. Maybe I can't. But what I might be able to establish is that Jude-the-attorney has some connection with the school where my two girls were kidnapped from. That has to be the case. It's no coincidence that the Woody I saw in the photo in Mary-Margaret's garage had the same license plate numbers as the Woody the nuns have described as being the kidnap vehicle. The only difference is that the kidnap vehicle had California plates, the Woody in the photo had New York plates."

"You don't think Uncle Jude kidnapped those schoolgirls do you? I mean, why would *he* do such a thing?"

I said, "Does your Aunt Mary have any connection with the convent?"

"I have no idea. Do you want me to go back and ask her?"

I shook my head. "She'd deny it. But I have no doubt she or Jude or both fed the Woody's license plate number to someone at the convent. No wonder no records of that plate number show up in Sacramento. For all I know, the Woody the nuns claim to have seen is a phantom, too."

"Why did they do this? I mean, why did they go to the trouble of covering up Morgan's death?"

"Good question, Randall. Next time you see her, ask your Aunt Mary. The initial motivation was probably family pride. Maybe they were fearful that everyone else at the party would think to themselves 'My God, what a pathetic bunch the Crowders are.'"

"Or maybe think it out loud," Randall said.

I nodded. That was certainly likely.

"But now they'll have people thinking even worse of them," he said.

"No denying that," I said.

From Mary-Margaret's house we drove to the junkyard where my Biscayne rested. After examining her one more time, I had to admit she was a gonner. Poor thing. So I asked for a recommendation from the yard's crusty owner, on where to find a good used car at a reasonable price. His nametag read "Bonzer". I wasn't in the mood to ask where that name came from.

"Try Buster's Buggies. I forget the exit number, but you'll see a big billboard on the right-hand side of El Camino."

"Is Buster a relative of yours?" I asked.

"Of course he is. I wouldn't trust anybody who isn't."

We missed seeing the billboard. We found out after finding Buster's that he had only paid for one month's worth of advertising and that month had occurred five months ago. Buster himself greeted us before we even had a chance to open our car doors.

"Howdy there. Buster Flagg's my name. Welcome to my horsepower corral."

I wasn't in the mood for cutesy, but I shook his hand anyway.

"What kind of beast is your mind set on?" he said.

"I just lost a Chevy Biscayne. I'd like to replace it with something similar," I said.

"Lucky you. I just had a great little, low-mileage Biscayne traded in two days ago."

Before he could show me his Biscayne, I asked, "Why did the owner trade it in?"

"He got a promotion and wanted something a little snazzier to reflect his new standing."

Great. That was Buster's backhanded way of telling me a Biscayne was only for low-class people. Maybe he's right. Gumshoes are usually imagined to be bottom-of-the-barrel types.

"Okay. Show me the Biscayne."

After performing the ritual of kicking tires and raising the hood, I shrugged and agreed to the asking price. I'm not a haggler. Even when I go to Tijuana I don't actually haggle in any common sense of the notion. I make no counter offers. I simple glare at the peddler until he lowers his price to one I am willing to pay. Then we arranged a wire transfer from Amanda's business account. That settled, Randall and I formed a two-car caravan to the Santa Clara police station.

Detective Prendergast told us, "Any more digging out there and we might trigger an earthquake." By *out there* he meant the site where Randall and I had begun to dig, looking for the skeleton of Morgan Crowder.

"So, we have nothing to charge Mary-Margaret Crowder with. Given that, I fail to understand why she and her padre friend were so eager to chase you away."

"Morgan's body is somewhere, and I bet she knows where," I said.

"Right now I have better things to look into. You two are free to go back to Santa Maria, Santa Julietta, the dark side of the moon. Morgan Crowder remains a missing person of interest, but our interest goes back to being miniscule. Good day, gentlemen."

And so Randall and I headed south, stopping for a meal at the white-trash diner in Soledad, then refueling our cars and heading south down Highway 101.

26

When I turned off the freeway at my exit in Santa Maria I hoped Randall would continue on toward Santa Julietta. He didn't. He followed me. I parked in front of my house and he at least showed the good sense to park behind me instead of parking in front of Germaine's house.

"How much trouble are you looking for?" I asked him when he stepped onto the curb in front of me.

"I just want to take a minute to see if Gemmy is all right and to tell her I'll call her as soon as I get home."

"You're making two mistakes," I said. "First, don't see her now. Her parents are home and Fowler will try to kill you the instant he sees you. Two, don't call her when you get home. She needs some time as well as space. An abortion is a mind-shattering event. Even if you choose to have it. You should never have taken her to The Byrds concert. Now stop compounding your errors."

He grinned. "Why don't you add, 'Put a condom on them, Randall.'"

"This is not the time for humor, young man."

"When is?"

"Never."

"Go straight home and just hope there isn't more trouble waiting for you there than you can handle."

He ignored me.

"Gemmy's dad won't come near me."

"You think not?"

"I know he won't."

"Why not?"

"Because of what I know and what I may spill to Gemmy's mom."

I wasn't sure that I wanted to hear what he might say next, but it was too late. When I just glared at him, he laughed hysterically.

"You're sweet, kindly, church-going neighbor Fowler C. Payette raped his daughter." Another hysterical laugh. "And that is why she insisted on having an abortion. She wasn't sure who the father of her child was. Me or her daddy."

"Has Germaine told her mother?" I said.

"Not yet. But it won't take much for her to blurt it out."

"Or you?"

"Yeah. Me."

This was turning into Hell on Pine Street and there was no way I could avoid being sucked into its fiery vortex.

"Don't go to the Fowler residence. Please." I hated pleading, but I had to stop him. It was not his place to point a finger, to shatter Sarah Payette's world, to throw added fuel into Germaine's emotional turmoil.

"Don't try to stop me."

My sucker punch to his midsection doubled him over. My thumbs' pressure on his carotid arteries caused him to pass out. Before he could come to I carried him into my house and dropped him onto my bed and removed his shoes. From my dresser I pulled out a pair of handcuffs and shackled him to my headboard.

Sitting in my bedroom Lazy-Boy, I watched Randall breath deeply and tried to emulate him while I imagined what to do next. Nothing sensible came to mind. I lost track of how much time passed before my front doorbell rang.

My next-door neighbor Mary Ann Chase stood there when I opened the door. I sensed that she wasn't paying me a visit to borrow a cup of sugar.

"Stu, I saw you punch that young man and then carry him into your house. And by *that young man* I mean the fellow I've seen dating Germaine Payette recently. I don't know his name, but I recognize his car."

She pointed toward Randall's Cadillac.

"Come in, Mary Ann. I'll tell you all about it."

And I did, trying to keep my narrative as concise as possible. I omitted Germaine's claim that Fowler had raped her.

"My word, Stu Fletcher, you have had a wild, scarcely credible couple of days. Until now I never did know the young man's name. Where is Randall now?"

"Out cold on my bed. I knocked the wind out of him to stop him from charging over to make a scene at the Sarah and Fowler's house."

"Aren't the Payettes Catholic?" Mary Ann asked.

I gave Mary Ann an ambiguous facial expression.

After a long pause, she said, "I'm sure they are. And I know who the Crowders are from my seeing numerous articles in the Santa Julietta newspapers telling of A.C. Crowder's making quite sizeable donations – hundreds of thousands of dollars -- to this and that local and regional Catholic charities."

I nodded.

"Which leaves me to wonder what prompted Germaine, I suppose with Randall's consent, to have an abortion."

My gesture – palms up, shoulders shrugging – was as good as a lie. But damned if I was going to paint Fowler to be a rapist, based on a third-hand rumor, however trustworthy Germaine and Randall might be otherwise. True or false, the rumor would leave neighborhood relations in total shambles forever more. I was choosing not to be the spark for that dynamite.

"What can I do to help, Stu?"

Good question.

After puzzling for a moment, I said, "When Randall wakes up, it could work better for a saintly wise woman to speak with him about how a young female might currently be feeling, immediately following having had an abortion. Far better than for me to try to do it."

"Saintly wise?" she said. "I've never before been accused of holding that status. Why, thank you."

"You are one mighty damned sharp old lady, Mary Ann, and you know perfectly well that you have more than an inkling that you are."

"Thank you. You are most kind. So, of course, I shall be willing to speak to the young man."

While waiting for Randall to come around, I brewed some tea and listened to Mary Ann tell me about her ailing parakeet, Calico Jack, named after a famous early 18th Century Caribbean pirate Calico Jack Rackham. She had owned the bird ever since I had known her, so his ailment was likely simply to be old age, though I had no idea what the average life span of a parakeet might be.

I had finished my tea and was working on a Budweiser when the doorbell rang again. I hadn't been this popular since I bought the house. My newest guest was Angie, who said she had delivered Germaine and had taken Stephanie to Santa Julietta, neither time leaving her car.

"I just kicked each girl to the curb and took off. I didn't want to get involved in any family wars," she said as she took my beer bottle from me and drained the remaining contents in one swallow. "Got another one of these? Working for you makes a gal thirsty."

After Angie stepped inside I introduced her to Mary Ann as a friend of a friend of mine. While in the kitchen fetching Angie a beer, I heard Randall begin to make noises. So I checked on him and found him with his eyes open, but unsure where he was. I took a beer to Angie and whispered to Mary Ann, "Time for you to do some soothing."

After all the driving she had done, Angie insisted on standing.

She told me, "I did the cowardly thing and at both Germaine's house and then at Stephanie's I kicked a lady to the curb and sped off as fast as I could drive."

"Don't feel guilty. All I asked of you was to deliver them."

"Yeah, but still---. I felt kinda guilty."

"Guilty of not facing the storm awaiting each of them?"

"Misery loves company?" she said meekly.

"Your presence would only have added fuel to each blaze."

"Are you saying this just to make me feel better?"

"No, I mean it."

With her beer bottle Angie gestured toward the bedroom. "What's that all about?"

"Mary Ann is such a sweet woman. She has a calming effect on everyone she meets. I'm hoping she can soothe Randall. He was adamant that he was going to barge into the Payette's house."

"I'd best be going. I'm short of sympathy for guys who knock their girlfriends up, then whisk them away to some back-alley coat-hanger shop, although I must admit that place in San Jose isn't exactly back-alley. Still…."

I hustled Angie out the front door before she could share her lack of empathy with Randall. I handed her two twenties and asked her to bring back some Mexican fast food for four. I had mixed feelings about abortion and the sordidness surrounding most sites conducting the procedure didn't help. But what was I hoping for? A sterilized magic wand in place of the cliched coat hanger?

As a philosopher my talents were rather meager. On the question of when life begins I was a doubter regarding the pat answer: at conception. That moment, to my mind, was merely one step along the way toward becoming a living creature. Female eggs and male sperm also represented stages. Why didn't the destruction of either of those stages rile those who insisted potential life must be allowed to become life? Clearly, to some, not all stages of potentiality are equal. When a potential person becomes a realized person is not, I think, a philosophical matter so much as it is a socio-political matter. But then what do I know?

Back inside my house I found Mary Ann and Randall sitting in my living room. I walked to where Randall was seated and held out my hand for a peace-making handshake.

"Sorry I punched you, Randall, but I felt I had to stop you from seeing Germaine right then."

He pushed my hand away, more with a sense of submission than of anger. "I guess I deserved it."

"Germaine's standing with her parents is extremely delicate at the moment. When you add a lemon to a glass of iced tea, you have to sit back and allow the lemon time to sink. I hope that's not too stupid an analogy."

Randall nodded. "Your neighbor lady said something similar. But God, I want to see Gemmy, Mr. Fletcher."

"I know you do. But now is not the right time."

His glare didn't soften. But I was saved from having to think of what to say to insure he would not step off my porch and dash headlong toward the Payette house by Angie's telling him, "You march straight to your car, young man, get in it, and drive non-stop to Santa Julietta. I didn't nurse that poor girl all the way from Santa Clara just to have you ruin my efforts. Now git."

And, by golly, he did exactly as he was told to do. Angie and I stood on my porch and watched his Cadillac until its taillights were out of sight.

Turning to me, Angie then said, "Damn it, Fletcher. It's high time you offered this girl a mighty strong drink. I done for the day with telling spoiled college kids that it's time to grow up."

"Yes, ma'am. Glad to oblige."

Inside, I poured Angie two inches of Jim Beam straight, and, after only a moment of hesitation, poured myself one of the same.

27

Angie stayed the night, leaving for home after fixing me a three-egg omelet filled with cheese and spicy sausage bits. Our love-making had been of that existential kind one only imagines when believing the apocalypse has arrived and we were the only couple left alive. But afterwards she changed. Her words suddenly came in torrents.

"Germaine's abortion shocked my whole system, Fletcher. I tried to suppress everything about it, from the moment we arrived at the clinic and I suddenly realized what the place was and why we were there.

"I tried not to freak out when we were walking toward the Avalon, looking for her. But when we found her I nearly screamed. Maybe I should have. No one would have heard me amidst the music and the noise. Finally, by the time I was driving down Highway 101 it all came roaring back to me."

I anticipated what *it* was and held her hand.

"In high school my boyfriend, Royal, and his pals gang-raped me after a football game. By the time I realized I was pregnant, we had broken up, most of my girlfriends began to shun me, and my parents were in the middle of a nasty divorce. The one girlfriend I had left helped me do the coat-hanger thing. It worked, but I became serious infected and nearly died. The hospital surgeon felt sorry for me and told my parents I had had a uterine tumor. He knew better, but he told me he had a daughter two years younger than me. My parents still don't understand why I don't get married and have children. I've never told them I can't have children. I hope someday Randall and Gem can have babies."

"Did you speak to any authorities about your boyfriend and his buddies?" I said.

"His dad was a cop," she said, as if that explained everything.

"Did you ever try to take any personal revenge?"

Her eyes brightened and she chuckled. "All these years later he can still only walk by usin' a cane."

"What about his friends who raped you?"

She shook her head. "I guessed that they all could figure out I had done the damage to Royal, even though they couldn't prove it. I reckon each of the others spent the next few months lookin' over their shoulder, watchin' out for Hellbent Angie."

It was a Russian chess grandmaster, Savielly Tartakower, who famously observed: *Sometimes the threat of a move is far more intimidating than the move itself.* I didn't ask, but I wondered if Angie played chess.

Angie had no sooner driven off than my doorbell rang again.

"How much do I owe you, Fletcher?"

Fowler Payette.

"You owe me nothing, Fowler. I'm glad I found her. She had no business going to that concert, but don't tell her I said so."

"I see you also found that kid who knocked her up. I won't thank you for finding him."

"Germaine is home. She's safe once again. Resting, I hope."

"That's it. Change the subject," he said as he pulled out his wallet.

"I said you owe me nothing. I don't want your money. Consider my efforts to be a neighborly gesture."

"Like lending Sarah two eggs and a cup of brown sugar? Oh, come on. You at least had some expenses."

I nodded. "Two eggs and a cup of sugar. Brown sugar."

"Very well. By the way, Sarah would be here to thank you, but she's afraid to leave the house for fear Gemmy will run away while she's gone."

"I understand."

"How did you know to go to…to…that place where we met you?" Fowler said.

"I consulted my Ouija board."

"Please, Fletch. Don't be flippant with me."

"Okay. I have a friend in the south end of the Bay Area who had an abortion a couple of years back. I explained my situation and asked her to give me the names of the most reputable ones."

Fowler made a choking sound before repeating, "Reputable? Jeezus, Stu. That's like asking for a reputable rapist."

"Sorry. But you know very well what I meant."

"Yeah. Kinda."

"I hope I saved you a small bit of grief by getting there first," I said.

"I suppose you did."

I said, "Let me ask you how you knew Germaine would be going to The Byrds concert."

"Sarah worked up the courage to phone the Crowders. She spoke with the young daughter."

I nodded.

Fowler asked, "Did your Ouija board give you that information, too?"

"No. I got that from the same source Sarah did. I had the concert site pegged before I left Santa Julietta. What was troublesome was finding out Germaine had gone to the clinic and then felt well enough to want to attend the concert. I went to the clinic merely to find out where it was and if Germaine was scheduled for a procedure. I was taken aback to find out she had already been there."

"She's a tough young girl, my Gemmy is. Good genes. By the way, how did my daughter pay for her…her procedure? Do you know?"

From my closet I fetched Germaine's Ping putter and handed it to Fowler.

"You mean….?"

"It's worth a lot and she knows it. The abortionist also knew and agreed to take it as payment."

"Then how did you get it back?"

"I offered the doctor three times what it's worth, plus a Ping sent to him directly from Mister Solheim himself, along with a letter with Solheim's signature on it, congratulating him on his purchase. He thought about it for a few seconds, then agreed."

"Christ! How much did that set you back?"

I said, "A well-known golf pro in Scottsdale owes me a favor. He knows Mr. Solheim. As for getting the money, the attorney I work for in Santa Julietta owed me for work I'd done, plus she gave me an advance on work I will be doing for her."

Flower said, "It's not fair that you should pay. The money ought to come out of that little shit Randall Crowder. Either from him or his old man."

I shrugged. However fair Fowler's notion might seem, it was never going to happen.

He asked, "Do you have any more business with the Crowders? Sarah and I have never met them. I was taken aback when Sarah worked up the courage to call them. I imagined she would have to elbow her way through three sets of servants to get to talk to someone with real Crowder blood."

I said, "They're not our class, Fowler, but they're not that much higher up the pole than we are."

"I guess I supposed they only speak to bishops, popes, and God."

"Not quite."

"I couldn't imagine Gemmy marrying that Crowder boy, even if she had decided to…Well, even if she had made a different decision."

"From being with him for a couple of days I judge Randall Crowder to be a likeable young man."

"Yeah, but he didn't take advantage of your daughter."

I didn't want to get into an argument with Fowler over whether his daughter had been taken advantage of or not. So, I simply said, "No."

He chuckled. "Ouija board. I like that. I didn't know you relied on consultations with the other side."

"I don't, really. I'm not a fan of any kind of magic. Folks who indulge themselves in magic never seem to be able to explain what, if any, the limitations on magic are. Why some things are above and beyond science, but others aren't. Appeals to magic never seem to be boundless, yet believers won't or can't tell me why x, y, and z are beyond explanation, while a, b, and c are not."

"I was never much for magic shows when I was a kid," Fowler said.

Fowler was a good Catholic, which meant he believed in all kinds of magical happenings that I, as a faithful heathen, dismissed as gibberish. He even believed in many things that any Protestant would disclaim.

I said, "You still have your bits of magic and I have mine, though my bits a different from yours."

"As a heathen, what bits of magic do you believe in?" he asked.

"Strong hunches, for a good example. My father's advice, for another, that is, when my father's advice went against all reason. 'Trust you instincts', he used to tell me. I don't even know what an instinct is. Maybe it's no different from a strong hunch. Guesswork, but not quite. When unsure, I ask myself what my dad would do, and often I have to make a guess about that."

"You're confounding me now, Fletcher."

"Meaning I'm not making sense, right?"

He shrugged. I could tell he didn't want to insult me, even if that meant agreeing with me after I had insulted myself.

I slapped him on a shoulder. "Go home, Fowler. Hug your wife and take comfort that your daughter is now home and safe. A lot of folks' daughters are neither."

Misty-eyed, Fowler nodded, shook my hand, and left.

28

Reed Mackenzie seemed pleased to see me, but I might have been wrong. While he started out being surly, reminding me he hadn't seen me in eons, grouchy that bail had been denied even though he was not accused of murder, pissed that the Church had allowed authorities to find him and arrest him, he also made clear my presence was better than his having to share his current life with nothing other than jail guards and cockroaches.

"Your accusers are coming home this weekend, Amanda tells me. I plan to ruin it for them. I now even have a judge's order to wave at them – and their parents – should they act disinclined.'

"Disinclined? My, you are one uppity gumshoe. Where did you learn a word like that?"

"Probably from hanging around Amanda Reynolds too much."

"She'd better be as good as people says she is. Otherwise, I'm going to be bending over in Soledad, finding myself on the wrong end of the bugger stick."

He was right about that. To take his mind off his potential plight, I said, "Tell me what you know, if anything, about the Convent of Santa Franchesca Ornella."

The priest's head snapped back, and his gaze bore into mine.

"You're not involved with anything there, are you?" he said.

"I am."

"May God have mercy on your soul."

"Why is that?"

"I hear that the Mother Superior is… what phrase am I looking for?"

I suggested, "Hell on wheels?"

"Precisely."

"What else do you know about the convent?"

Father Mackenzie smiled. "I know the diocese sends all of its horny nuns there, to be straightened out by the abbess."

"Tell me more about that."

He laughed. "Why? Because it will further my case or because you just like to listen to smut?"

I said, "Two young girls were kidnapped from the school's playground."

"Yes. I read about that in the *LA Times*. But I doubt if any of the nuns on the teaching staff kidnapped them. However, if the kidnappings had been of virile young men, you might be wise to question all the creatures wearing black habits."

I remained silent, hoping he would tell me more.

Finally he continued. "I am told that Mother Agnes holds classes at night once a week for her female flock. She lectures them on the virtues of holding fast to the straight and narrow. Not a single one of the sisters under her tutelage is a virgin, and by that I don't mean they have each been seduced by God Almighty. Oh, no. Each of them has succumbed to temptations of the flesh, succumbed *after* having taken vows of chastity.

"You may recall, Fletcher, from any Roman history that may have passed through your head that vestal virgins who yielded to temptation were, immediately after being found out, put to death in one manner or another. However, within the Diocese of Los Angeles, nuns are, instead, sent to serve under Mother Agnes. Now, you may judge for yourself which is worse. Death or Mother Agnes."

"Interesting, because I didn't find her to be draconian. At least in dealing with me. A bit brisk, yes. She certainly has a basilisk stare. But the one sister who came into her office, didn't tremble in her presence."

Father Mackenzie threw open is arms. "Maybe she's changed, but I doubt it. Every Catholic priest and nun is taught to be on his or her best behavior in the presence of a non-Catholic, especially someone like you.'

"What is there about me?" I said.

"For one, you are not only a non-Catholic, but also a non-Christian. Not only a non-Christian, but a non-Everything. You eschew the embrace of God. Hence we must be on our guard, fearing that you may be an agent of the Devil."

"You look rather too relaxed to be on guard against me."

"Oh, I am wary of you, all right. I just am masking my fears. I must, must I not, pretend to be at ease with you, given that you are allegedly slaving on my humble behalf?"

"Let's talk about that, shall we? That is, talk about my slaving efforts," I said.

"Slave away."

I made brushing motions to have him slide over on his bunk to make room for me to sit.

"Tell me again why you think these young men have conspired to make up a nasty story about you?"

"I honestly do not know. At basketball camp I behaved entirely professionally toward them. No hug, no embraces of any kind that anyone later might interpret as squalid. I didn't shower with them; I didn't kiss them goodnight. No verbal endearments, no untoward looks. Nor did I transform myself into some alluring creature, as did Zeus dozens of times in Greek mythology. I treated them exactly the same way I treated all the other boys assigned to my care at that camp. Fairly and from a distance – at all times."

"So why did they rush home to mommy and daddy and say you forced them to have sex with you?"

"I haven't a single clue, Mr. Fletcher. Like King Lear, I am far more sinned against than sinning. In fact, I sinned not at all. I taught them how better to play basketball. And that is it."

I asked, "Have you every ministered in a parish where you might have been their pastor?"

"Not to my knowledge."

"And you don't know either of the parents otherwise?"

"No."

"Why do you suppose the Church failed to ask them not to file charges against you? Maybe offer to move you to the other side of the country? Banish you to Mississippi or Alabama?"

He let out a huge sigh. "Pardon the expression, but 'God forbid' I be sent to such hellish places."

"Maybe the diocese wants to nail you to a cross, make an example of you, serve as a warning to other priests."

"Why me? Why me?"

"Admit it. Your past lechery is now rather legend. And it is not of the sort that they wish to see on the front page of any newspaper, let alone a nationally prominent one."

"I am not alone in my transgressions, you know. I could name at least a dozen others just within this diocese who are my equals in this category of sins."

"Well, I am going to have to try to find out who has singled you out to stand trial before Caesar. I'm guessing at this point that the notion did not simply pop up in the parents' minds."

I stood up, having decided I had to get away from him lest I become seduced by his words. I wanted to believe him, but I also knew that Catholic priests, especially Jesuits, could make black appear to be white. They were verbal magicians and I had to escape before any spell was cast.

The notion had not occurred to me previously that nuns could be just as lustful as priests, and just as eager to find ways to indulge their lusts. I doubted Mother Agnes's evening classes reminding her female flock they must resist temptation would deter so much as one of the women who listened to her. Lust is not conquered by sermons, even the ground-shaking sermons I was certain Mother Agnes was capable of preaching.

While I was in Santa Julietta I thought about stopping in to check up on Randall and Stephanie Crowder, but first I need to report to Amanda Reynolds.

29

I simply cannot believe you bought another Biscayne. What *were* you thinking?"

"Let me ask you: Why do you wear the same pair of brass knuckles into the courtroom every time?" I said.

"Smartass."

"No. You wear them because you are comfortable with them. So it is with me. I am comfortable driving a vintage Biscayne. I am able to drive without thinking about driving."

"Okay. Okay. So you are next going to park your Biscayne in front of the Ledbetter's house."

"I am." I hadn't even looked up their address yet.

"How do you propose to proceed when you confront them?" Amanda said.

"With a bludgeon."

She laughed. "That's a given. What I want to know is which bludgeon, among your many, do you intend to use?"

"I imagine I'll ask them why they chose to pick on a poor, harmless priest."

"Then what?"

"I'll tell them I am recording their answers and then remind them that they will likely be asked later in a formal, sworn deposition many of the questions I intend to ask them."

"And if they wonder why they have to answer the same questions twice and slam the door in your face?"

"I'll wipe the blood off my nose, go home, and harass them with repeated phone calls."

She laughed again. "I adore your tenacity."

"Thanks. Some people don't. Instead, they call it harassment."

"Well, stay tough and carry on. Keep me informed."

"Yes, ma'am."

"And take better care of this Biscayne. Try not to park next to bad guys' Cadillacs."

"For sure," I said, saying this to a woman who has gotten rich keeping bad guys from getting convicted, allowing them to walk away, to drive away in their Cadillacs, and park them somewhere that I'll be sure to find and park next to them."

I had some luck with the Colliers, but luck is transitory, as I was soon to find out.

"That's brassy of you to come here ready to defend that monster of a priest," Alma Ledbetter said when I told her and her husband who I was.

I responded, "Well, yes. In my humble profession being brassy sometimes gives me an edge. However, I can see that isn't going to work today."

My saying that much managed to get me past the door.

After I sat down I said, "I'm hear to listen. I want your side of the story. I've already listened to Father Mackenzie."

"Have you talked to our sons yet?" Brent Ledbetter asked, as he motioned for me to seat myself on the sofa.

"No. I'm waiting for them to return during a break to Santa Julietta. I understand they'll be home this coming weekend."

The Ledbetters looked at one another, indicating neither parent was aware of their sons' plan to come home.

"How did you find that out?" Mrs. Ledbetter said.

"I prefer not to divulge my sources," I replied. *Sources*, plural. A tiny lie.

"What do you expect to learn from us?" Brent said.

"Have you tried in any way to verify your sons' claim against Father Mackenzie?"

Alma Ledbetter smiled. "We'd prefer not to divulge our sources."

"Touché."

Her smile turned into a smirk.

Brent Ledbetter said, "Alma and I both have a solid positive relationship with both of our sons. On a matter such as this neither of them would even begin to think about lying to us."

"Did you ask for details from either of them?"

Alma became indignant. "We did not lock them in an interrogation room and make them sweat."

"I take it that's what happened to them after you reported their accusation to local authorities?"

Alma raised her voice. "They were treated as though they were the perpetrators, not the victims. I was livid when the boys told me how they were treated. Still am, for that matter."

"I'm sorry. I agree that such treatment was unnecessary."

She said, "'Unnecessary' doesn't begin to account for the multitude of sins imposed on our sons, just because we and they tried to do what is right. It shouldn't matter that the man who assaulted them is a priest. He committed a crime. And that is what I told the lawyer from Los Angeles, the man representing the diocese."

Brent Ledbetter added, "Don't forget the two bishops from LA. They both tried to dissuade us from pressing formal charges. They tried to assure us that Father Mackenzie would be relocated to the Church's equivalent of Siberia and that he would never again be given any opportunity to…to do what he did."

I said, "Why did you reject that offer?"

"Because I wanted to see that man punished and sending him to some remote outpost of the Church is hardly what I call punishment. I told the lawyer that we demanded that Father Mackenzie be defrocked," Alma said.

"As well as spend time in prison," her husband added.

I would have liked to have said, "See him nailed to a cross," but I didn't. My guess was that their only sources for the alleged crime was their sons' claims against the priest and now the parents were operating more on certitude that certainty. Nor was either of them going to be shaken from their belief. I needed to talk with the sons.

I rose and said, "I hope you believe me when I say my sole interest is in finding the truth. If my findings lead me to think Father Mackenzie is guilty, I will say so openly. I am not here in any effort to whitewash a crime."

I failed to declare that my prime interest was to look for evidence that might tilt the case in Father Mackenzie's favor.

30

Having learned nothing particularly useful from the Ledbetters, I drove to the offices of Shaffler, Klein & Reynolds in downtown Santa Julietta. I was told Amanda was in court for the remainder of the day.

"No doubt saving some poor sewer rat from getting a well-deserved whiff or two of cyanide," I said to Amanda's much-too-lovely secretary, Callista.

"Watch it, buster. If the boss hears you talk that way about one of her esteemed clients, she'll kick you in the crotch so hard and fast, you'll be doubled up and cross-eyed for a week."

I held out my palms in a don't-shoot-me gesture.

Amanda walked in.

"So who has the better of it in this jousting match?" she said, dropping her briefcase on Callista's desk.

"Gumshoe here was just making demeaning remarks about your noble client," Callista said.

"We'll see how noble he is in an hour or two. The jury is sequestered and I'm hoping they ignore Judge Wilson's instructions to them, which basically amounted to telling them to hang my client high."

"You didn't object?" I said.

"No, no. His reasoning – in quotes – will give me plenty to base an appeal on." She motioned for me to follow her, then told Callista, "Whatever you had for lunch smells good. Order me some."

Callista pointed to me.

"No. He'll be long gone by the time it arrives."

I made a sad face and shrugged.

"So the doting parents believe anything and everything their boys told them. Right?"

I nodded and took a seat across from her in her office. "I plan to interview the guys separately right from the start. Afterwards, I'll feed each of their discrepancies back to them. Again, separately."

"Want me to play good cop?" she said.

"No. I'm still pretty good at playing disappointed good cop the second time around."

She said, "Do you have any feel for Mackenzie yet?"

"I think he's holding back something important."

"Do you have any clue as to the nature of his holdback?"

I smiled. "I don't think he's queer."

"Whoa! That'll turn the case on its head. I love it! So, how are you going to find out for sure that he's not a flippy wrist?"

"Catch him in bed with Mother Ages?"

"You've got to be kidding."

"Unfortunately, I am. But I'll think of something."

"You've got time. The court calendar currently overfloweth. So the padre is going to be cooling his heels for two or three whiles yet."

"No bail?"

Amanda laughed. "Are you going to put up the money? Because the good cardinal is content to let him rot."

"I'd go bail except I don't have time right now to follow him because I've got a lead on my kidnap case that I want to follow up on before it unravels."

"May I help in any way?" Amanda said.

"Yes. Maybe you can. Who is the diocese attorney that might have tried to warn the Ledbetters away from pressing charges on Father Mackenzie?"

"That's easy. Jude Crowder. He often represents the cardinal himself in touchy legal matters."

I said, "Do you know anything about his younger sister, Mary-Margaret? Or her boyfriend, a man everyone calls Father John?"

"Nope. You're on your own with them."

"Thanks. And, oh, by the way, next time you get together with Mackenzie, have Callista present. Watch how he reacts. Keep her there the whole time."

"If you say so. I'm sure she'll love it. Is she allowed to try to flirt with him?"

"That's a must."

On my way out I said to Callista, "You're soon in for a treat."

"Wow! Do you intend to take me to Brascoe's for dinner?"

"Oh, it's better than that."

"How soon?"

"Soon."

"What shall I wear?"

"Nothing at all would be perfect."

"Mmmmm! Yummy."

"Boss Lady will tell you all about it."

So Jude Crowder was an *eminence gris* to Cardinal James Francis McIntyre, the crusty conservative head of the Diocese of Los Angeles, which included Santa Julietta County. In 1964 the good cardinal had suspended a priest who had called for McIntyre's removal for failing to support the civil rights movement with adequate ardor. More recently he engaged in a nasty quarrel with the Sisters of the Immaculate Heart of Mary. The good sisters not only started promoting liberalism but additionally abandoned their traditional discipline, which included casting aside their habits in favor of "street clothes".

Their battle with the cardinal landed at the feet of the pope, who sided with the cardinal and ordered the sisters to restore their former practices or else request a dispensation from their holy vows. A huge majority of the sisters opted for dispensation and recently formed their own organization independent from the Church.

For me the deepest insight into the cardinal's mind was that in order for the priests within the diocese to learn more about the nature of communism he sent them to the John Birch Society for their education. Rumor was that, behind closed doors, the cardinal had to be reprimanded repeatedly regarding his frequent use of racial slurs.

Understanding the cardinal's character gave me more than a trifle insight into the mind of Jude Crowder. Uncle Jude to Randall, Stephanie, and Theodora, advisor to the Convent of Santa Franchesca Ornella, magician who made a Woody disappear. A Woody with a license plate bearing the identical numbers of the Woody used in the kidnapping of two girls from the convent's orphanage. And the Woody that disappeared once belonged to Morgan Crowder, cousin to Aloysius, Jude, Francis, and Mary-Margaret Crowder.

My job now was to try to find the links between Jude Crowder and the two sisters at the convent – Sister Melda and Sister Carmen – who reported the license number of the kidnap vehicle to authorities. My obvious suspicion was that Jude had fed the numbers to the sisters. In fact, my belief was much stronger than a mere suspicion. Nothing else explained how that precise string of numbers ended up as a non-existent California license plate series, but rather the numbers on a license plate assigned to Morgan Crowder's Woody by the state of New York. So what was Jude Crowder's sway over one or both of those sisters? *That* was for me to find out.

31

Praise be for curtain-twitchers! Arriving home tired and hungry, I had scarcely opened my refrigerator door when Mary Ann Chase knocked on my back door.

"Sorry, Mary Ann. All I have to offer you is beer and cold meatloaf."

"I'll accept the beer; pass on the meatloaf."

I fetched another cold Bud for her and motioned for her to sit down at my kitchen table. We clinked our bottles together. "Salud!"

She nodded and took a lengthy pull on her beer.

"What's going on?" I said.

"Someone has been watching your house. Make that two someones."

Her description of the car and the people in it made clear my house-watchers were Father John and Mary-Margaret Crowder.

Mary Ann said, "First they knocked on your door, then, when no one answered, they returned to their car, drove it around the block, and parked it in front of Lloyd Mallory's house.

I nodded. Lloyd lived on the other side of North Pine Street, four houses north of mine.

"When did they arrive? When did they depart?"

I knew that Mary Ann could tell me to the precise minute the answer to both my questions.

"They knocked on your door at 2:33 and watched from 2:47 until 5:09."

"Did you offer them cookies and coffee?"

Mary made a face. "I most certainly did not."

"A can to pee in?"

"No, but the man kept squirming, as though he might have needed a urine depository." With that remark Mary Ann smiled and left.

I had no idea why the priest and Mary-Margaret felt a need to watch my house. Looking for Randall and Stephanie? They could call A.C. Crowder's house to find out that the two had returned home. So they obviously wanted to find me. Why? It's possible they suspected I was putting two and two together regarding the photo of the Woody and its New York license number.

But that would mean they were somehow in on the disappearance of the two girls from the convent. Or knew about it. But how? That was the connection I did not understand yet. How did the convent sisters have the number of the alleged getaway car, a number that matched the numbers on Morgan Crowder's Woody? The sisters had to be fed the numbers by either Mary-Margaret or Father john, or else by Jude Crowder, a lawyer heavily involved with Monsignor McIntyre's diocese, which included the Convent of Santa Franchesca Ornella.

I decided to make a phone call to Jude Crowder's law office. In the Greater LA phone directory, a copy of which I keep in my kitchen phone nook, I found him listed as a member of Crowder, O'Brien, and Byrne on Wilshire Boulevard just west of the Beverly Hilton. Nice address, if you can afford it.

Although Father Mackenzie didn't know it, he served as my entry ticket to Jude Crowder's law office. I explained to the woman who answered the telephone that I needed to consult with Mr. Crowder because I was the research leg man for the woman who is presently the defense attorney for Father Mackenzie.

When she sounded confused I said to her, "Think of me as the equivalent of Paul Drake to Perry Mason." That immediately enlightened her.

"Sooner is better," I told her when she asked me how soon I wanted to see Mr. Crowder. Her hesitation made me add, "We wouldn't want to make Cardinal McIntyre twitchy, would we?"

With that I was on Jude Crowder's calendar for 1:00 p.m. the next day.

I found Wendy Ellen Sheldon doing laundry when I arrived at her house in Santa Julietta.

"Without the girls here doin' laundry takes less than half the time. Can I offer you a beer? Without CPS breathin' down my neck I've gone off the wagon. In fact, if I remember rightly, you drink 'em two at a time."

"You remember correctly."

So we sat, side by side, on her living room couch, with four Falstaffs lined up on the coffee table.

"I suppose you're here to tell me there's no good news yet," she said.

I mulled whether to tell her about the license plate number, but instead said, "You're right. There is no good news."

"So, how many fucks do I owe you for tryin'?"

"You don't owe me any."

"Damn! I was hopin' you'd say 'A hundred'."

I let that pass.

"I'm going back to talk to the convent sisters one more time."

"That's a waste of shoe leather."

"Then I'll go there barefoot."

She grabbed a beer and handed me one.

We clanked the bottles together in a toast.

"To barefoot gumshoes!" we said together.

After taking a long slug of beer, she said, "My laundry can wait. In fact, I might as well throw in everything I'm wearin' right now."

We finished drinking our beers, then headed off to her bedroom. An hour later I dressed, kissed Wendy Ellen goodbye, and drove to the convent.

32

I was hoping to get to Sister Melda before Mother Agnes saw me. I failed and Agnes gave me a look that made me glad she didn't have a whip in her hand.

"Mr. Fletcher, I think we have already seen quite enough of you here. Now turn around and march right back to your car."

I didn't know yet if Mother Agnes was in on the chicanery being promulgated by Jude Crowder. I suspected she was. Not much got past her. So, I figured that if she wasn't part of the kidnap misdirection, she would have flogged Sisters Melda and Carmen until they confessed to whatever the two of them were up to. But my impression of the two sisters was that neither of them had any lash marks on their backs.

I turned, but over my shoulder I said loudly, "Please tell Sister Melda and Sister Carmen that I have some news about the Woody automobile and its license plate."

If Mother Agnes wasn't already pale from lack of sunshine on her coif and wimple, I could swear she turned ten shades whiter.

"Stop!" she said. "What do you mean by that?"

I turned to face her. "Just what I said. I have solid leads on both the kidnap vehicle and its driver."

"Have you told the police?"

"Not yet."

"Oh, I'm so happy. Carmen and Melda will be ecstatic."

I nodded. Then I waited, and waited, and waited. But she seemed to possess no curiosity about the whereabouts or condition of Eileen Sanchez and Melissa Hargrove.

Finally I said, "After such a long time I'm betting that news of the young girls won't be as good. So brace yourself."

"Oh, Mr. Fletcher, I refuse to believe that serious harm has come to the girls. Somewhere God is watching over them."

"Where was He when they were taken? On a coffee break?"

When provoked Mother Agnes takes on both a look and stance that reminds me of a monument I saw in Fukushima, Japan at the end of the Korean Conflict. We were told that the troop ships taking us back to the States were two days late arriving in Tokyo harbor. So, after we offloaded at the port of Nigaata, the battalion's orders were to dawdle on our way to Tokyo. Hence, we were given a day of liberty in Fukushima.

Four of us GIs hired an English-speaking guide and set off looking for fun. The only reason we came across this monument was because it was on the way to a little restaurant that served American beer. The monument was a statue of a woman named Nakano Takeko. She was, according to our guide, the only known female samurai in Japan's history.

During a Japanese civil war in the year 1868 Nakano fought at the Battle of Aizu, where she was wounded, taking a shot in her chest while leading a charge against the Imperial Japanese Army. Fearing that her enemies would capture her, defile her body, and make her head a gruesome war trophy, she asked her sister to cut off her head and bury it. Her sister obliged and Kaneko's head was buried beneath a pine tree at Hokai-ji Temple in what is now modern-day Fukushima. And today a monument stands near the temple, where girls come each year to honor her.

I left Mother Agnes and felt her glare burn a hole in my back. My car was across the street and I moved it to where I could see the main entrance to the convent but would not be noticed by anyone going in or out. Knowing that the Sisters of Mercy all lived inside the convent, I supposed I was wasting my time. And, after two hours of stakeout I was convinced I had indeed frittered away my time.

But then, as darkness fell, a man parked his car in front of the convent and quickly went inside. Moments later he emerged with a nun clinging to his arm. He held the car door open for her, then he climbed behind the wheel and they came my way. I slide down in my car seat just far enough to see over the edge of the driver's side window. As the car passed I was unable to see the nun and unable to identify the man. Damn!

The next best thing to do was for me to follow them. In the dark I tried to keep near enough not to lose them, far enough behind not to be spotted. The traffic was moderate, so my car did not stand out. Even so, I nearly lost them when their car entered the 101 freeway and headed for LA. But then they exited onto Cabrillo Boulevard, heading for the beach area. Shortly after passing Higgins Wharf they turned into the parking lot of the Pacific Beach Retreat Hotel.

After parking, the man led the woman into the hotel. I didn't recognize the man, but I was sure the woman was Sister Carmen. What she was doing going into a hotel I could only imagine. I jotted down the license plate of the car he had driven. California plates: 22 DMW 376.

I went into the lobby to see if Carmen and her male friend were still there. They weren't. So I used the public pay phone to call in a favor from a friend in Sacramento who worked in the Department of Motor Vehicles.

"Ray, this is Stu Fletcher." Pause. "Yes, you guessed it." I read him the license number. It took him a while, but when he came back on the phone he told me, "Blue Mercedes, right?"

"Right."

"It's registered to a Jude Ignatius Crowder, with an address in Laurel Canyon. That's…."

"I know where it is, Ray. Thanks. Now I owe you one." Ray Van Osterman was a drinking-buddy classmate of mine at Long Beach State. As a poor kid from the blue-collar east end of San Diego, Ray's booze preference was Rheinlander beer, because we could buy it at Lucky's Liquors for 99 cents a six pack. It came in eleven-ounce bottles and tasted great, better than Olympia or even Coors, which another classmate of ours, Willie Lancaster, imported from Colorado during quarterly breaks, because, as the owner of Lucky's, Ned Mueller, told us Coors Brewery lacked distributorships in California and seemed to be in no hurry to establish any.

Ray now had a working wife and had become a middle-management employee for the State of California. His taste in booze had jumped several notches, so now I owed him a twelve-bottle case of Napa Valley Chardonnay, which would cost me roughly fifty-dollars. To be mean I would see that twelve bottles of Rheinlander, worth a buck ninety-eight plus delivery fee, showed up on his doorstep a day ahead of the case of white wine.

Meanwhile, I slipped the hotel desk clerk a twenty-dollar bill plus the number for my answering service and asked him to let me know what time Mr. Crowder and his guest checked out. The clerk said he was off duty at midnight.

"If they have not checked out by then, I want to know that, please."

"Yessir. I'll call you, if they have checked out; I'll also call you if they haven't."

"Thank you."

"No, sir. Thank you," the clerk said, pointing to the money barely poking out of his vest pocket.

33

Pro bono means *for the good*, not, as most people seem to think, *for free.* In the case of the girls missing from the convent, I hoped my efforts were for the good, because monetarily I wasn't even breaking even. I had no insurance on my stolen gun and the car insurance payout for my blown-up Biscayne was not going to cover what I had borrowed from Amanda to buy a replacement car. Wendy Ellen's bedroom treats were nice, but not convertible into cash.

Oh, well, I was far from broke.

In the morning, back in Santa Maria, when the phone rang I hoped it was my answering service. It was.

"Mr. Fletcher I had a call from a hotel desk clerk who said I must phone you first thing this morning. I hope he wasn't lying."

"No, Jennifer. That was my instruction to him."

"Oh, good. So, his message for you is: *She hadn't left by midnight.* Does that make sense?"

"Yes, it does. Thank you."

So, Sister Carmen was serving herself up as Mystery Man's cupcake. I wondered if Mother Agnes has signed off on this little assignation. How else could Sister Carmen walk through the front door of the convent? Or was there a back door? Did Mother Agnes count heads at bedtime like a prison guard? I wouldn't put it past her, indulging herself in a bit of nightly nose-counting.

The basketball boys would be home for the weekend by now. Time to see if I could shake them up. But first I needed to check in with Amanda to see that we're on the same page regarding those boys.

"So, how do you propose to try to poke holes in their stories, Stu Fletcher?"

From her tone I guessed Amanda thought I would not be able to trick the young men into altering their narratives. Usually she showed more faith in me. Now it was clear we were not on the same page.

I finally said, "I'm going back to visit Father Mackenzie one more time and press him about my feeling that he's not queer."

"What if he lies to you, telling you he's not a faggot when he truly is?"

"How do I know he's lying either way? I'll do what I used to do with suspects in interrogation rooms. Make them repeat their stories so often that the story finally falls into a dozen pieces."

"Want me to go along and play good cop to your bad cop?"

"No thanks. As a defense attorney you've spent your entire career playing bad cop. You can play that role, if you like. But then Mackenzie may lose confidence in you as his courtroom defender."

"You're right. I'll stay here. Good luck."

That's what I like about Amanda Reynolds. She leaves her bullshit shovel in the hardware store. Who you see is who you get. Now we were on the same page

McKenzie Mackenzie was asleep on his bunk. So, I poked him gently a couple of times, bestirring him from some feverish nightmare.

"Oh, it's you, Fletcher. Good to see you," he said, sitting up.

"I'm back because I'm puzzled by something." I sat down beside him on the bunk and scooted up close, crowding his personal space.

"Puzzled?"

"Yep."

"Ask away."

"Why do you affect so many homosexual mannerisms when you're not really queer at all?"

"Do I do that?"

"Absolutely."

"You're way off course, Fletcher. Queer is as queer does."

"I think not."

"You egged those boys on. But not because you're queer. So why?"

"I'm sorry, but I fail to see where you get off insisting I'm not a homo. Show me some proof."

"You're a poor actor. Not poor poor. Just poor. It's not that you don't fool anyone. But you certainly don't fool everyone."

"If you're right – and you're not -- what about me is it that doesn't fool you?"

"You try too hard. Let me tell you something. When I was in high school my father was a flight instructor during WWII. Besides teaching flying, he had two passions. Well, three if you count my mother. The other two were sailing and directing amateur theater productions, before, during, and after the war."

"So?"

"I used to watch him direct plays and I saw him turn bad actors into good ones. Maybe not Hollywood quality, or better yet, not into British stage actors, but with his help he got people to become believable."

"So you're saying I'm not believable?"

"That's what I'm saying."

"You've scarcely had occasion to observe me. You've been here how many times? Two? Three?"

"The first time was enough to plant the doubts in my mind. My second visit watered my doubts, let them germinate."

"You're wrong. I'm as queer as a nine-dollar bill."

"No. I think it's a game for you. You turn queerness on and off, like a water spigot. One must watch very closely, but that's what happens. Now I'm asking you to tell me why. Do you get a kick out of cock-teasing young men?"

The priest sat silent for a while, then said, "What is the difference between real flirtation and fake flirtation? There is none. In fact, fake flirting is an oxymoron."

"From my father's directing techniques I came to know the difference between someone who was good at playing King Lear and who wasn't. No one becomes King Lear. The question in acting is how close can an actor come? You don't come especially close to being Priest Queer. Your mannerisms are too forced. You're like an actor who doesn't quite know all his lines and must peek at the script now and then. It's those tiny pauses that throw you out of character for very brief moments. Then you have to adjust your shoulders to ease back into your role."

"Nice try," Father Mackenzie said, visibly agitated. "But a good Lear and a bad Lear still amounts to someone acting at being a king. One cannot act like he is a flirt without becoming a flirt."

Maybe he was right.

34

The Ledbetter parents weren't home, but their sons were. Maybe the young men's folks didn't want to be home when I showed up. I know that, if I were the father of Tyson and Bryson Ledbetter, I would want to hide out in a mall while some asshole detective questioned them.

"Do you drink beer?" Tyson asked me before we sat down in their too-frilly family room. Mrs. Ledbetter must have pilfered her decorating ideas from Victorian magazines.

"I do, but not while I'm working," I said.

"I hope you don't mind if me and my brother do," Tyson said, already holding a can of Old Milwaukee in his hand.

Me and my brother. What are they teaching in secondary schools these days?

"Drink away. In barley water *veritas*, eh?"

I knew I would get puzzled looks from both of them. Another piece of wasted cleverness. So, I sat down and pulled out my notebook, as though I might actually write something down.

"Bryson, without interruption from your brother, tell me what it was that caused your parents to have Father Mackenzie arrested."

"You mean his playing grab-ass with us?"

I nodded.

Bryson took a deep breath, then said, "The second week of our four-week camp, Father M, as we all called him, asked Tyson and I to stay in the locker room after everyone had showered, dressed, and headed back to their room for a rest period prior to going to the chow hall. We were sitting on a long bench with lockers on either side. He walked behind Tyson and put his hand on my brother's left shoulder, touching a dark red bruise and asked, 'Does that hurt?' It was an old bruise mark and Tyson shook his head. So next he ran his hand down Tyson's ribs, saying 'Tell me when it hurts.' Tyson didn't say nuthin', so when his hand got to Tyson's hip, Father M pinch my brother, pinched him hard."

Tyson interrupted. "I didn't squeal or shout. I can handle pain."

I pointed to Bryson. "Go on."

"Well, then Father M let his hand wander forward, stroking his thigh."

"Just his thigh?" I said.

"No, no. His hand kept sliding slowly forward, towards Tyson's crotch."

Tyson's face turned red and he said, "Then he grabbed my cock and asked if I had any trouble urinating. I told him no. So he said, 'That's good. Some of the other guys are complaining that it hurts when they pee. So I'm just checking. Next thing I knew he was stroking me with his thumb and forefinger. And rolling his finger like he was rolling a cigarette."

I said, "You know how to roll a cigarette, I take it. Do either of you smoke?"

Bryson said, "Hell, no. We're college athletes. Smoking ain't healthy for us."

I wanted to say: Bad grammar ain't good for your grade-point average either. But, as he said, they were college athletes. Nobody was going to bench them for bad grammar.

"Did he touch you inappropriately, too, Bryson?"

"He sure did. But no foreplay with me. He went straight for my cock. He even sat down between us on the bench and fondled us both at the same time."

"Tell me how each of you responded to that."

Tyson said, "Do you mean, did either of us get a hard-on?"

"I meant, did either of you brush his hand away?"

"No way," Bryson said. "He might have given us bad marks on our final report."

Tyson interrupted. "A bad grade from him might have caused our college to…to re-re-…cancel our scholarships."

"So you let him play with you."

"Yeah. We didn't like it, but what were we gonna do?" Bryson said.

"The man's our coach," Tyson said, as if that explained everything.

"How often at camp did he try to fondle you?" I said.

"As often as he wanted," Tyson said.

"Which was how often?"

"Mostly after lights out at the end of the day. He made us stay behind in the gym, while everyone else had to shower and go to bed after the final pre-bedtime light workouts."

"Did he do anything beyond fondling you?"

The two looked at each other, before both shaking their heads in the negative.

"Did you tell anyone at camp about this?"

Two more negatives.

"Why not?"

"We didn't want to get in trouble," Tyson said.

"You thought the two of you would be the ones in trouble if you spoke up?"

"Hell, yes." Bryson said. "Everybody likes Father Mackenzie. For that matter, we still liked him. He's a cool guy. So, yeah. So everybody at camp would assume we invited him to be queer with us and neither of us wanted that."

"But you told your parents."

A pair of affirmative nods.

"What did you suppose they were going to think?"

Bryson said, "We knew they weren't going to think Ty and I are queer, or that we would gladly put up with that sort of activity from a priest or from anyone else."

"Did you expect your parents would contact the police?" I said.

"We sort of hoped they would," Tyson said.

"Did your parents react as you expected? By that I mean did they think badly of either of you because you allowed Father Mackenzie to continue doing what he did?"

Bryson explained, "They realized we were in a tough spot. If we let him keep on doing it, we would look com-...com-...."

"Complicit?"

"Yeah. That's the word I was lookin' for. It would look like we were okay with it."

Tyson's turn. "But if we said something to the camp's directors we would look bad by turning in a man everybody respected. They would assume we were lying, not that Father M was a dirty old man."

"So, were you lying?" I said.

I received the pair of dirty looks I expected.

"You don't believe us?" Tyson said.

"I simply asked you if you were lying. I'm a professional detective. I have to ask unpleasant questions sometimes. I like to think I can keep my own beliefs aside when I'm working. My question wasn't meant to suggest I believe you were lying." Of course, I didn't believe any of that. I was bluffing – with a weak hand.

"No, we weren't lying. And if we tell you we were lying all along, we'd be the ones in big trouble, right?"

I told them, "I don't know." Another bluff. "If you were lying, do you suppose your parents will forgive you? Will the police forgive you? I don't know the answer to those questions. Do you care if you're forgiven or not?"

The two young men looked at each other, unsure how to answer. And if or when they did answer, they wanted to be certain they both gave me the same answer.

Tyson finally spoke. "There's nothing to forgive, because we've been telling the truth all along."

35

I drove away from the Ledbetter's home convinced the brothers were most certainly lying. Their answers were too pat, too well-rehearsed. Abbott and Costello couldn't have played it smoother. They even managed not to smirk at one another in the middle of their routine. But, though I was convinced they were pinning false charges on Father Mackenzie, my problem – or more likely Amanda's problem -- was going to be how to break the boys down, get to them admit they had made the whole story up, or, more importantly, to get a jury to see through the young men's cruel effort to put Reed Mackenzie behind bars for a long, long time.

I drove straight to Amanda's office and gave her a play-by-play account of my visit with the Ledbetter twins. She agreed with me that the boys had been much too glib.

"Now let me send you to someone else who was in the summer camp with the twins. I'm sure he'll have an alternate account of what went on. His name is Midas Ballerion. He goes by Ike. Here is his address. He should be there any time after four o'clock."

"Are you going to provide me with his sexual orientation? Or do I have to play Twenty Questions with him to figure it out for myself?"

She said, "I don't think it matters, but I could be wrong."

"Midas?"

"His dad's a professor of classics at the university."

"Even so, couldn't the old man calculate how much nasty ribbing his son would take over the years?"

Amanda grinned. "He could have named his son Bellerophon."

I said, "Bellerophon Bellerion. I like it."

"Get out of here before you become totally out of control."

"Yes, Ma'am."

"No wait," Amanda said. "After talking to the Ledbetter boys, do you still think Mackenzie might not be queer?"

"I'm now guessing that those two get it on with each other. As for Father M, I don't know, but I'm going to press him again."

"Okay, but please deal with Bellerophon first."

"See? You like it, too."

"Don't you dare ask his father if he, at some point, seriously considered Bellerophon."

"I promise."

"I may have to put Midas on the witness stand. So don't tease him and piss him off. I don't intend to question him as a hostile witness. Okay?"

"I'll wear my best set of manners when I talk to him. Promise."

She opened a desk drawer and pulled out a check for me. "This makes us even through today."

I looked at the check and wondered if maybe I should have become a short-order cook at Denny's.

Amanda said, "Don't look so glum. Just remember who bought the car you are now driving."

"Objection, Your Honor."

"Sustained."

"Good thing I didn't ask for upgraded tires."

"Before you leave, give me a solid reason for thinking Father Mackenzie is not queer," she said.

"Sure. While Father M and I were sitting on his bunkbed, a female prison matron walked by, leading a female prisoner. You know how the jail is so Byzantine that women prisoners have to be led through the male sector to reach the women's cell block."

"Yes. I know that."

"Well, as the two women walked by his cell the good father gave each of the women a long, hard stare. Both the matron and the female prisoner were good looking, and he zoned in on them like your average horny, heterosexual male would."

Amanda smirked. "You mean like you would, and probably did."

"Yeah."

She said, "Imagine what would happen if I put you on the witness stand and asked you to repeat that event to the court. Why, the judge would laugh himself out of his robes. But not before he would order me into his private chambers and give me an earful for wasting court's time with those kinds of shenanigans."

I shrugged. "Maybe he would but think about this. You've stood in a crowd on the mezzanine at the university's concert hall at intermission many times, right? And you could tell which guys were eyeing your ass and which ones weren't, right again?"

"I believe the phrase is they were 'undressing me with their eyes'," she said.

"Okay. Yeah. So, unless your judge is too ugly ever to have had that happen to her, she would understand what I would be saying."

"Fletcher, bring me some better evidence, just in case the judge Mackenzie draws is too ugly to grasp the idea. Okay?"

"I'll try. If nothing else comes to mind, I'll plant a bunch of dog-eared Playboy magazines in his rectory."

"Don't you dare!"

36

Before I drove out to interview the basketball camper with the golden first name, I decided to see Father Mackenzie once more. I found him on his knees, on the floor of his cell, praying, his hands folded together on the edge of his bunk. I waited quietly until he had finished.

"So much for communication being a two-way street," I said as he rose.

He turned. "Just because *you* cannot hear the Lord doesn't mean He's not speaking to me."

"Okay. What's His message?"

"Patience and I will be exonerated."

I said, 'I'd like to think He's right, but getting there is going to require a little more cooperation from you."

"How little?" he said, gesturing for me to sit on his bunk.

"Let's start by your confirming for me that you are not a homosexual."

"Must I?"

"Yep."

He sat down beside me and stared off into the middle distance, which meant a plain gray wall in this case. I waited, silent beside him.

At last he said, "I don't want anyone else dragged into this. I'd rather go it alone and take my punishment."

"How noble of you. But if those boys are lying, I'm inclined to think you owe it to the world to expose them as liars, their parents as too gullible."

"My saying anything, and I mean anything, is not going to alter the characters of any of the Ledbetters. They are who they are; are what they are."

"You mean none of them will fall off their donkeys and have epiphanies?"

"Exactly," he said.

"I thought Christians were believers into character-altering. Isn't that what having non-believers come to Jesus is all about?"

Father Mackenzie shook his head. "I'm not one of them. I believe character is built well before a young person finishes high school. From then on we all put on masks."

"In that case, I'd still like to unmask the boys, at least. So who will you harm by speaking up about you not being queer. As Amanda's alter-ego in your case, you and I have attorney-client confidentiality privileges."

He shook his head.

"Look, Mr. Fletcher, whatever I tell you or don't tell you, I'm going to be damned either way. If I keep my mouth shut, I'll get convicted and spend several years in Soledad or San Quentin. If I tell you the truth, perhaps I'll walk out of court a free man. Only I won't be free. The Church will make my life more miserable than if I remain behind bars."

"Explain that to me."

He stood, walked to the other side of the cell, turned, and faced me.

"Why do you suppose the archdiocese has moved me here, there, and everywhere?"

"Because you bugger acolytes and choir boys, same as dozens of other priests within Cardinal McIntyre's kingdom do? No. So tell me the real reason."

He shook his head slowly.

"No. You are right. I have never fondled or buggered any young man anywhere anytime. But what I have done to incur the wrath of the Church, Cardinal McIntyre, I refuse to tell you, because if I tell you, my life will be in serious danger."

"Why, why, and why?" I said.

He shook his head again.

"You do not know what other evils go on within the diocese, evils I have long been part of, and for me to divulge that secret would be to put a rope around my neck."

"Can you even tell me if these evils are crimes within the civilian penal code?" I said.

He had to stop to think before saying, "In my case, the answer is unequivocally no, but for others it would be a crime. Wait. I take that back. Or take it back to this extent. I doubt if any prosecutor would be interested in going to court. However, these evils would definitely be sins in the eyes of the Church. "

"Now you've lost me."

He smiled. "Good. Let's keep it that way."

"Okay."

As I started to leave, Father Mackenzie waved for me not to call for the prison guard yet.

"Sit down, Mr. Fletcher. I have a serious question for you."

I sat.

"Are you a heathen? A non-believer?" he said.

"Do I believe in your god? Any god? Is that your question?"

He nodded.

"Think of it this way, Padre. In the history of mankind there have been hundreds of gods, maybe even thousands. The Aztecs, for example, had gods whose names we can't even pronounce. Accounting for all the gods in Greek mythology requires a thick text. But now the difference between what you believe and what I believe amounts to a trifle when you think of it in terms of me believing in only one god less than you do. Then again, where you believe in a myriad of saints and angels, I believe in leprechauns and tooth fairies."

"You mock me."

"Yes. I do. But it's not as though you don't deserve it. And, as a side note, I've convinced myself that your faith has grown weak after what you have spent years observing as an insider."

The priest ran a thumb across his fingers, caressing an imaginary set of worry beads. Finally, he said, "Weaker, but not weak. I truly do believe my God works in mysterious ways. Whenever I cannot fathom His plans, His intentions, the failure is mine, my inability to recognize the far bigger picture."

"You assume there is a bigger picture."

"Don't you? Do you suppose this vast, complex universe is here *ex nihilo*? Or that it just spins on and on to no purpose?"

"Why not? To assume it was brought into being by Something and that Something has a final destiny in mind is no triumph of reason. It's fantasy fiction. Plus, once you posit a Creator, you must then account for where this Creator came from, and so on back in an infinite regression. Or, if you proclaim the Creator has always just been, or was self-created, then you must allow that the universe itself can be self-created."

"Must I?"

"I'm speaking of the must of a logical entailment, not the must of your consent."

"A philosopher," he said.

"Not me, but my father consumed philosophy texts the way some people read thousands of mystery novels in their lifetimes. During sailing voyages, whenever we dropped anchor for the night, we would sit in the cockpit of our rented sloop, stare up at the stars, and he would introduce me to the enduring ideas and questions of the philosophers he had read. While you were a pupil in a Jesuit seminary, I was my father's pupil."

"History is full of philosophers who were not atheists," Father Mackenzie said.

"True. But several philosophers have proved at which point every theistic argument fails," I countered.

He changed the subject.

"Why did Miss Reynolds agree to take my case? Why are you going to try to help me?"

"It was you, Father Mackenzie, who asked around, wanting the best defense attorney available. I believe you initially wanted one of the big-name lawyers from San Francisco, until someone told you the best was closer to you."

"Something like that, I guess," he said.

"A question for you."

He nodded and said, "Go on. Ask."

"Why did you not want an attorney the archdiocese would have provided you."

His eyes narrowed. "Because I know who the cardinal would send to save me."

"Who is that, if I may ask."

"A man named Jude Ignacious Crowder."

37

When I rang the doorbell, no one came to the door at Midas Bellarion's house. On my way from the county jail I had stopped to buy two bags of chips and a refill on my coffee thermos. So, I parked down the street from Midas's house where I could see both his driveway and his front door.

The neighborhood had a post-war look to it, a wide street, ranch style homes, and tall streetlamps lining the sidewalks. Some yards were better manicured than others, some were scattered with plastic toys. The area was near enough to the ocean that on cool winter mornings fog did not burn off until nearly noon.

The election was over, Hubert Humphrey's rally fell just short, and, depending on one's point of view, we were stuck with, or blessed with, Richard Nixon's five o'clock shadow for the next four years. Or longer. Fog had dampened political yard signs and the thin cardboard placards had all begun to curl.

After losing his 1962 race to become California's governor, Nixon had churlishly snapped that the press wouldn't have him to kick around any longer. I hoped that by now he had discovered a better means of reading the future. If not, then California, the nation, and the world were in for a bumpy, bumpy ride.

I had no idea what kind of hours a professor of the classics kept. Or his son. I also wondered what Mrs. Bellerion did to pass the time each day while her husband lectured to barely interested students on the Quest of the Golden Fleece, the main protagonists in the Trojan War, and the tragedies befalling the House of Thebes. Perhaps, the sound on her TV was turned up too high to hear her doorbell, her attention fixed on *The Days of Our Lives, Search for Tomorrow, As the World Turns,* maybe even *Dark Shadows,* and reruns of *Queen for a Day.*

By early November the sun set so early darkness fell by five o'clock, making the Bellarion house's entry way difficult to see. Earlier, when I rang the doorbell, I noticed an absence of a porch lamp, as well as no lamp over the garage door. and, though a streetlight lit the lawn, the pathway from garage to front door was obscured by shadows.

So, I called it a day, though that didn't mean I drove the seventy miles back to Santa Maria. I could have camped out in one of the three upscale apartments on Shoreline Drive near the Maritime Museum that Amanda's law firm maintains primarily for out-of-town witnesses. However, Wendy Ellen Sheldon was home and I saw no reason to turn down her offer of allowing me to spend the night with her.

Before going to Wendy Ellen's house I decided to stop at the Pacific Beach Retreat Hotel. The clerk to whom I had offered $20 the evening before was back on duty

"Your couple has not checked out. So I'm assuming they'll be here for another night's lodging," the clerk told me.

I gave him another twenty. "Call my answering service at midnight to tell the service whether the couple I was interested in had checked out or not.

"Glad to be of service to you, sir."

I'm sure he was, but I wasn't quite so sure how Amanda was going to feel when she saw forty dollars as an item on my expense sheet entitled *bribes*. On prior cases when I had had to shell out money to buy information I had used the terms *enticements, inducements,* and *gratuities*. But no matter the description, Amanda always ground her teeth and gave me a look that said: *I hope it was worth it.* It usually was.

"Thanksgiving and Christmas are going to be rotten without my little girls," Wendy Ellen told me, while fixing a plate of cold cuts for me. "I'm not even going to put up a tree to decorate. What's the point?"

"Maybe Santa will bring the girls back to you," I said before recognizing how crass that sounded.

"Not funny," she said.

"You're right. I apologize."

"Don't you have any leads, Stu?"

"I do. I think I have a good lead on the car used in the girls' kidnapping." That wasn't exactly a lie, but several shades darker than the truth.

"Can you tell me?"

"I'd rather not. I don't want to get your hopes up." Or mine either.

"Even if I offer to cook Christmas dinner for you?"

"Not even. The lead is too iffy, Wendy."

Wendy curled her lower lip into a pout.

"What I know now may even be dangerous to whomever knows it," I said.

"Whomever? Where'd you learn that fancy talk?"

"From my mother."

"You've never talked about her."

"She is the exception to my disbelief in saints."

"I wish I could say that about mine."

"Where did you grow up?" I said.

"In Bakersfield. The asshole end of the San Joaquin Valley. My folks ran a small diner at the north end of town, catering to oil riggers and carrot pickers. They had me peeling potatoes before I could walk. I must not have peeled them fast enough because they reached a point where they couldn't cover the rent. Coffee was still a nickel a cup, with endless refills."

"What then?"

"Mom borrowed money from her brother so Dad could buy a camper truck. We drove around to where Mexican carrot pickers took their lunch breaks. Dad and I sold sandwiches Mom had made. Doing that didn't pay the rent on the tiny apartment we had. So they both got warehouse jobs, packing carrots. Don't ever offer to buy me or make me a stew that has potatoes and carrots in it."

I said, "Compared to you, my life growing up was all strawberry ice cream. My father worked as the pilot scheduler for American Airlines at LAX. My mother worked in the library at USC. I went to Torrance High and then Long Beach State. I finally ended up as a detective for the Burbank PD. It was my library assistant mother who taught me when to use *who* and when to use *whom.*"

"Tell me about your first girlfriend."

"Sally Lynn Dickenson in the first grade."

"No, no. In high school. When you were old enough to have seriously naughty thoughts – and do something about them."

"That would have been Roxanne Linnzicki, a brown-eyed blonde, the assistant chief of police's daughter. Mike Linnzicki, Roxy's dad, was the one who first got me thinking about becoming a copper."

"Tell me more about Roxanne."

"Okay. I'll cut right to what you're dying to know. Roxy was a backseat dry-hump delight. And she always insisted on being on top. It was not my backseat to begin with. I didn't have a car of my own until I was a senior and had saved enough for a down payment. Danny Weinstraub had a Ford station wagon. So, at the Torrance drive-in Danny would have Lori Dortmund sit on his lap, I would have Roxy in the back seat, then Butch Gordon would curl up around Veronica Peyton in the cargo area behind the back seat."

"Was Roxanne your first fuck?"

"Please, let's change the subject, darlin'. A man must retain some secrets. Okay?"

"So tell me about this car you've got a line on."

"I think I know where the missing Woody went. I may have to apply brass knuckles to somebody's teeth to confirm my suspicions, which is why, for the moment, I want you to remain in the dark about the details. I'm sorry, Wendy, but I don't want to endanger you."

Wendy Ellen nodded, but I didn't detect much of an honest assent in her nod.

"I'll take you up on your offer of Christmas dinner. If you make up a grocery list, I'll take you shopping and pay the tab."

"Now that's the kind of man I like. Done deal. I'll let you know when I'm ready for a trip to Von's. Turkey or ham?"

"Lady's choice."

38

In the morning I almost regretted not having driven home the previous night, rather than spending it with Wendy Ellen. Not because of anything Wendy did wrong, just I dreaded driving the extra seventy miles home in the morning, then having to retrace my way to Santa Julietta before heading down to LA.

Sometimes Amanda Reynolds calls me "Gaviota Man", because of the pass between Santa Julietta and Santa Maria that goes by that name. In Spanish *Gaviota* means *seagull*. Historians claim the first Spaniards exploring north from LA killed a seagull near the pass. History books also say that, during the 1846 Mexican War, the Mexican army set an ambush for the forces of John C. Fremont coming south, but Fremont got wind of the ambush and took the mountainous route up into the Santa Ynez Mountains, eventually capturing Santa Julietta.

Heading south on Hwy 101, just before reaching Gaviota Pass, lies the steepest grade of the freeway between San Francisco and LA. Northbound eighteen-wheelers are told to keep to the right. Otherwise the pass is memorable because there is a brief, northbound-only tunnel engineered through a mountain as the mountain descends to the sea.

Home again, I repacked my well-worn suitcase, a gift from my parents when I started college. I was expecting to have to stay overnight in LA after I my visit to Jude Crowder. Despite Amanda's willingness to overlook some of my more dubious claims on the expense account details I turn in to her, I make myself stay in moderately priced hotels whenever I'm obliged to stay overnight doing work for her. The nearest hotel to Jude Crowder's law firm was across the street from UCLA's Botanical Gardens, a ten-minute drive away.

Decorations of pumpkins and turkeys covered the walls of the reception area of Crowder, O'Brien and Byrne. However, there were no depictions of Pilgrims in this office full of Catholic lawyers. The Pilgrims had been separatists from the Church of England, but not advocates of a return to Catholicism. The receptionist was a freckled redhead wearing glasses with oval lens and red frames. Perry Mason's Della Street she wasn't. Nor was there a bust of Voltaire along the wall next to the entryway as Perry had. However, a large photo of Pope Paul VI hung next to the door that I presumed led to the offices of the three attorneys.

"Mr. Fletcher?" the receptionist cocked her head and added a smile to her query.

"Yes."

"Please, have as seat. Mr. Crowder will be with you shortly." The name on her desk bar read: Jennifer O'Brien. A niece perhaps to one of the partners. I guessed she was in her early- to mid-twenties. She had a lovely voice and lacked a wedding ring, likely meaning she was too picky to have found the right man to marry yet, rather than because she was a divorcee. Women who have cashiered one or more husbands emit powerful, silent men-beware waves. Jennifer didn't.

I took a seat in a corner by the magazine stand and scanned the covers of the three issues at the top of the pile: *Liguorian, Catholic Digest*, and *The Angelus*, each a monthly magazine, each directed toward a Catholic audience. Deeper in the pile were quarterlies dedicated to UCLA athletics, upscale interior décor, and to the LA Dodgers baseball team. One bore a cover photo of Vin Scully, the best play-by-play announcer ever and an ardent Catholic.

I had just started to read the article on Scully when a side door opened and a man emerged who introduced himself to me as Jude Crowder. He was tall and thin, with sandy blond hair and a tan to make Hollywood swoon boy Tab Hunter jealous.

"Mr. Fletcher, I'm pleased to meet you. Jude Crowder, Randall and Stephanie's uncle. Follow me."

Nice sky-blue-and-yellow tie. UCLA colors. Firm handshake. A small scar at the right edge of his chin. My research on him told me he was a member of Hollywood director John Ford's camera crew when that group filmed action at Midway Island in June, 1942, when US Navy carriers ambushed a Japanese task force headed by four carriers as the Japanese attempted to capture the small US garrison in the middle of the Pacific Ocean. Jude Crowder had been hit by a piece of shrapnel as the film crew crouched behind sandbags atop a runway observation tower. Because he was a civilian he didn't merit a Purple Heart, but, after the war, his present-at-Midway stories enhanced his reputation as a gutsy, give-'em-hell attorney.

His private office had been decorated by a minimalist. Bookshelves of law texts, a blown-up photo of himself standing between John Ford on one side and Clark Gable and Ava Gardner on the other on the movie set of *Mogambo*. To the left of that large photo hung smaller photos, several of empty Hawaiian volcanic beaches plus a photo of him with a woman I presumed was his wife.

He gestured for me to take the seat in front of his large oak desk. He sat on the edge of the desk, next to the photo of him and same the woman in the photo on the wall. Hard as I tried, I was unable to convince myself that he was the man who had spent the night with Sister Carmen at the Pacific Beach Retreat Hotel in Santa Julietta.

"How may I help you, Mr. Fletcher?"

I came right to the point.

"Your cousin Morgan Crowder owned a vintage Woody automobile when he went missing. According to what I've read, he left the Woody behind when he and his roommate, Lennie Camden, vanished and at some point you had custody of that vehicle."

Jude gave me a blank look that might have told me he hadn't been listening to me. Finally, he said, "Is that an assertion or a question, Mr. Fletcher?"

"A question."

"As best I can recall, I drove Morgan's Woody from the site where we all attended the soiree from which he and Leonard vanished, drove it directly to the Santa Clara police station. I drove it there at the request of authorities who wished to examine it further. Having complied, I left the station with my sister, Mary Margaret, who followed me. That is the last time I saw Morgan's car."

I said, "While I was at your sister's home up north I had occasion to see a couple of photos of the Woody parked under the wing of a small aircraft."

"Oh, yes. Morgan was an avid flyboy who introduced Mary-Margaret to flying Pipers. She even got good enough to race in a couple of Powder Puff Derby events."

"As you surely know, a Woody was allegedly used in the kidnapping of two young girls from a convent school in Santa Julietta. My research tells me the license plate letters and numbers might very well match those of your cousin's car. Do you have any insight into how that might be?"

A shrug. "As I say, once the Santa Clara police took custody of Morgan's Woody, I had no further acquaintance with that vehicle. It is odd though, I agree, how that car went from sitting in police custody to perhaps being used in a kidnapping a couple hundred miles away. Have you inquired of the Santa Clara police what became of the car once they had no further use for it?"

I lied and said, "Santa Clara police records indicate the car was turned over to your sister once they were finished examining it."

He tried to remain calm but I could see my answer flustered him. However, he recovered quickly. "I assume you've spoken to Mary-Margaret about this."

"I tried. She ducked."

"Very well. I did see the Woody again. Took possession of it from my sister several months after Morgan vanished. Until I took it, the Woody sat in Mary-Margaret's garage. However, its presence on her property made my sister twitchy and she complained to my brother A.C. that she wanted the car moved. In turn, A.C. ordered me to get rid of the damned thing."

I said, "Ordered?"

He laughed. "The pecking order in our family would be impossible for anyone outside the family to sort out. It's highly complex. How it devolved into what it is, I cannot begin to explain. But yes. When my oldest brother even suggests some course of action be initiated by someone else in our family, be it little Teddy, Mary-Margaret, or me, we take that suggestion as an order, an order not to be questioned."

"So what did you do about the Woody?"

He said, "I brought here to LA and sold it to a Mexican dealer who's business is to purchase used automobiles here in southern California and take them across the border for resale. Sometimes he takes them whole, other times he...."

Jude struggled to find the word he wanted, so I filled it in for him.

"A chop shop."

"Yes. I believe that is what the locals call the dismantling of a car in order to sell its parts off."

"Do you remember the name of the dealer you sold it to?"

"I'd have to look in the phone book. The name doesn't come to my mind immediately."

"I'd appreciate your helping me out here."

"Of course. If the car was used in the commission of a felony, I certainly want to be of all the help I can be." He reached over and pressed a button on his telephone console. "Jennifer, would you come to my office, please?" Looking over at me, he said, "Jennifer will be able to find the file of the man I sold it to."

I said, "He obviously required no proof of ownership."

"No. I knew he wouldn't. Ironically, I defended this man on charges of dealing in stolen cars. So I know how the man conducts his business."

"Was your defense of this man a success?" I said.

"As a matter of fact, I did get the man off. The reason.... well, reason has little to do with it. The jury found the prosecutor highly offensive. They acquitted the man after only twenty minutes of deliberation. Shortly thereafter, the DA dismissed the man from his staff."

Jennifer entered without knocking and Jude Crowder explained what I was in search of.

Without taking her eyes off of me, she said to her boss, "I'm sure I can find the man's file somewhere, but the search may take a while. Would you mind coming back near our closing time. I should be able to find it by then."

"Sure. What time do you close?" I said. *May take a while.* All of two minutes was my guess.

"Five o'clock."

How about I swing back by here around four thirty?"

"Make it ten till," she said.

39

Jennifer O'Brien was waiting for me outdoors, on the steps of her law firm's building.

I asked, "Do you have what I'm looking for?"

She feigned astonishment. "Wow! That's a saucy question."

I knew it was, but I said, "Oh, really? What makes it saucy?"

"You know perfectly well the built-in the sexual overtones of your question."

"You're seeing something that isn't there. Allow me to rephrase my question. Do you have the name of the man to whom Jude Crowder sold his cousin Morgan's Woody automobile?"

Jennifer glared at me. "Are you going to ask me to dinner or not?"

"I could do that. Is that the price of answering my question?" I said.

"Part of the price."

"And the other part or parts?"

"Whoa! Don't rush things. We hardly know each other – yet."

I wasn't entirely sure what game she thought she was playing. Or who thought the game up.

"You make me nervous, Miss O'Brien."

"Is that all I make you?"

"Where do you suggest we go for dinner? I'm not familiar with this part of LA."

"The Peking Empress. It's across from the main entrance to UCLA. Hot and sour soup to die for. Their House Special Chicken is their signature dish. You'll love it."

So I found myself sitting at a dark corner table of a Chinese restaurant. Next to me, closer than decorum dictated for a first date, Jennifer O'Brien nattered on about her life as a UCLA coed, talking to me as though she had been my girlfriend for longer than she had worked in her uncle's law office. Longer than two years.

The object of this game remained a mystery to me, but I played along. Or rather I remained passive while she auditioned for the role of drama queen. *Passive* included allowing my right hand and arm to remain limp when they became the objects of her firm clutches, doled out as exclamations to the points she was making.

Finally I asked her, "What do you know about your uncle's partner, Jude Crowder?"

155

She didn't answer immediately. I could almost see the gears turning inside her head. At last she said, "Jude makes my uncle uncomfortable at times. I think he does it deliberately, if you know what I mean."

"No. I don't know what you mean."

"Well, Jude is very mysterious, and my uncle says he knows that Jude breaks the Lord's seventh commandment – Thou shalt not commit adultery -- and breaks it often, with more than one woman. Uncle Robert doesn't know what to do about it. He's afraid to confront Jude because, Jude has an awful temper and Robert fears Jude will attack him. And Father John, Jude's sister's boyfriend, has told my uncle to ignore Jude's behavior, ignore it because the time will come that the Lord Himself will confront Jude about his philandering and punish him as He sees fit."

"Tell me more about Father John," I said.

"Father John lives in the Bay Area. San Jose, I believe. I don't see him often. Do you know him?"

"I've met him."

"Isn't he cool?" Jennifer said, gushing. "Father John is funny when he tells stories about all the beatniks in Bay Area. San Francisco and Berkeley. John once confided in me that more than once he has smoked marijuana, not because he likes it, but to get closer to those young people. Most of them are almost my age, you know."

And some even older. Jack Kerouac and Lawrence Ferlinghetti for examples.

That was a side of Father John that I would not have guessed existed. But then I had only seen him in the company of Mary-Margaret Crowder, and I didn't suppose for a moment that Mary-Margaret danced about bonfires with flowers in her hair and a marijuana joint dangling from her lips. On the other hand, perhaps her obvious devotion to Father John may have led her down the garden path toward huppiedom.

"Tell me more about Jude Crowder."

"I must confess I don't know him that well. I pay him little attention. But that's because he has never tried to flirt with me." Clutching my arm, she added, "And I have never tried to lead him on. I mean, after all, he's so much older than I am."

"Has Jude confessed his adulteries to your Uncle Robert? Or has…."

"Heavens no! But, once, to confirm his suspicions, Uncle Robert had one of the detectives who works for the agency our law firm hires to do…. Well, you would know all about what sorts of sordid things gumshoes do to catch out the kinds of lowlife behavior Uncle Robbie suspected Jude Crowder of engaging in."

Yes. I would know all right. *The sordid things gumshoes do.*

Jennifer continued. "I overheard Uncle Robert telling my father about what the detective reported back to him. It was wickedly delicious! Why, I couldn't take my ear away from the keyhole."

"Did the detective happen to attach a name to Jude's lover?"

"No, but he reported something even better than a name."

"Better than a name, eh?"

"Yes. He reported what she was wearing, Rather, what she had been wearing before Jude helped undress her."

"What was that?'

Jennifer giggled, then leaned in close and whispered, "A nun's habit."

"Was this a Halloween costume?"

"Oh, no, it was the real thing. The woman was a genuine nun."

"Was this detective able to attach a name to this nun?"

Another whisper. "Carmen Armenta."

"Any details on this Carmen Armenta?" I had not yet attempted to find out Sister Carmen's last name.

"Only that she is a member of the Sisters of Mercy and works at a hospital in Long Beach. This was a couple of years ago, when Jude had a big case down in Long Beach, defending an accountant who was accused of embezzling more than a hundred thousand dollars over several years from a hospital's operating funds. The hospital was the same one where this Carmen woman worked as a nurse."

I couldn't wait to look into whether the Carmen caught in a dalliance with Jude Crowder in Long Beach was the same Carmen who now worked as schoolteacher in a convent in Santa Julietta.

40

I asked Jennifer, "Why does your uncle tolerate Jude's womanizing?"

"Because Jude is such a great courtroom lawyer. He dazzles juries, and he drives prosecutors mad. Plus, he's won some huge class-action cases. Wow! Did the money roll in those times."

I nearly forgot that we had placed our order. When it arrived I was amazed at how good it all looked and how hungry I was. Jennifer dazzled me with her chopsticks dexterity. I stuck to using my fork. The house special was indeed excellent. Shrimp Szechwan style was superb. Jennifer ordered another round of drinks.

When the fortune cookies arrived with the check, they turned out to be so ambiguous as to be meaningless. *You will catch lightning in a bottle.* Even Jennifer was disappointed by that. Mine read: *Nowhere will the world be brighter than at home.* Feh! That was always the case.

"You do plan to invite me into your bed, Mr. Private Eye?"

"My dear, I hardy know you."

"What better way to achieve that goal, eh?"

I had no comeback to that.

She added, "I won't disappoint you. I promise."

"And if you do?" I said.

"In that case, you'll have to give me a chance to make it up to you."

Fair is fair.

As it turned out, she wasn't bad, but, even so, she insisted on a rematch. I agreed, given that I might learn even more about Jude Crowder from her. But we didn't set a date for another cavorting under the sheets. I only hoped this whole affair had not been a setup for Jude to make me disappear, the way he made Morgan Crowder's Woody vanish.

My trip was a success, at least insofar as my having an initial opportunity for sizing up Jude Crowder. Still, he now knew I was looking into his role in feeding Morgan Crowder's license plate number to the Sisters to use in falsely identifying the car used in the abduction of the two convent girls.

What action he would now take I didn't know. Well, in theory, he could bring the entire Archdiocese of Los Angeles crashing down around my head. I needed help, so I headed back to Santa Julietta.

Police Captain Wade Septazelli, one of the really good guys on Santa Julietta's city police force. He had left a message for at my answering service. When I called him from Amanda Reynold's office, he told me sister Carmen had received a phone call to go to one of the main charities the local Sisters of Mercy help out. A Sister Rachel volunteered to go in Carmen's place. As Sister Rachel walked to her car, another car jumped the curb and ran over her. I was betting the phone call to the assassin came from the offices of Crowder, O'Brien, and Byrne.

Amanda was puzzled.

She said, "Why is this hot-shit lawyer for the Archdiocese so keen on keeping you from learning more about the kidnapping of two children? Why ask those sisters to make up a story about the kidnapping car? Okay. It's because a car that he supposedly got rid of was used. But there is obviously more to it, if you think he ordered this Sister Carmen silenced. He claims he sold the car to a guy who may or may not run a chop shop. Do you know if the cops ever questioned the chop shop owner?"

"They did not, because, even though the case was, and is, so high-profile that everyone in southern California knows about it, Jude Crowder never came forward to announce that he possessed important information about the car that was used."

"Now why is that?" Amanda said, as if she couldn't guess.

"Because he is somehow involved with the kidnapping. But why?"

"I currently don't know of any rings trafficking in children that age. Do you?"

I said, "No. And, by the way, I filled Captain Septazelli in on much of this, and he decided to put Sister Carmen under police protection."

"That's a sensible idea," Amanda said.

"Any thoughts on who killed Sister Rachel? You have more inside knowledge of local thugs for hire."

She grimaced. "Thanks a lot."

"Well, it's true."

"Even so, it's impolite to point it out."

I said, "There's a good chance that whoever ran over Sister Rachel may be the same thugs who kidnapped the two girls."

Amanda said, "Why hasn't Jude come forth to admit that he sold his cousin's Woody and admit why. Admit to whom he sold it. And now for the big follow-up question: Why would he not provide authorities with the correct license plate numbers of the Woody? Instead, he obviously allowed authorities to struggle with the partial numbers the nuns saw. And, as for the wrong color of the plates… what's behind that?"

I said, "Maybe you should insist Jude be arrested, so he can answer your questions."

"Am I missing something?" she said.

"Not that I can see. Unless Jude himself is running a child-peddling business."

"Or the Church. God knows Rome itself is into a variety of shady businesses and practices."

"God knows?" Amanda's heathen instincts exceeded my own.

"That's a figure of speech, Fletcher."

"On the other hand, if there is a God and God knows, why doesn't He put an end to them?"

"God only knows, Fletcher," she said with a wide grin.

Wendy Ellen was watching a sitcom when I arrived at her place. Talking over an annoying laugh track, I filled her in on what had happened, in LA, at Santa Julietta police headquarters with Wade Septazelli, and in Amanda's office. Only when I finished did she turn the TV off.

"I bet that priest you're seeing in jail knows something. Rough him up, Fletcher. Make him talk."

"I don't think I could get away with laying a hand on him. Why do you think he knows anything about the kidnappings?"

"Doesn't even Mother Agnes have to go to confession regularly? She knows more than she's letting on. Maybe she spilled the beans in the confession box."

"It's a thought. But I have no idea whether Father Mackenzie was hearing confessions from the Sisters of Mercy, and even if he was, priests are sworn to secrecy regarding what they are told in the confession box. If a serial murderer were to tick off all his victims to his priest, the priest is forbidden from going to authorities with what he's heard."

"That's dumb!" Anna said.

"Dumb or not, that's the way it is. I imagine priests lay awake unable to sleep some nights after hearing what they hear in the confessional."

Wendy Ellen sneered. "Yeah, but I bet a lot of those guys get off on what they hear. I bet they love giving some of their parishioners nasty looks when they see them later. I know I would. I'd keep a little black book of all the dirty linen people let hangout when they confess, and I wouldn't take my book with me to my grave."

Hearing Wendy say that allowed me to tell her about Francis Crowder's diary and how it had led me on a merry chase in the Bay Area.

"Mary Chase. Isn't she your next-door neighbor in Santa Maria?"

I couldn't help but laugh. "Yes, Wendy. She is."

41

I decided to try to isolate Sister Carmen and confront her with what I now knew about Morgan Crowder's Woody and its license plate numbers. I wanted to be the one to instill her with fear for not telling me who put her up to lying. I didn't want to walk into the convent and have Mother Agnes present when I confronted Carmen because it was possible Mother Agnes was in on some kind of coverup regarding who really kidnapped Melissa Hargrove and Eileen Sanchez.

I was sure I could frighten Sister Carmen out of her starchy black nun's habit merely by hinting that I knew about her evenings spent with Jude Crowder at the Pacific Beach Retreat Hotel. Whether Mother Agnes knew about Carmen and Jude, I wasn't sure. Agnes ran a mighty loose ship if she allowed any or all of her Sisters of Mercy the equivalent of three-day Navy furloughs.

I had to think long and hard about a way to lure Sister Carmen away from the convent, draw her away on her own, without arousing suspicion. I settled on asking Jennifer O'Brien to phone Sister Carmen and tell her Jude Crowder wanted to meet with her, that he was already on his way up to Santa Julietta. The rendezvous was to be at The Shady Lady bar in downtown Santa Julietta. I didn't know if any of the sisters owned a car, but there was a city bus route stop only two blocks from the convent. I checked to be sure the route ended somewhere near downtown. It did.

As for why Jude didn't want to pick Carmen up at the convent, I told Jennifer to tell Carmen that he had come into possession of some nasty information about Mother Agnes and didn't want the abbess to know Carmen was meeting him. Jennifer agreed to make the call, but only on condition that I would reward her with another opportunity for her to be my boudoir playmate, as she put it. I made her a solemn promise to fulfill her wish.

The Shady Lady bar was not new to me. Amanda had taken me there shortly after I first met her. She had explained to me that the place was considered too lowbrow by the county prosecutor's attorneys. So she didn't have to worry about being overheard by the opposition when discussing details of a case. I had no objections, so long as the bar was well stocked with cold bottles of Bud.

Sitting in the back at a table for two, I was near the jukebox, where a pair of middle-aged strumpets wearing too much makeup and clothes that were too skimpy fed their loose change into the jukebox. Moments later Hank Williams, playing "Your Cheatin'

Heart" came through the ceiling speakers, followed by another Williams song, "I'm So Lonesome I Could Cry". I wondered if Jesus was listening in and thinking about Sister Carmen, who may still have been wed to God, but she definitely wasn't being faithful to Him..

I was nursing my second bottle of beer and munching peanuts when the woman I thought was Sister Carmen arrived and began looking around for Jude Crowder as soon as her eyes adjusted to the tavern's dim lighting. She had left her habit at the convent and was wearing a long-sleeved blouse and blue jeans. I recognized her as the same woman I had seen entering the Pacific Beach Front Hotel.

I stood and waved for her to join me. Of course, she didn't recognize me. She looked startled and took a quick glance toward the exit. So, I shook my head and mouthed, "No, No! It's okay."

I could see she was torn between joining me and fleeing. So, I hastened toward her as she turned toward the front door.

"Sister Carmen. It's all right. I'm a friend of the Crowders." I deliberately didn't provide her with my name. "Join me while we wait for Jude." Little did she realize that waiting for Jude was going to be like waiting for Godot.

"Who are you?"

"My name's Stu. We haven't met before, but I know a little bit about you."

Her eyes narrowed. I was afraid she might make a scene.

So I said, "Come. Sit down. We have a lot to talk about before Jude gets here. It's important. What would you like to drink?"

"Wine."

"Red or white?"

"Rose."

I motioned for the bar maid and pulled back a chair for her.

"Where's Jude?"

"He'll was delayed. He'll find his way here. Something about a huge pileup just past Thousand Oaks. He exited to take surface streets, but so did everyone else."

Her wine came and I again told the server I was still okay nursing my second Budweiser.

"What is your name? You are not familiar to me."

"Fletcher. I work mostly in Orange County. I'm here because word is the FBI is going to interview you again. We want to make sure you remember everything you need to remember to keep them off-track. Do you require a fresher session on anything?"

She shook her head. "I still remember the car description and the partial license plate letters and numbers that Jude gave me."

"We just want to be sure. After all, it's been a while," I said.

"Sister Melda is the one you should worry about. She barely survived the first round of interviews. She's not as bright or as tough as I am."

"We intend to give Sister Melda a refresher course. Will she do better if you are there to coach her?"

"She has to steel herself. She knows they will put her in a small room with two of them and her, all by herself. What has come up that the FBI thinks a second round of questioning is necessary?"

I gave her a slow shrug. "We don't know the details. Just that they want to get together with you and Sister Melda again."

She laughed. "The best way to make sure Melda knows her lines is to have Mother Agnes put the fear of God in her."

"I expect Jude will ask Mother Agnes to do just that."

Carmen said, "Will Mother Agnes be interviewed, too?"

"I expect she will. But, of course, we have no doubt she will have no difficulty backing you up, even though she was not on the playground."

"Are you an FBI agent, trying to trip one of us up?"

"Would I admit it, if I was?"

"I suppose not. It was stupid of me to ask?"

"Stupid to ask, but not stupid to think it."

She drained her wine glass and gave me a long, hard stare, trying to read me.

"Another glass of wine?"

She grinned. "An effort to get me drunk?"

"No. I simply figured that staring at me as hard as you are might make you thirsty."

She shook her head. "No more wine."

I decided to jolt her. "Are you spending the night with Jude again at the Pacific Beach Front Hotel?"

"You are an FBI man."

"No. As far as I know, the FBI knows nothing about your trysts with Jude. The real issue is: Does Mother Agnes know?"

She flinched so hard she nearly fell over backwards off her chair.

"Well? Does she?"

"No. And neither does Sister Melda or anyone else at the convent. I am capable of being very discreet."

I wanted to say, "But not as discreet as you think you are," but I didn't. Instead, I said to her, "You are wed to Jesus and now you are cheating on him. I tossed her a quarter and added, "There's a song on the jukebox called 'Your Cheating Heart'. Play it. It's your song." I then stood and said, "Jude should be along shortly. I have other errands to run. It has been a pleasure to meet you, Sister Carmen."

Her jaw dropped and she braced herself against the table. "You're going to leave me to sit here by myself, with all these…these men?"

"I am. I'm sure you can fend for yourself. If not, you have God to protect you.."

I left a two-dollar tip on the table and walked away without looking back.

42

I returned to my car and sat, mulling. Was my using Sister Carmen to bait the bear, Jude Crowder, a good idea? Probably not, but the deed was done. Too late now to undo what was likely a blunder.

I now had no doubt that Jude Crowder had coached Sisters Carmen and Melda into providing authorities with a phony account of the kidnap vehicle. But why? Was he involved in the abductions? Nothing else made sense to me. But why would he abduct the girls? Or be a part of having them abducted? Why were the two sisters willing to go along with the subterfuge? Who else in the convent knew? Maybe all of them, including Mother Agnes? It was all very strange.

What I was certain of was the likelihood Jude or someone working for him would now come gunning for me. Perhaps, literally. Sister Carmen would certainly give Jude an earful about me when they finally linked up. Okay. I told myself I would be ready for them. I even checked that my under-the-dashboard .38 to be sure it was loaded.

More and more the abduction of the two girls was somehow connected to the disappearance of Morgan Crowder and his roommate twenty years earlier. The only thing the two events had in common – at least the only connect I could fathom so far – was the Woody. The car belonged to Morgan and apparently was hijacked by Jude Crowder, although I doubt if he would acknowledge what he did was a hijacking.

Why did Jude provide Carmen and Melda with the Woody's license plate numbers? Did he want to conceal the real abduction car's plates? And if so, why? Had he abducted them? If so, did he use his own car? I tried to imagine where Jude would hide the abducted girls. That would depend on the motive for taking them and I lacked that.

The last time I spoke with Sheriff Cuddleston I asked him where the FBI was. I thought by now I would trip across at least one FBI agent. Cuddleston's reply was, "They're all up in the Bay Area, mostly at Berkeley, building dossiers on every kid waving an anti-war poster. There may still be one or two in LA, looking into child-kidnappings there to see if one of those bunches had branched out. But that business is a black hole. The FBI doesn't have any Hispanic agents. So they're not going to be able to infiltrate any of the gangs, and that is the only way to get a bead on them."

Southern California gangs were known to abducted young girls occasionally, most always the motive was revenge for something another gang had done. If you steal my cocaine, I'll steal your girlfriend. That sort of thing. Occasionally too, children of high-profile rich families were abducted for ransom. But Melissa and Eileen were orphans, kidnapped from a Catholic orphanage. There had been no ransom note and even if there had been, to whom would it be addressed? Cardinal McIntyre? The pope? And who would be expected to pay?

Jude Crowder was playing a bizarre game, but to what end? I was baffled. And angered to know a man of his standing could stoop to such crimes. I had an urge to find Jude and shove the barrel of my pistol into his ear and demand answers.

But then I took a deep breath and calmed down.. Men of Jude Crowder's standing in nearly every community stooped to heinous crimes. I had witnessed that fact time and time again as a member of the Burbank PD. On the homicide detective squad we never had a shortage of cases.

Yet, men and women of Jude's standing were seldom punished. At most they got their knuckles rapped. Two years ago Amanda Reynolds told me of a prominent attorney in Ventura who could not resist the temptation of several hundred thousand dollars one of his client's fiduciary accounts. The money was being held there, contingent on the client's being found guilty of stealing the money or whether it was money he was due for services rendered.

Instead, the attorney removed the money from the fiduciary account and spent it on himself, buying clothes, theater tickets, home furnishings, and a new car. When caught, the attorney served no jail time. He wasn't even formally charged with a crime. He was disbarred, but only for one year. He also had to make restitution to the fiduciary account, which he did by stealing his parents credit cards and using them to withdraw the maximum cash allowed on each card.

Amanda thought the whole affair was funny. I didn't.

I decided to let the Jude-and-Carmen soup pot simmer for a while and headed for the county jail to see if I could rattle more information out of the wily priest. When I arrived it was chow time so I cooled my heels by sitting in my car and listening to the radio. The dial was set to country music station KHAY and I let it remain there. I was in the mood for more cry-in-your-beer music. My visit to The Shady Lady must have set my C&W neurons to vibrating.

Johnny Cash was singing "Folsom Prison Blues". The follow-up to that was Waylon Jennings' "Something's Wrong in California" and I found myself chuckling until Dolly Parton and Porter Wagoner made me stop by soullessly making a hash of Tom Paxton's "The Last Thing On My Mind".

Hoping mealtime was over for the jailbirds, I passed through Sheriff Huddleston's flimsy security checks and was taken to Reed Mackenzie's cell, where I filled the padre in on what I had been up to.

When I finished the padre patted his blanket, urging me to sit next to him.

"Ah, Fletcher, if only you had known then what I'm going to tell you now, you would have gone about things differently."

"How so?"

"What is your opinion on literary irony?" Mackenzie said with a smirk.

"Same as with any other form of irony. I find it amusing. Now tell where this is going."

"Eagerly. You see, the reason Cardinal McIntyre and his minions transferred from LA to Santa Julietta was because I was screwing eight or ten – I've lost count – nuns in various convents in LA parishes within the archdiocese. But only one nun counted. Carmen Armenta."

"Go on."

"Jude Crowder was also screwing Carmen and he wanted exclusive dibs on her. Hence, my transfer. It had nothing to do with my have a yen for choir boys or acolytes."

"Sister Carmen, eh?"

"Are you familiar with Aldous Huxley, Fletcher? I know you told me you graduated from Long Beach State, but you didn't mention when you studied there."

"I've read *Brave New World*, which I found entertaining, and *Point Counter Point,* which makes for a great sleeping pill."

"What about *The Devils of Loudun*?"

"Yes! One summer I wanted to pick up some extra credit hours so I signed up for a class about Reformation and Renaissance philosophy, taught by a man who had a reputation as a brilliant teacher. His name is Harvey Bernstein. And one of the required readings was Huxley's *Devils*. I found it hilarious."

"It is that!" Mackenzie said.

I said, "Bernstein's course centered on French skepticism, the mainstay of which was Rene Descartes, of course. But we also read some Nicolas Malbranche, Pierre Bayle, and Erasmus as spokesman for the Counter-Reformation. Huxley's *Devils* was a side dish to all of that, but what a tasty one it was. It gave us students a far better understanding of the cultural milieu in which the philosophers were arguing back and forth."

"Well, the church was not amused when *The Devils* was published."

I said, "I can see why."

My recollection was that the Church, to try to save face, declared that all the promiscuous nuns were, in fact, seduced by the Devil and would be obliged to undergo exorcism.

Father Mackenzie said, "In any case, the cardinal saw in me another Urbane Grandier, the priest who screws every nun within a radius of forty miles of his parish."

"Where is the irony?"

"I'm getting there," he said. "The cardinal sent me here to Santa Julietta, at the outer edge of his dominion, but then, unbeknownst to him, a couple of abbesses got together and shipped Sister Carmen here, not knowing I had been exiled to this city."

"I see. Indeed! How amusing. Amanda will be excited."

"You seem to know a bit about this fellow Jude Crowder."

"Yes. I'm beginning to see him at the epicenter of another case I'm struggling with."

"Let me assure you, Jude is a wicked bastard. Devious as the Devil Himself. Beware!"

"So you were fucking Carmen Armenta."

He laughed. "I take it you know her, too."

"Yes."

"Jude Crowder does not like sharing his toys," the padre said.

"Yet, you and Carmen Armenta both end up in Santa Julietta?"

The priest said, "The cardinal consulted with Jude about moving me. But the Sisters of Mercy in LA hustled Carmen out of town without consulting anyone. That she and I ended up in the same place and for the same reason surely proves God has an incomparable sense of ironic humor."

No doubt about it. A classic case of the right hand and left hand not knowing what the other was doing.

I said, "Well, now that Jude knows you are both here, his plan is to send you off to Soledad."

"I imagine he leaned really hard on the Ledbetter family to file charges against me, to put me here in jail, and he'll likely work hard to keep me incarcerated at least until I can no longer get an erection."

I should have been making written notes, but I told myself I could remember all the salient details long enough to tell Amanda Reynolds.

"He's in the safest place he could be," was Amanda's first reaction when I repeated Father Mackenzie's story to her.

"Except he wants bail, as soon as we can arrange it," I reminded her.

"Let him simmer," she said. "Better that he's disgruntled than dead."

"Right, because Jude will be rolling into town soon, if he hasn't arrived already."
One of Amanda's paralegals, a young woman named Jane Appleton, interrupted us.
"Mr. Fletcher, we have received an urgent call from your answering service."
Jane handed me the note.
It read: *Teddy Crowder has gone missing.* Signed. *Randall Crowder.*

43

At the Crowder mansion the gate guards opened the wrought iron gates and waved me through. They had clearly been alerted that I had been summoned. A.C. Crowder greeted me on his front porch and introduced himself. I was a bit stunned by his obsequiousness.

"I appreciate your coming so quickly, Mr. Fletcher." His looks were not what I had expected. He was not tall, no tan, no thick white main of hair, no horn-rimmed glasses. Just the opposite. He was short, balding, pale-skinned, and wore wire-framed granny glasses.

We shook hands and he ushered me into his living room, where his wife, Randall, and Stephanie sat on the sofa.

"Allow me to fill you in," A.C. began.

The story was Theodora had not come down for breakfast. She was invariably the first one at the table when the family sat down daily at 7:00 a.m. for a traditional beginning of the day that always included each member of the family declaring his or her plans for the day.

"Naturally, we searched the house and gardens for her, enquired of the gate guards" A.C. said. "She hadn't left the premises yet wasn't anywhere on them."

"Surely you have a rear entry onto your land," I said.

"We do, but the trade entrance can only be opened and closed by a buzzer by the kitchen door. I also have a series of cameras aimed at the gates, the delivery driveway to the house, and the pathway leading to the rear gates. I've run the tapes and the result is nil. Same with tapes of the front gate and we've had no visitors since my brother Jude was here last night. And Teddy stood with the rest of us to wave him adieu."

Trade entrance. Adieu. How very upper class. Rather British, I thought.

"So none of you have any ideas about how she vanished."

All heads shook negative simultaneously. "No other security tapes aimed at anything on the premises?" I said.

"No need," A.C. said. "As you already know, our perimeter walls are quite high."

I looked to Randall and Stephanie. "Did she have any favorite hiding places inside or out?" Every kid worth his or her salt had such cubbyholes.

Stephanie said, "Randall and I checked those already."

Mrs. Crowder sat fiddling with an empty candy wrapper.

I spoke directly to her. "What is it you have to add?"

She looked up at me and said, "Teddy has a duffle bag she packs whenever she goes somewhere overnight. The duffle is not where she stores it."

Something concrete at last. I also noticed that, from the looks on their faces, this piece of information came as a surprise to A.C., Randall, and Stephanie.

"Mother! Why didn't you tell us?"

Mrs. Crowder gave them all an embarrassed shrug.

I asked, "No notes telling you she was going somewhere?"

Head shakes all around.

"Where might she go?" I said.

Randall said, "Nowhere without telling one of us."

Until now, I thought.

"With your permission, I would like to review your tapes. I know. It sounds insulting, and maybe it is. Still, that is where I would like to start. May I assume you are hiring me to find her?"

"Most certainly," A.C. said. "What's your fee and how much do you want up front. I'll write you a check, unless you insist on cash."

"Money can wait," I said and quoted my usual fee, a hundred and fifty dollars a day plus expenses.

A.C. led me to his private office on the second floor. In one corner a movie projector sat on a card table. He turned it on, opened a cardboard box filled with tapes. He fed on reel into the machine and pressed a button.

"Have a seat." I sat down on a fold-out card table chair and wondered why a man of his means possessed such a cheap setup. His screen was a bare wall. How frugal of him, I thought. No. Not frugal. *Flinty* was the word I wanted.

"By the way, aren't you the detective who was looking for those young girls who were kidnapped from the local convent?"

"I still am looking." I wasn't going to tell him that I was convinced that his sister, Mary-Margaret, his brother Jude, and the other convent sisters, include the convent's abbess, were involved in those girls' kidnapping to some degree or another.

We watched the most recent days' tapes that covered the rear of his property. Nothing unusual jumped out at me. Next he ran tapes of the front areas, including tapes aimed at the gate guards themselves. He also had tapes of the driveway and of both directions of the road leading to the turnoff into his property.

"Stop. Back that tape up, will you, please?" I said, as the tape was playing of the road that passed his entryway and guard gate.

A.C. ran the tape backward until I said, "Stop! Freeze that frame."

I stood and walked toward the wall. "Do you have a magnifying glass? Any kind will do."

From a desk drawer he withdrew one that was right out of a Sherlock Holmes story. When he handed it to me I felt like Basil Rathbone ready to look at threads in a carpet. The object at hand, however, was not a bloodstained carpet. It was an automobile that appeared in many consecutive film frames, as though the car was parked. I was certain I recognized both the car and its rear license plate. The car was a Buick; the license plate told me that the Buick belonged to Mary-Margaret Crowder.

"Are there any more tapes from this camera?" I asked A.C.

"Yes. Why do you want them?"

I showed him the automobile parked alongside the road, a hundred or so yards past the main gate.

"I see it. What about it?"

"If I'm not mistaken, that car belongs to your sister."

"You think Teddy climbed the fence and went with Mary-Margaret?"

"That would explain her absence," I said.

"But why?"

"We're looking at two pieces of *your* family. You tell me."

A.C. put his head in his hands.

"Where might they go?" I asked.

"I own a cabin up at Arrowhead."

"Cabin?"

"Well, okay. A six-bedroom retreat on ten acres. I make it available to anyone in the family."

"How do you suppose Mary-Margaret contacted Teddy? Your gate photos and your guards attest to Mary's not having been on your property recently."

A.C. let out a sigh before saying, "It's the bloody damned telephones. Two-years ago I relented and indulged each of my children by allowing them to have their own private telephone line in their bedroom. For all I know, each of my children has a Wall Street stockbroker and calls the broker every morning. Hell, I trust my children. I never look at their phone records. I don't not invade their phone privacy. Maybe that's stupid, but I do not spy on my children."

However admirable, his hands-off policy may have come back to bite him on his ass. I said, "Let's speak to your wife. I want her input on all of this."

At first he gave me a nasty glare, but quickly the glare melted away and he finally nodded his agreement.

44

From my previous encounter with Mrs. Crowder – I didn't even know her first name, -- I had judged her a pretty straight forward woman, and without any airs, which had surprised me. Santa Julietta and nearby flossy communities were full of wives who thought the sun shone out of their asses—or their husbands'.

She hadn't given much of a tell about what she thought of A.C., or, in his absence back then, whether she was cowed by his presence. I imagined A ,C. could be a kick-in-the-teeth bully even toward his wife. Having money does that to most men. Having lots of money, such men think, entitles them to double down.

I hit her with, "Does Teddy get the urge to run away from home often, Mrs. Crowder?"

A.C. immediately stepped in. "What the hell kind of question is that?"

I calmly said, "It's the kind of question I ask the mothers of intimidating fathers, especially fathers who not only are capable of intimidation but wallow in it."

"Why you…."

"There. You see? The perfect reaction to what I am saying."

He backed off, but I could tell that the steam coming out his ears wasn't going to be enough to lower his internal pressure.

"You may call me Evelyn, Mr. Fletcher." Turning to her husband, she said, "Now, Al. Please. We've asked for this man's assistance in finding Teddy. So let him ask his questions." Back to me. "Go ahead, Mr. Fletcher."

"My question is about her fantasies of running away from home. Where? I mean, where in California? Your husband has already told me about your cabin at Big Bear."

She said, "Nowhere in particular in California. No, wait. More than once she's spoken of wanting to go to the San Diego Zoo. We live so close, yet we've never been there. None

of us." She looked at her husband as though to shame him.

"Beyond our state?" I said.

A.C. spoke up. "France."

173

Evelyn nodded and offered a wan smile. "Yes. We took her to Paris last year and, from the moment we returned to Santa Julietta, she has spoken repeatedly about wanting to return."

A.C. again. "Bah! Mary-Margaret isn't going to take her to Paris, for chrissake. I think Big Bear is our best bet. Teddy really loves going there. That's the first place I'd look."

That made sense. Still, we were facing a ten-year-old needle in the vast haystack that is Southern California.

I told them, "Let me phone Sheriff Cuddleston and convince him to contact authorities in San Bernardino County. Give me the address of your cabin at Big Bear Lake."

Evelyn Crowder went to fetch a notepad and returned quickly with the address written on it. Meanwhile, A.C. began to pace the length of his large living room.

I said to him "Does either Teddy or Mary-Margaret know where you hide a key to your cabin?"

He stopped pacing and glared at me. "How would you know whether there is a key hidden anywhere?"

I said, "You'd be the odd duck out if you didn't stash a backdoor key under a planter box or somewhere similar."

He gave me an I-gotcha look. "It's under the *front* door ceramic statue of a cocker spaniel."

"Teddy knows this, too?"

A nod.

With permission to use their phone, I called Sam Cuddleston and told him I needed a favor. When I returned, one of the gate guards was standing at the front door, handing Evelyn Crowder an envelope. She thanked the guard, turned, and, looking ashen, brought the envelope to me. The postmark was Palmdale, which lay on State Road 18, on the way toward Big Bear Lake.

It was addressed to Crowder Family and the return address in the upper left-hand corner said Theodora. Inside the envelope was a brief hand-written letter using purple ink.

> Mom and Dad,
> Auntie Mary and her friend Father John are taking me to
> Las Vegas to do early family Xmas shopping. I will call home
> when we get there. Don't worry. I will be OK.
> Love, Your Teddy Bear

"Nice penmanship," I said to break the palpable tension.

"Isn't it though. She works hard at it," Evelyn said. A centuries'-old psychology trick: Focus on a triviality to ward off relief struck dumb by shock.

A.C. took the letter from his wife. His hand was shaking as he read it for himself. Evidence there were human parts lurking behind the tungsten-plated hide of an oil-well industrialist.

"Can anyone of you tell me more about Mary-Margaret's friend called Father John?"

Again A.C. deferred to his wife.

Evelyn said, "Mary met him eight or nine years ago at Alma College in Los Gatos. Alma is a Jesuit seminary. In fact in February it is moving to Berkeley and changing its name to the Jesuit School of Theology at Berkeley."

A.C. added "Oh, yeah. She and Jude drove up there together. John was a participant in a colloquium and afterwards, according to Jude, bold as Billy, Mary charged up to ask him some questions and ended up getting invited to go to lunch with him."

Randall said, "I've had a few conversations with John. He's a Dominican friar and specializes in the teachings of St. Augustine and Thomas Aquinas."

Stephanie said, "Aunt Mary and Father John are definitely not Platonic lovers. I can tell you that."

"Stephanie! How dare you!" Evelyn said.

More calmly, A.C. said, "How did you come by this titillating tidbit, Steph?"

"One time when Mary came to visit us, she insisted on staying at the Windjammer Hotel down on the waterfront. Remember? One morning I went to pick her up and drop her off at Dad's office and when I rapped on her hotel room door, Father John answered, wearing a hotel-issue bathrobe."

Evelyn said, "I've never heard that story." Turning to A.C., she said, "Have you?"

A.C. nodded with a smirk.

"Why, you people! Why am I always left in the dark?"

45

Before leaving the other Crowders' efforts to mollify the family matriarch, I placed a second call to Sheriff Cuddleston filling him in on the note from Teddy Crowder to her family. He reminded me that the way from Santa Julietta to Las Vegas lay along the same route that led to Big Bear Lake. In each case, a driver first had to reach I-15 at San Bernardino.

After finishing with Sam Cuddleston, I phoned my answering service and found out Skip Prendergast of the Santa Clara County police had left a message for me to call him. I decided to wait until I was on neutral ground before returning his call. So, after excusing myself from the Crowders' company, I headed for the nearest pay phone, which turned out to be at a 7-Eleven on Soldier Canyon Road.

"We've found a body up at Steven's Canyon Country Club. As it turns out, shortly after the club opened for play, the club members decided they wanted to reverse the nines, meaning what was planned to be the first hole became the tenth and so on. So, the original third hole became the twelfth."

"Just one skeleton?" I said.

"Just one. And luckily, we were able to match the dental records we had on hand from the original investigation. We had a set of dentals from each missing man, sent by their dentists."

"Keep me in suspense, Lieutenant."

"We found Lennie Camden."

"Great. Keep digging," I said.

"We already have. No other skeletons turned up and we dug until the club threw a fit."

I thanked him and, when I hung up, I wondered where Jude Crowder had buried his brother and why elsewhere? In any case, the hunt for Francis Jerome Crowder's diary or diaries was going to go on in earnest. Maybe that was why Mary-Margaret wanted to take her niece "X-mas shopping". One problem with supposing Teddy was kidnapped to get at the diary was that, from what Teddy had told me, Randall was the one who has last possession of Francis's diary.

So what do I do?

Using Carmen, I baited Jude. Now I realize that was a mistake. I had to remind myself how dangerous Jude could be. Apparently, he was the one who came up with the idea of killing Lennie and burying him along with Francis. Only he changed his mind for some reason. He, Francis and Mary buried Lennie and Jude went south with Francis in the back of the Woody.

Were Mary and Father John using Teddy to lure me after them? I had to decide whether to remain in Santa Julietta and face Jude or to chase after Teddy. I needed help and for that I settled on Sheriff Sam.

But how to go about that and do it quickly? Sam wasn't Catholic, and, rather than draw Sam into the story of a drunken dead cousin being hidden from authorities, I could more easily make him buy a ravished-nun story. And for that Father Reed Mackenzie could help me. I could turn Sam's puritan sex attitude against Jude.

An hour later, sitting in Sam Huddleston's office, I finally shared my secret of seeing photos of the missing Woody, how it came to disappear, and how the license plate letters and numbers matched those of the alleged vehicle used to kidnap Eileen Sanchez and Melissa Hargrove. Next I watched Sam's eyes grow big as I told of my seeing Jude and Sister Carmen entering the Pacific Beach Retreat Hotel. Strange that my own eyesight became sharper with this telling and I claimed I had no doubt who Jude's paramour was. I fudged by claiming the desk clerk had confirmed my identification.

"So what exactly are you asking me to do, Fletcher?" Sam said when I had finished.

"Help me by keeping an eye on the convent, particularly on the sisters' quarters. I've told Sister Carmen what I've told you and I expect Jude Crowder will come looking for me to do me harm, try to silence me just as he had no qualms about killing Lennie Camden."

"You say authorities in Santa Clara County have found one of the skeletons and have matched dental records?"

"Yes."

"Looks like we have enough reasons to hold Jude Crowder, but no reason to hold Sister Carmen. Lifting her skirt may rile the pope and God, but whether she fucks and who she fucks is no business of the State of California."

"Agreed."

Sam said, "How do propose to retrieve the young Crowder girl? It's not clear she's been kidnaped and I'd have to dig pretty deep into the Juvenile Code to see what her aunt and her padre friend could be nailed on. There's probably some statute against an underage kid waltzing off like she did without her mommy's consent."

"Are you willing to deputize me?" I said.

"Why not? We'll haggle over who pays what expenses. Just don't lose a bagful of quarters in the slots then try to get the citizens of Santa Julietta County to cover your losses."

46

You can't get there from here. Look at a map of Central California and having a direct airline flight from Santa Julietta to Las Vegas makes great sense, especially given the millions of dollars in loose, leisure, entertainment money rattling around in Santa Julietta piggy banks. But no. Unless a would-be gambler in Santa Julietta owns his own airplane, he must drive south on Highway 101 to Burbank, where commercial airlines fly daily roundtrip to gamblers' paradise.

Wagering money on the turn of a card or the roll of a pair of dice holds no thrill for me, but Las Vegas casinos attract like nowhere else those thrill-seekers knowingly facing uphill odds when they sit down across from a stone-faced dealer or a unsmiling slot machine. My odds of finding Teddy Crowder popped when Sheriff Cuddleston sent a description of Mary-Margaret's gray Buick and its California license plate, courtesy of Sacramento, to the Nevada highway patrol and Las Vegas authorities. I remained puzzled why Teddy wanted to go to Las Vegas to Christmas shop.

The plane out of Burbank was full and I had opted for a window seat in the back row. Thankfully, the kid who plopped into the seat next to me was skinny. I couldn't decide whether I was bravely hastening toward Teddy or cravenly running from Jude Crowder.

In a class at Long Beach State called "The Psychology of Logic", my young professor explained that philosophers from Plato to Freud all argued that the human mind was akin to a quarreling committee, and that reason was always the most feckless member of that committee. By the time I landed at McCarren I had once again reminded myself that emotion trumps reason.

I still could not fathom why someone would want to kidnap Melissa and Eileen. It made no sense, especially since no kidnap request had shown up. To whom would kidnappers deliver a ransom note to? The convent? Certainly not Wendy Ellen. But if not to ransom the girls, then what? I knew there was underworld sex-trade trafficking in young girls, but most of that occurred in LA, almost exclusively by Asian mafias, and nearly all of the girls who had been recovered alive were busty, slim-hipped, white high school girls.

And why were authorities fed phony license plate numbers, numbers that matched the numbers on Morgan Crowder's Woody? Was it Morgan's Woody that was used in the kidnapping? Was Jude involved in the child-sex trade? Was the Church? The Catholic Church had no history in that. At least that I knew of. I wouldn't have put it past bishops,

179

cardinals, and even a few popes stooping that low. But in the 1960's in Southern and Central California such a practice would be something novel.

The Archdiocese of Los Angeles could raise money for its many causes in many ways, both legal and not-so, without peddling young girls' flesh to fill its coffers. That would be too novel for an institution steeped in centuries of gouging money and valuables from the laity. But maybe Jude Crowder was acting on his own in this venture, not fronting for the Church in his role as one of its leading advisors, for both legal and non-law-related affairs.

My own read on him was that he was dangerous, but not especially imaginative. I supposed that, whatever the reason for kidnapping of two young orphans, it was not his idea.

Enter Mary-Margaret and her boyfriend.

Mary, I had decided, was both bright and imaginative, having no need to be egged on, either by her boyfriend or an older brother. Maybe she was running the show. If so, I might need help.

The contact in Las Vegas that Sheriff "Cuddly" had given me was a sergeant with the NV Highway Patrol named Aeneas Timmons. I learned he got his first name because his mother was a high school Latin teacher. Aeneas fought in the Trojan War and, on the Trojan side ranked second only to Hector. When Troy fell his mother helped him escape from the Greeks.

"Your trio has a room at the Aladdin. Do you want us to maintain a vigil?" he told me as he stopped me from hailing a taxi and ushered me toward his patrol car. "We flattened a rear tire on their car. So they won't be going anywhere soon."

I asked Aeneas to go with me when I knocked on their hotel room door. He agreed.

Father John opened the door, took a quick glance at me then peered over my shoulder. When he saw a man wearing a flat-brimmed hat standing behind me, his shoulders drooped, and he opened the door wider. When I stepped in I saw Teddy, seated on the floor watching cartoons on TV. Mary-Margaret looked up from the sofa, where she had been reading a glitzy local promo magazine. From her angle she was unable to see the state cop behind me.

"Don't give up, do you, Fletcher?"

"I try not to."

She looked at Father John. "Call house security and have him removed, John."

John shook his head just as Aeneas Timmons stepped into the room.

Mary asked, "What's this about?"

Timmons said, "You and your padre friend here are wanted for questioning in Santa Clara County, California."

She didn't even ask why. "Turn the TV off, Ted."

Teddy turned and saw both me and Timmons.

"Are you a real policeman?" she said.

"Yes, young lady. I am. Nevada Highway Patrol."

"Was my Aunt Mary speeding on our way into Las Vegas?"

"No, but policemen in California want to ask her and her friend here some questions."

"You mean about where they buried their cousin Morgan and his roommate a long time ago?"

Timmons shook his head, astonished. "That's right. You are certainly one smart cookie."

"Yes. I know that." Looking at me, she said, "Does this mean I won't get to do any Christmas shopping?"

47

Mary-Margaret and Father John were now in custody and almost ready to be escorted away to Santa Clara by Nevada Highway Patrol deputies. Teddy had insisted that her aunt hand over the room key to me. I had already been on the phone, arranging for side-by-side seats on a return flight to Burbank the next day and letting Teddy's family know what was happening.

South of the Aladdin Hotel & Casino a dozen shops hawk Las Vegas-themed souvenirs, including sweatshirts, tee-shirts, drinking mugs and glasses, and, of course, cards and dice. For shopping purposes Teddy had brought along her own cash stash. Ere long she had spent her wad and was hitting me up for twenty-dollar bills.

"Don't you worry, Mr. Fletcher. My dad is good for whatever I borrow. He'll probably even toss in an extra hundred or two for chaperoning me.."

Laden with booty, we returned to the Aladdin, where Mary-Margaret had booked the room for two nights. We feasted at the Aladdin's buffet, then turned in. Or rather, I did. Teddy curled up on the floor in front of the TV. With a blanket, two pillows, and a room-service milk shake, she settled in to watch a marathon of Bugs Bunny cartoons. In the morning I found her curled up, asleep on the floor, the TV showing a test pattern.

Back in Santa Julietta that afternoon I told A.C. Crowder he could stop counting out hundred-dollar bills when he reached fifteen, even though my wallet was capable of holding more. The entire family hugged Teddy as if she were a thousand shares of oil stock.

While Teddy's mother smothered her youngest child in love hugs, A.C. took me aside, took me into the kitchen.

"What's this business of Mary-Margaret being detained by Las Vegas authorities."

"You are aware, are you not, of the entries in your late brother Francis's diary, wherein he claims that when your cousin Morgan died at a party, he, Jude, and Mary-Margaret decided to hide his body and not tell authorities he had died.?"

"Oh, Jesus," A.C. said. "I know the story about Morgan and his roommate disappearing, allegedly having run off. I never credited the story. I mean, both those men were in the middle of an academic quarter at Stanford. No one would run from that, unless he or she was failing miserably and didn't want the parents to find out."

I continued, "They not only planned to hide Morgan's body, but they also decided to kill Morgan's roommate who showed up unexpectedly and saw Morgan's body. The place they decided to bury the two dead men, according to Francis's diary, was behind the tee box on one of the holes of a new country club that was under construction, Stevens Canyon Country Club in Los Gatos."

"Well, did they? Bury them there, I mean," A.C. said.

"According to the latest news, police found only one body buried there. It was Morgan's roommate, Lennie Camden."

"So where the hell is Morgan?"

To tell or not to tell, that was the question I put to myself.

"No one knows," was my answer.

"So that's why Mary-Margaret was detained?"

I nodded.

"What about Jude?"

"What about him?" I said.

"Is he being detained?"

I said honestly, "I don't know."

"You say they killed Lennie Camden?"

"That's what Francis's diary says."

"Where the hell is that diary? How come I haven't heard any of this before? Who has the diary? Who has read it?"

Stephanie entered the kitchen. 'Dad, Teddy has presents she wants to give us. She says she can't wait until Christmas. I mean, it's not even Thanksgiving yet."

A.C. said to her, "Stephanie, I gather someone found a diary my brother Francis kept. Have you seen it? Read it?"

Stephanie stared at her shoes.

"Well? Have you?" A.C.'s voice became louder.

"Yes, Father."

"Yes, you've seen it? Or, yes, you've read it?"

"I've read parts of it."

"The part about Morgan and his roommate?"

Stephanie nodded.

"Tell me what Francis wrote."

She looked him in the eye. "Uncle Francis wrote that Uncle Jude, Aunt Mary, and he killed Lennie Camden after Lennie saw them loading Morgan Crowder's body into the back of his station, his Woody. Then your siblings took the two bodies to a golf course, where they buried the two men. Francis says he did not go along to the golf course but was in on the decision to bury the two men there."

"Holy fucking Jesus! Where is the diary? I want to read it for myself. I do not believe my siblings would have been capable of such wicked chicanery."

"Teddy has the diary," Stephanie said, looking sheepish.

"Teddy?" A.C. barked. "My God! Why her?"

"She wanted to keep it from other prying eyes, to use her own phrase," Stephanie said.

"Other prying eyes? I assume that includes me." Now A.C. was in a high simmer.

He paced from one end of the room to the other, then back.

"Daughter, do you realize that makes you, your brother, and your little sister...." He turned to me. "What's the legal term, Mr. Fletcher?"

"Accessories after the fact," I said.

"Accessories. That means you are all involved in murder and…and what else, Mr. Fletcher? Corpse desecration?"

"Close enough," I said.

Evelyn Crowder entered the room. "What's going on in here?"

"Your children are about to become jailbirds. All three of them," he said.

"What!" She looked to me, then back to her husband.

"Whatever are you talking about, Husband?"

"It's a long story, Ev. Fix us all some coffee and we'll try to piece it together for you. All of it, I promise."

"You make the coffee, Al. Then we'll all sit down and I'll be all ears," she said.

I said, "If you don't mind, I'll excuse myself. I'm not sure I can bear hearing the story again. However, I would like you, as a family, to keep that diary safe, if Teddy has it, as she says she does."

Evelyn said, "Diary? What diary? How much of this story have I missed?"

"All of it, I'm afraid, Mrs. Crowder. All of it."

48

I left the Crowders as Stephanie took her mother aside to fill her in on the story she had missed out on. From the Crowder mansion I drove straight to Wendy Ellen's house, hoping Wendy would allow me to take a short nap on her waterbed. In serious need of flipping my switches to *off,* even if only briefly, I decided Wendy's bed was my nearest wind down site.

"You're no closer to finding my little girls?" Wendy Ellen said as she welcomed me.

I shook my head. "Sorry."

When I finished telling her what I knew, she slumped into a kitchen chair.

"What would a lawyer be doing snatching my girls?" she said, watching me help myself to a beer from her fridge.

"I doubt if he kidnapped them, Wendy. He brought the car from Santa Clara to LA, or at least as far as Santa Julietta. My best guess is that he sold the car to some Mexicans and the Mex gang used it to grab the girls."

"If that's so, Stu, you had better stop. I don't want you getting mixed up all by yourself with any gangs of Mexicans. You'll get yourself killed."

"Sheriff Cuddleston told me the FBI in LA is looking into Mexican gangs' involvement. Whether that's true or not, I hope it is. You're right. I'm not about to take on any of those gangs by myself."

"What would Mexican gangs do with…. No, wait. I don't want to know," she said, and began to cry.

The further question was, why would any LA gang kidnap kids this far from LA. More likely the kidnapping was done by a local gang. I knew that there was at least one gang operating here. Two years earlier I had a run-in with a gang run by a man named Roman da Silva. He was Central California's version of a mafia don except he was a Hispanic from Costa Rica.

From local people I know and mostly trust, word is that Roman was killed while visiting friends in Cuernavaca, Mexico. Whoever is now running his gang of thugs I do not know. I no longer eat and drink at Jocko's, a small tavern outside Santa Maria, in the town of Nipomo. The man in Roman's gang I used to use for inside information, a thug named Little Ivory Turpinza, vanished during my investigation into a local murder. The assumption everybody made was that Little Ivory died and was buried in an unmarked grave, courtesy of Roman da Silva.

I was beginning to think I needed to make a trip to Jocko's again to see if anyone still in that gang knew anything about the kidnapping. Roman's replacement was a man named Ricardo Novato. Rumor had it that he could often be found at Jocko's. There was no harm in trying to find him there. Or so I fondly supposed. Ricardo's right-hand man was one Chico Ladera. Like Little Ivory, Chico owed me a favor for my helping him years earlier in Burbank.

I first met Chico amid the dumpsters behind the Empire Shopping Center. In 1960 I had been a homicide detective in the Burbank PD and happened to be near the shopping center because a week earlier two white women were robbed and brutally murdered after dark in the parking lot of the center. Witnesses claimed two men committed the crimes and one of them fit Chico's description from his mile-long rap sheet.

When my partner, Alex Durrea, and I arrived at the dumpsters Chico was already bleeding and on his knees. The man he was up against was a Mexican gang leader by the name of Alberto Montebello, short, wiry, and full of machismo. Streetwise, Alberto knew he would lose no face by dropping his switchblade when I pointed my service revolver at him.

To Chico I said, "Do any of these guys belong with you?"

Chico pointed to one young man. "Sebastiano."

I said, "Good. I want you and Sebastiano to climb into the back of my cruiser.

"Why? We ain't done nothing wrong."

"Do as I say and maybe you'll get to do nothing wrong again tomorrow as well. Eh? Or would you prefer my partner and I drive off and pretend we saw nothing happening here."

While my partner wrapped Chico's arm with a bandage and a sling made of Chico's sweater, I sat in the driver's seat of the cruiser with the door open and with my gun in my lap, aimed in the general direction of Alberto, who had collapsed his knife and stood staring at me defiantly, hands on his hips.

When Alex finished he jokingly told Chico not to bleed anymore on the cruiser's seat or else he, Chico, would have to pay the city of Burbank to have the seat cleaned. Chico was not amused. He was, however, thankful to be driven a mile from the shopping center before we dismissed him and Sebastiano.

Before I let him walk away, I said to Chico, 'Remember my name, *Señor*. Someday you will owe me a favor. Understood?"

He nodded. "I will not forget, *Señor* Fletcher."

The bartender at Jocko's was new to me. I was not sure if he knew the protocols for passing messages to gang leaders, so I asked. His nametag read: Buster K.

"Buster, I'm looking for Chico Ladera. Has he been around?"

Buster stared me down until I slid a twenty-dollar bill under my empty beer schooner.

"He may be around tomorrow night."

"This is more urgent than 'tomorrow night'."

He gave me a deep shrug. So I added another twenty.

Buster took my money and said, "Sit tight. I'll make a call."

He didn't even ask for my name. When he returned he said, "Sit at that back table next to the rack of pool cues. I'll bring you another beer. It may be fifteen minutes. So just signal when you need another brew."

I picked up my beer, looked at my watch, and headed for the corner table. Fourteen minutes later Chico walked in via the back door, saw me, and headed my way.

"*Señor* Fletcher, we meet again. I am guessing that you wish to collect on the debt I owe you. If so, it cannot involve Alberto Montebello. He died last year in a knife fight, of all things." Chico grinned and gestured, asking if he might be seated.

I said, "Order a drink first. It's on me."

A minute later he returned, holding a bottle of Pacifico.

He sat and took a swig of his beer. "The air is so much better to breathe in Santa Julietta, is it not?"

I nodded and said, "I'm looking for a kidnaper. Maybe more than one even."

He nodded. "The two unfortunate girls who lived in the convent, *si?*"

"Yes. That is the reason I invited you here. In Burbank you were a man who heard things that most other people did not hear. I am hoping that you still have that special way of listening than brings you news missed by other…"

Chico interrupted me.

"By *other* I assume you mean both local police and the FBI. You are going to ask me if I have heard about who kidnapped these poor, unfortunate girls and maybe also what the kidnappers have done with them."

"Exactly, *Señor.* You have read my mind." I tapped my head.

"I must apologize, *Señor* Fletcher, but I know nothing about this kidnapping except for what was in the local newspaper at the time. I say I know nothing, but by that I mean I have heard nothing spoken of in the local Mexicano community, nothing pointing to or suggesting that some member or members within our community has ripped these two girls from their beloved nuns."

I said, "Do you happen to know any of the nuns in the convent?"

"I do not." His answer was too quick and too emphatic.

"Sister Melda Torres, maybe? Or Sister Carmen Armenta?"

He shook his head but averted my gaze.

"Tell me who in Santa Julietta might be able to help me with this, Chico."

"Have you asked the local padres?"

I gave him an oh-come-on look.

"Are they not bound by the sanctity of the confessional?" I said.

"In a case such as this, one or more of them would find a way to allow such information to…to seep out under the doors to the confessional."

"Seep out to whom?"

"Someone who could bring justice to this crime."

"Do you have any particular padre in mind?"

"Try Father Spannard."

"The priest for the youths?"

"*Si.*"

"Anyone else?"

"Father Benedict."

I asked, "Is that his first or his last name?"

"His last. His first name is Tomaso. He is the priest who hears the confessions of all the nuns at the convent. I believe there are seven. Oh, and the Mother Superior. He hears her confessions as well."

"Does he in particular have a reputation for allowing some confessions to leak out under the confessional door?" I said.

"You can only hope."

"Another *cerveza*?" I said.

"*Gracias,* but no. I must be going. Is there anything else I can help you with? Is my debt to you paid in full?"

"I'll call it even. Okay?"

"*Gracias* again." With that he drained his beer bottle and left.

49

Father Spannard was tall and athletically built – a weightlifter, I guessed. Pince nez glasses perched at the bridge of his nose. Piercing blue eyes looked out as I took a seat in his church's priory. With his bass voice, he could be a narrator of historical documentaries on TV.

"Sorry, Mr. Fletcher. I cannot discuss the contents of any confessions I hear. You surely know whatever is spoken to me inside the confessional booth is sacrosanct."

"Not even if what you have been told there could save an innocent person from going to prison? Or could convict a guilty person of a heinous crime?"

"Not even." He bowed his head and muttered an apologetic "Sorry."

I stared at him.

"Men and women have been hanged or beheaded when what was said to a priest might have saved them."

He shrugged.

"I don't see how you can sleep at night with that knowledge on your conscience."

"It's God's way. So it's not mine to question."

"It seems to me there are a great many of your god's ways that ought to be questioned."

"That is not our way," he said.

"I know. What I'm suggesting is this. Your way is in serious need of fixing. You surely realize that anyone not wearing a cassock would be jailed for withholding valuable evidence."

"We have a long and successful history in this world, sir. Our way has withstood the test of many turbulent times."

"You clearly have subjected your sense of privilege to very, very flimsy tests. I suggest you give yourself a few extra lashes at bedtime for failing those kidnapped girls. And perhaps, too, for failing Father Mackenzie."

Father Spannard balled his fists but refrained from throwing a punch at me.

"Think about this, padre. Suppose it was you who was arrested for kidnapping those girls or for molesting the Ledbetter boys, and some priest could prove your innocence by sharing with authorities what he had heard in the confessional, how would you feel about the sanctity of the confessional then?"

"The Lord would find a way to save me without my having to rely on another priest, or even me, to divulge what he had heard in the confessional."

"So far your God is providing very little evidence to help us find those girls, find who harmed them. Nor is He helping Father Mackenzie prove his innocence."

Father Spannard gave me a pitying look, then turned and walked away.

If there is a textbook on how to conduct surveillance, Sheriff Cuddleston's boys neglected to read it. When I turned on Calle del Caballeros de Santana, the street that fronts the Convent Santa Franchescha Ornella, I had no trouble making the county cops, two of them slouched down in the front seat of their grubby-looking unmarked Chevy. When I parked my car in front of the sidewalk leading to the convent's entrance, the two deputies slid lower.

After getting out of my car I waved to them as I thought a coy senorita might flash a handkerchief at a group of ogling high school boys, as much to embarrass them as to gain their attention. Just then a man on a bicycle came racing around the corner of East Yucca Street and nearly ran into me. I held out my palms defensively.

"What do you expect to see at that speed?" I said to him – a man in his forties, breathing heavily.

"What do you mean?" he said and took a quick glace toward the surveillance car.

"You and the two men in the Chevy over there are keeping watch on the convent, noting who comes and who goes."

A shrug. "Okay. So? What of it?"

I said, "Why don't you hang a sign in the yard, a sign that says: We're cops and we're here to take notes on who comes and who goes."

"So we're that obvious, are we?"

I gave him my best John Wayne look, hitching up my trousers, cocking my head, and saying, "You nailed it, partner."

"Well, shit. You must be that guy from San Diego who irons his own corduroy, carries a long-barrel .22, and makes top-of-the-line honchos snarl and curse."

I said, "You mean there's somebody who can accomplish all of that? Wow! he must be a Somebody, with a capital S."

He laughed. "Is that you way of saying that's not you?"

"I hope not."

"What have you done to piss off all the brass, Mister?"

"You mean the bigwigs are upset?"

A chuckle. "Hell, yes.! Just grab the mike over at the Chevy and call into HQ that a certain wicked ex-cop from out of town just broke up our surveillance and is wondering why the spy team consists of nothing but a bunch of amateurs. Then stand back and listen to the howling to begin."

"Sounds like your bigwigs are a tad twitchy."

"Twitchy?" The man doubled over with laughter loud enough that both men in the car sat bolt upright.

The man atop the bike held a handout for me to shake. "I'm Jesse Hamilton, and I'm in charge of this all-too-obvious bunch."

I shook his hand. "Stu Fletcher. How long have you lived in Santa Julietta, Lieutenant? I haven't seen you around."

"I'm new. Just moved up here from Riverside to take over for Captain Megara, who retired. Well, actually not moved here. I have taken an apartment in Ventura so as not to sully the local landscape. By the way, folks call me Smudge. You may do so as well." He rubbed his very black skin. "I've got to tell you, 'Hey, Smudge' beats "Hey, Nigger.' Gotta give folks that."

I nodded without smiling.

"Tell me, Mr. Fletcher. It's the weekend. Should there be some parents coming to pick up their son or daughter?"

"Okay, Smudge. Well, the reason you don't see any parents coming to or going from Santa Franchesca is because all the children here at Santa Franchesca Ornell are orphans. Except for the two who were kidnapped. They were foster children, ripped from the arms of their loving foster mother. Didn't anyone tell you this?"

The lieutenant said, "I'm not entirely sure why we are staking out this place. Can you fill me in?"

I said, "Yes, I can." And I did.

When I finished, he said, "Whew! What a tangled web that is."

He looked puzzled.

"You're not a fan of Sir Walter Scott, are you?"

"What?"

"Tangled web. It's from Sir Walter."

The lieutenant arched his eyebrows. "Oh. I would have bet it's a line from Shakespeare. You're well-read for a gumshoe. "

"Not especially. I was forced to read Scott in an English Lit class at Long Beach. The professor was fond of Scott."

The lieutenant looked around. "I guess I'd better move my boys, if they're so obvious. How did you figure me for a cop?"

I pointed toward his shoes. "You're English shoes. Chief Fry's niece holds the local monopoly on that brand."

"Oh. No doubt our surveillance subjects will know that."

"No, but they might wonder why a pedestrian is standing in the middle of the street talking to a bicycle rider.

"Let's move, shall we?" I prided myself, perhaps too much, for not saying *a black bicycle rider.*

"Where are you headed? he asked.

"I'm headed into the convent to make a further nuisance of myself Charlie-Chan-style. Are you familiar with Chan?"

"I am. I wish there was a TV channel devoted entirely to running his movies. I'm sure it would make me a better detective."

"Who do you prefer to play Number One Son?" I said.

"No one."

"You probably don't need one."

"I don't know about that. Chan's sons may be bumblers but in their bumbling they always trip across seemingly innocuous stuff through which Chan sifts and sorts, always discovering a useful, even necessary clue. And then senior Chan pauses to enunciate a witticism."

I said, "Wow yourself! 'enunciate a witticism'. You must be a college boy, too."

"U-C Riverside. Philosophy. And please don't ask how a black philosophy major ends up being a policeman on a bicycle."

"Long story, eh?"

"Twisted is more like it."

I said, "Tell you what. I'll go in the front door and you can check out the back door. Maybe you can stumble on to something."

"Will do."

"I'll give you a couple of minutes before I stir the penguins."

"Okay," he said, giving me a thumbs up. "I'm off, but let's leave the sleeping dogs lie." He pointed toward the Chevy with its two occupants.

<h1 style="text-align:center">50</h1>

With some of the money I earned working for Amanda I had bought myself a new police-band scanner to put in my Biscayne. I knew there were better models than the Motorola, but it was all I could afford. When I returned to my car the scanner was broadcasting a call for all available cars to converge on an address I recognized – the Crowder estate. The call warned officers to be on watch for an armed man who had kidnapped a young girl.

Teddy Crowder again, I imagined. Before the dispatcher could name the alleged kidnapper I knew from the description of the man it was Jude Crowder. He wanted his brother's diary and may have imagined that without Francis's diary, prosecutors would have a much harder time making a case against him. So Jude had convinced himself he needed to destroy the elusive diary.

Teddy had already outfoxed Mary-Margaret and Father John. When those two kidnapped her she let her aunt think she was bringing the diary with her. But when the three of them arrived in Las Vegas, Teddy changed her story, telling Mary-Margaret and Father John she had heard often from her father how Las Vegas hotels were full of thieves, breaking into rooms and stealing hotel guests belongings. And, for that reason, Teddy had announced, upon the threesomes' arrival in Sin City, that she had left the diary hidden safely back in her house.

Apparently, Mary-Margaret had telephoned Jude before the Nevada authorities and I knocked on her hotel room door to tell him this. Thus, as soon as Jude learned Teddy was back home again, he made his plan to kidnap his niece, making sure, before flitting away with her, that Teddy actually had the diary in hand.

I decided my best chance of finding Jude and Teddy was to threaten Sister Carmen with my own version of hellfire and damnation and hope she didn't laugh at me.

"Men are not allowed in here, sir."

The door had barely closed behind me when a sister I had not had the privilege of meeting stepped into the hallway and saw me.

"I'm looking for Sister Carmen," I said.

"You may look for the devil for all I care, but not in here. Now leave before I scream."

I held up both my hands. "I apologize, but it is imperative that I find Sister Carmen. A young girl has been kidnapped and Carmen may be the only one who knows how to find her."

The young nun stared at me, obviously trying to guess if I was telling her the truth.

"She's not here. She just left."

"Which way?" I said.

"That way." She pointed down a long corridor.

I took off running, leaving here in my wake.

"Sir, you can't go down there!"

I kept on running until I reached the end of the hallway.

To my right a sign pointed to the entrance to the nuns' dormitory. I frightened two other sisters as they stepped out into the hallway, saw me, and screamed. I held up my hands as a signal of apology and kept moving down the corridor until I reached a self-locking double door. Overhead was an exit sign. I opened it to see where it led.

I saw a long narrow pathway that led toward the foothills. Hedge, taller than I am, lined the left side of the pathway. Chain link fence even higher lined the right. Dried mud marked dozens of bicycle tracks. I loped the hundred yards or so to where the path came to a wide alley. To my left I saw no one; to my right I saw Lieutenant Hamilton peddling toward me.

"I lost her," I said to Hamilton.

"Let me peddle ahead. If she came this way, I should be able to catch up with her," he said.

I nodded and tried to re-enter the sisters' quarters, but the door had locked behind me. I banged hard on it and one of the sisters opened it. "Who are you looking for, mister?"

"Sister Carmen."

She gestured for me to come in. "She may have gone down the main corridor. Go through the open double doors halfway back and turn right.

"Where does that lead to?"

She said, "The first door down that corridor leads to our classrooms, plus the children's dorm is on the second floor, above the classrooms. At the end of the corridor is where Mother Agnes's office and quarters are. The door at the far end opens onto the play yard. The door on the right, beyond the door to the classrooms, is another passage that leads to the gymnasium and to the chapel."

I thanked her and retreated to the corridor she described. That hallway was empty, but if Carmen had turned that way, she had a choice of several ways to elude me. As I stood pondering my choices, Mother Agnes emerged from her office.

"Mr. Fletcher, whatever are you doing back at my school?" she shouted.

I waited for her to walk closer, then told her, "I'm looking for sister Carmen."

She threw her head back and yelled at the ceiling, "Do you hear that, Lord?"

To me she said, "You have no business being in this sanctuary without my permission, Mister Private Detective. No business for any reason. Do you understand me?"

"Sister Carmen is involved in another kidnapping, Mother Agnes. Sheriff's deputies are outside, hoping to trap her. Now if you saw her come this way, you had better tell me or run the risk of becoming an accessory to that crime."

"Which one of my children is it this time?" she said, her voice returning to a sensible level.

"The child is not one of yours. Her name is Teddy Crowder, and she is Jude Crowder's niece."

"Why? Why would Carmen want to kidnap her?"

"Because a diary pointing to two murders many years ago is now in Teddy's possession, a diary that names Jude Crowder as the murderer of his cousin Morgan and of Morgan's Stanford roommate."

"What does any of this have to do with Sister Carmen?"

"Come now, Mother Agnes. I'm sure you are well aware that Carmen is Jude Crowder's lover."

"How dare you!"

"How dare I what? Suggest that Carmen is Jude's lover? Or suggest that you know all about it?"

"Both!"

"I already know for sure Carmen is Jude's lover. Or one of his lovers. And I'm becoming more and more convinced that you became aware of that quite some time ago."

"Get out of my convent. Get out before I call the police."

"You need only step outside to summon them, Madam. But first, tell me which way Sister Carmen went."

She came at me with both fists clenched. The punch she threw came from the shoulder. I wondered where she had learned to box. While she was stationed on the Navy hospital ship off Okinawa I supposed. The punch never landed, but if it had, she might have broken my jaw. I blocked her right-hand jab with my right palm and clenched her wrist with my left hand and twisted her arm.

"You're hurting me!"

I loosened my grip and her arm dropped. She didn't try to hit me again, but I kept my guard up in case she changed her mind.

"Carmen. Which way?"

She glared at me, clenched her teeth, hissed at me as if I were an agent of the Devil. I shoved her aside then trotted down the hall toward doors that led to the convent's classrooms and children's dormitory, the gymnasium, and finally the chapel.

From behind me I heard her yell, "God will punish you for your iniquities."

My iniquities? Right. My sins were as numerous as any man's but finding Sister Carmen wouldn't be counted among them.

When I threw open the door to the hallway leading to classrooms and the cafeteria, I saw a wide stairway I judged led up to the children's sleeping quarters. Too many rabbit holes to peek into, I thought. I can always return to check them out. To the right was a thick double door that, when I flung it open, exposed a gymnasium full of children playing, but no Carmen.

The last door, at the end of the hallway, opened into the convent's chapel. The chapel appeared to be empty, but I looked carefully between each row of pews as I walked toward the pulpit. Once there, I saw what looked like a stairwell to my right. A closer look revealed a polished wooden staircase curving down toward a spooky darkness.

At the head of the stairs I found a light switch. Flipping it lit up a basement filled with stacks of wooden stairs, beyond which was a stack of long tables. But again…no Carmen.

On the far side from the pulpit was a locked door. As I was deciding how to open it, Father Spannard appeared.

"What's in here, Padre?"

He took a set of keys from beneath his cassock, chose a key, and unlocked the door.

"See for yourself, Mister Fletcher."

I saw only more accoutrements the Catholic Church found necessary in order to conduct its masses for the masses, and more. Candles, candle holders, rolls of velvet cloth, collection plates, baptismal bowls for holding holy water, acolytes' robes, and so on, into the darkness.

51

"Where am I going to find Sister Carmen?" I asked Father Spannard, trying to sound polite.

The slow, exaggerated shrug he gave me made me want to deck him, but I refrained, thinking I might need his assistance later.

"Did you see Sister Carmen come this way?"

"No."

Sister Melda came out of the gymnasium door just as I was there. Seeing me, she tried to duck back into the gym. Why hadn't I seen her before when I had peered briefly into the gym? She was in the women's locker room I supposed.

She turned to run. "No, no, no. You're going to talk to me." I grabbed her by her gym shirt collar and pulled her toward me until she could feel my breath.

"Please, Señor, I know nothing."

"Stop lying. Where is sister Carmen hiding?"

Her eyes widened. "They will kill me, Señor Fletcher."

"Who will kill you?"

"Señor Crowder."

"Jude?"

"*Si.*"

"Not if I kill you first."

"No, please, Señor."

"Where is Sister Carmen?"

"The last I saw of her she was heading to the outdoor playground."

"You're lying."

"No, Señor. Please. I tell you the truth."

If she went outside by the door behind me, Mother Agnes would have seen her. When I pointed this out to Sister Melda, she, too, gave me a shrug. Now, given all the time I had wasted threatening Father Spannard and Sister Melda, Sister Carmen would be too far away for me to catch her. Maybe Smudge Hamilton was having better luck.

Not knowing what to do next, I returned to the gym. The children were lining up in preparation to leave. I held the door open for them. The sister in charge of them didn't even thank me when she passed. After checking out the men's and women's locker room and finding no one, I returned to the chapel. I sat down in a pew and looked toward Jesus on the cross. Why Catholic art adores portraying Christ's bloody suffering in exaggerated detail, I didn't know. "The greatest suffering ever endured" Christians would like us all to believe.

I heard the door at the rear of the chapel open and close. I turned to see sister Melda coming toward me.

"You are a dead man, Mister Fletcher. Very dead and very soon."

"Would you care to expand on that, Sister?"

"The Crowders, they will kill you."

"I'm sure Jude will try."

"I hope he has much success."

"Thank you. What kind thoughts you express."

"Mock me, if you will. Soon I will watch Señor Crowder mount your head on a high pole and we will dance around it."

"What wonderful Christian thoughts you have, Sister."

From beneath her habit she pulled out a pistol and cocked the hammer. I put my head down and rushed her. I heard the gun go off just as I tackled her. Sister Melda's head banged hard against the floor and her pistol fell to the floor. I grabbed the gun and looked at the nun. She was out cold.

"Drop the gun, Fletcher." The voice of Lieutenant Hamilton. I complied.

"What the hell have you been up to?" he said as he picked up the pistol.

"I'm still looking for Carmen Armenta. Not only haven't I found her, but Sister Melda here also wants to make sure I won't."

"Whose gun is this?" the lieutenant asked.

"Probably Jude Crowder's."

"He's the fellow you supposed pulled off the kidnapping of the two girls?" the lieutenant said.

"Yup. He's the one."

"Kidnapped them during recess, eh?"

I nodded.

"What time is recess?"

I said, "We've all been told recess varies each morning and afternoon. So how would the kidnapper know when to grab the girls? Either he was told by someone here at the school or someone here phoned the kidnapper. But the FBI already checked the phone records. No calls were made within two hours either side of the time recess was held that morning."

"He was waiting and someone inside signaled him."

"Or he was waiting at a point where he could see the schoolyard," I said.

"But the phantom Woody has not turned up."

I said, "No, but it had to be the Woody I saw in the photos in Mary-Margaret's garage. I have a friend in New York state trying to check the New York license files to see if one of their Woodies is a match with Morgan Crowder as owner. But I haven't heard back yet from my friend."

"But you think Jude Crowder might now have possession of the Woody."

I said, "Unless he got rid of it. But I'm pretty sure damned certain he brought it down to Santa Julietta or maybe even as far as LA. But, in any case, he had possession of it at some time after Morgan disappeared."

Lieutenant Hamilton said, "They've found Morgan's roommate's body but not Morgan's."

"That's where the case up north stands as of now."

The lieutenant shook his head. "Why kidnap children who were under the care of an incompetent foster mother and now a handful of nuns?"

"The foster mother is not incompetent. She simply lacks the resources to be a good one."

"Why was she allowed to care for two girls if she lacked the wherewithal to manage the task?"

"Just one more day of bungling by the CPS," I opined.

"You jumped rather quickly at my calling the foster mother incompetent. Are you screwing her or something?"

"Or something," I lied.

Hamilton said, "Forget about everyone except the girls for a moment. Could the two girls have run away, and the convent is making up this kidnapping story to cover up their lax oversight that allowed the girls to run away on their own?"

"Where would they run that they wouldn't have been found by now?"

"If they walked quietly through neighborhoods, who would take them for runaways?"

"Someone would have noticed them and, when the kidnapping news hit the press, that someone would surely have come forward. But okay. Now let's try to picture them when they got beyond local neighborhoods. Where would they go?"

The lieutenant said, "Do you think they might have been picked up on the 101 freeway and, after all this time, no one reported them? There is enough traffic on the 101 that someone would have seen them trying to hitchhike, someone would have seen them getting into a car that had stopped for them. Yet, no one has come forward in over two months' time."

"Maybe they escaped by water," I said. If they stole a boat, the owner would have informed you. Or maybe a boat owner helped them."

Hamilton said, "We've questioned everyone who had a boat moored at the marina. Got nothing. One boat did go from Santa Julietta the evening of the day the girls went missing. That boat owner took his boat to Oxnard to have it hauled out for hull scraping and a bottom repainting. He said the Santa Julietta boatyard charged too much. He made a call to his wife as soon as he reached Oxnard so that she could drive down to pick him up. We checked his phone records, and a call did go from the boatyard's payphone to his home in Santa Julietta. The night manager at the Oxnard boatyard recalled seeing a woman pick a guy up. And he didn't see any young girls lingering about."

"It's still possible, but I admit it's a long shot. But long shots may be all we have. You know the stats better than I do regarding how many women and children go missing every year in the states. A large percentage of them never turn up."

Ignoring my pessimism, Hamilton said, "Oxnard PD asked every business near the boatyard if they had seen any young girls who met the descriptions we passed along. Results? Nada. So what's left? They grew wings and flew away?"

I said, "Someone is lying about something. We already know that two nuns lied about the plates on the car. What else did they lie about?"

Hamilton reminded me, "After you pointed out to them the fact that the plates they identified matched NY plates belonging to a Crowder relative who has been missing for twenty years our detectives grilled the nuns and asked your question: 'What else are you lying about?' They both gave the same answer: 'Nothing'. I have the tapes if you'd like to see them."

I thought to myself: What would you expect them to say? Liars lie about lying. So, I said, "That leaves us with Jude Crowder parked in front of the school, waiting and watching. And we have no motive for him wanting the girls abducted."

Hamilton said, "The nuns surely had to trust whoever got them to lie."

"Jude, making pillow talk."

The lieutenant winced. "No question but the Church hierarchy and their lawyers are a sworn-to-silence bunch – except, as you suggest, to each other."

52

Hamilton left to return his bicycle to the cop-beat shop on Padre Sierra Blvd. I wanted to talk to Sister Carmen and Sister Melda one more time. However, Mother Agnes came sweeping out of her eagle's nest, her black habit flying.

"Mister Fletcher, I must insist you leave. Your presence simply stirs up too much trouble. Now go!"

So I went. Back to Wendy Ellen's house.

"You look like you've been pulled through a knothole," was how she welcomed me.

"Worse than that. Sister Carmen left me running up and down empty hallways, almost daring me to catch her."

"Did you? Finally?"

"No."

"People tell stories about that place."

"Which people? And what kind of stories?"

"People who have lived here forever. Old people."

"Ones with rich imaginations, I suppose."

"Ha! You should talk."

"You're right. So tell me what kinds of stories these old people tell."

"Start with the graveyard out behind the chapel." Wendy Ellen paused to collect her thoughts.

"Okay. The graveyard." She sighed. "When a child at Santa Franchesca dies, the child is buried behind the chapel, without any kind of memorial service held at all. But, over many, many years, the number of children who have entered the school and have died there doesn't match the number of headstones."

"That seems like something anyone could easily verify – children versus gravestones," I said.

Mother Agnes's explanation is that they ran out of room for new gravesites. So they began to stack the corpses."

"So you think the two girls are buried there?"

"It's a possibility anyway."

So it was.

201

I said, "How do I get permission to dig? Up in Santa Clara County I gave police reasons to dig. Well, at least they had reason to dig in one spot. Francis Crowder's diary."

Wendy grinned. "Maybe you shouldn't bother getting permission."

"I'll lose my license for sure, if I try that."

"Even if someone else does the digging?"

"Not if I didn't urge anyone to go digging."

"Do you know anyone who might even be willing? And don't look at me. I'm terrified of graveyards," Wendy Ellen said and made a shuddering motion with her shoulders.

"Someone else might think he owes me." I was thinking of Murky Murtrans, a friend and a man whose bacon I had saved a year earlier. And, as far as I knew, Murky wasn't afraid of graveyards. Or of anything else.

I placed a call to Murky's ranch, out on the Sisquoc River. A woman with a heavy Latina accent answered and said, "Señor Murky, he has gone to Walsh-ing-TUN." She repeated the last word three times for me, but it sounded the same every time.

I said, "Washington state or Washington, D.C.?"

"Walsh-ing-Tun," three more times.

It didn't matter. Whether he was on Puget Sound or on the Potomac, he wouldn't be available for grave-digging duty. So I thanked the woman and hung up.

Next I called my answering service. I was told I had an urgent message from a Lieutenant Hamilton, so I phoned him.

He said, "You might want to head out to the airport." I was taken aback when he told me why.

Jude Crowder had kidnapped Randall and Teddy. And now he and Carmen Armenta were intending to hijack an airplane. Lieutenant Hamilton explained that, as a young Turk during WWII Jude had flown the Army's version of a DC-3, the C-47, back and forth between India and China. *Flying over the Hump* it was called, the Hump being the Himalayas – delivering food and weaponry to General Chang Kai Shek as the Chinese fought the Japanese. Then in 1948 Jude had again flown a C-47 during the Berlin airlift, delivering food and coal to residents of West Berlin from bases in what had become West Germany.

In Santa Julietta a group of former DC-3 pilots had formed a club whose primary purpose was to maintain and fly two DC-3s they had purchased at Army auctions of surplus goods back in the mid-1950's. Jude was a charter member of that club, called the KJ-3Club, KJ standing for Kachenjunga, the name of the third highest mountain in the Himalayas. Now Jude Crowder wanted access to one of the club's airplanes, wanted it fully fueled and otherwise ready to fly, in exchange for his releasing Randall and Teddy from captivity.

At Santa Julietta municipal airport I found Sheriff Sam Cuddleston, Chief of Police Wally Fry, and the local FBI agent, a condescending young man with a New England accent. His name was Calvin Horton. Calvin and I had butted heads in the local courtroom more than once. It took very little time for the two of us to reestablish our mutual disrespect.

"Who invited you?" he said After I had shaken hands with Sam and Wally.

"The name was unintelligible, though the rest of the invitation was quite clear."

Wallace Fry gave me a little head shake, warning me not to bait the young bull. I gave Wally a nod, then said to Calvin, "So what's your plan, General Horton?"

"The airplane is prepped, ready to fly. The club members are cooperating. Club records show that Jude Crowder has taken one of the two planes up three times in the past six months, each time with one of the other members acting as his co-pilot."

I said, "Do you plan to let him take off?"

"Not if the brother and sister, Mr. Crowder's niece and nephew, remain under his control."

"Do you expect him to release them?"

"No way of telling."

"Do you consider your second answer compatible with your first?"

At that moment the C-47 rolled out from a nearby hanger, pushed by several middle-aged men.

Agent Horton spoke into his walkie-talkie. "Billy, do you see the kids?"

Mixed with static, Billy's response was, "They're still onboard."

Horton spoke again. "Rifles ready. Aim at the tires."

I grabbed Horton's machine and yelled into it, "Delay that order. Billy, what was the last thing Jude Crowder said to you?"

"He said that he would release the boy and girl if we didn't try anything funny."

I looked at Agent Horton. "And you still want to try something funny."

"I'm in charge here, not you, Cowboy," Horton said.

"You're the cowboy, Mister," I said.

"I gave the order to shoot! Now shoot, Damn it!" Horton screamed into his walkie-talkie.

"No!" Wally Fry shouted. "Don't give Crowder any reason to start shooting. He's not stable, and so far he's only a thief – that we know of."

Jude Crowder taxied the plane out to the nearest long runway and turned it into the wind. When the pilot – I imagined Jude at the controls – revved both 1200-hph Pratt & Whitney engines, the sound became deafening.

"Shoot, shoot, shoot!" Agent Horton screamed to one of the men who became visible atop the hanger. It appeared as though he was armed with a high-powered rifle with a telescope.

"Shoot at what?" a voice on the walkie-talkie said. "We can't see the tires. They're protected by cowling."

"Then shoot at anything!" Horton called out, just as a cargo door on the C-47's port side began to open.

Sheriff Cuddleston shouted, "Cancel all orders to shoot at the plane! Someone is opening the plane's side cargo door."

We all watched as Randall and Theodora appeared at the cargo door. First Randall, then Teddy jumped to the tarmac. As the two of them waved to us, the C-47's engines revved once again, and the plane began to roll. I caught a brief glimpse of Carmen, wearing flight jacket and blousy trousers, as she leaned hard on the cargo door, making it slide shut.

"Now you can shoot!" Agent Horton yelled to his riflemen, and I heard several popping sounds. Duck hunters blasting away fruitlessly at a receding bird.

53

"I should arrest you for interference, Fletcher," Horton said to me, his self-importance sounding silly to everyone else standing on the runway.

"Take all the credit for rescuing these two," I said to the FBI agent as Randall and his sister approached us. "But stop being an ass."

Agent Horton's contemptuous smile told me he didn't require my confirmation of what he knew already. I took several steps away from him and watched the C-47 accelerate, lift off, and continue westward. From where I stood the plane looked as though it would fly straight into the sun.

The last time I rode in a C-47 the plane had a red cross painted on its fuselage. I was a wounded evacuee, being taken to a surgical hospital at a U.S. Army base in Japan to have my right leg either repaired or amputated. I had failed to nosedive into a foxhole fast enough when a woman with a red star on her cap unloaded her AK47 in my squad's direction.

By the time I refocused on Jude Crowder, his plane was out of sight. Randall entered my private space without asking and crunched me with a bearhug. Next it was Teddy's turn to hug me.

"Sister Carmen saved us," Randall told me between Teddy's sobs. "Uncle Jude was planning to take us along."

"To Mexico," Teddy said, after wiping her nose on her sleeve. Then she added, "I've never been to Mexico."

"Where are Mom and Dad?" Randall said.

I said, "Your mother wasn't up to being here and I had to agree. She was a nervous wreck just standing in her own kitchen."

"And Dad?"

I looked down at Teddy and gave her another hug.

"Why isn't Dad here?" Randall pressed.

"I bet I know," Teddy said.

"What do you know?" Randall said, too loudly.

"I bet he went to Santa Clara to be with Aunt Mary and Father John."

Randall looked at me.

205

I gave him a wan nod.

He took a deep sigh and pulled his little sister closer.

Despite pleas from both Teddy and Randall that they be allowed to ride with me away from the airport to, well, to wherever I was going, Sheriff Cuddleston and Chief Wally denied their supplications and whisked them away to be interrogated. I knew that nothing would change the coppers' minds, and I felt a wave of guilt wash over me for not protecting two of A.C,.'s children from an uncle hellbent on kidnappings and likely murders as well.

Before she left Teddy said nothing about Uncle Francis's diary, and I had no time to ask her. I assumed Jude had seen the part of the diary that implicated him, but whether he judged Francis's remarks damning enough that he would destroy the pages, I didn't know.

If I were Jude, I would burn them. But then Francis was not my brother and I was unsure whether Jude would hold his brother's written words to be sacred, no matter how damning. To burn pages of Francis's diary would be equivalent to burning a piece of Francis himself.

The world is full of people with bizarre notions regarding the sanctity of objects belonging to their nearest kin. It's not just relics belonging to famous people – a piece of Jesus's burial cloth, the envelope Lincoln used to outline his memorial cemetery address. A page from a brother's diary might be too honored to part with, damning or not.

I decided to head to the convent but was stopped by a green Jeep racing up to me. A tall man with a white goatee and wearing a Dodgers baseball cap stepped from the Jeep and ran up to me.

"You're Mr. Fletcher, the detective, right?"

"I am."

"I know who you are from listening to Jude Crowder rant about you. I'm Dr. Hal Gabridarian, a member of the DC-3 club. I was listening to the news on the radio as I came doe the 101 from San Jose. Which plane did Jude fly off with?"

I said, All I remember is the last two numbers of the plane's ID. Four eight."

"Shit! How long ago did he leave?"

I looked at my watch. "A little more than half an hour ago."

"I need to talk to him. It's urgent."

"Good luck. He's not responding to anyone."

"Here's the problem. I do repair work on faulty equipment in our planes' cockpits. Number Forty-eight's fuel gage isn't registering properly. It's stuck on *Full*. But my last estimate was that the tanks held no more than five percent of capacity. I had hoped to fix it before this weekend, but the parts I need have been delayed coming out of Dallas.”

“So Jude is flying on fumes about now is what you’re saying?”

“Where is he headed? Mexico?”

I nodded.

“Land or sea?”

“Fifteen miles out,” I pointed west, toward the ocean.

“Who is keeping radio contact with him?”

I said, “Our sheriff, Sam Cuddleston. And the Navy is going to send a pair of F-8s from Mirimar to intimidate him. The Marines still operated an airbase on a bluff northeast of San Diego.

“Did Jude release his hostages?”

I nodded.

The doctor’s face showed both surprise and relief.

He said, “Jude’s a psychopath, but then you surely know that by now.”

I nodded again.

The doctor said, I’d say, ‘Let him crash and sink’, but that would be a waste of a damned fine airplane.”

Dr. Gabridarian was a neurosurgeon and, by reputation, a good one. A ‘cool customer’, to used current hippie jargon. He possessed a steady hand when his hand held a scalpel.

Just then the sheriff drove up. So I introduced the doctor to the sheriff and let the doctor explain to Sam what he knew about the fuel gauge on Jude’s DC-3.

Cuddleston said to the doc, “Follow me. I’ll connect you with Jude Crowder and allow you to explain to him the predicament he’s in.”

I interrupted. “One of Jude’s demands was for the tanks to be full.”

The sheriff snickered.

“What?” I said.

“Our incompetent FBI man, Mister Horton, had the ground crew go through the motions of filling the plane’s tanks, but not a drop was added.”

I shook my head. “Maybe I owe Horton an apology.”

Cuddleston said, “Don’t bother. He’ll fuck up big time soon enough. We both know that.”

Whether I owed Calvin Horton an apology or not, I was beginning to feel a pang of sorrow for Sister Carmen. But I chided myself. Surely the world would be a better place without her. Likewise without Jude Crowder.

“Where are you headed, Fletcher?” the sheriff said.

“I’m still looking for a pair of orphans. Remember?”

Cuddleston said, “Do you trust those two Crowder kids?”

I nodded. “If they say the orphans weren’t on the plane, I trust them to have told the truth.”

Sam said, “I thought you were more cynical than you turn out to be. Beneath your scowl resides a peach-soft heart.”

“Peach soft, eh?” I laughed and walked away.

54

I returned to Wendy Ellen's house, thinking she might want to be with me when I questioned Sister Melda regarding the whereabouts of Melissa and Eileen. I was scarcely out of my car when I saw that much of Wendy's living room window was missing. I pulled out my .38 and approached the house cautiously. The front door was locked. So I stepped over the low hedges ling the front of the house and peered into the living room. Wendy lay on the floor, blood all around her. Using my gun, I hammered at the jagged glass, then stepped up onto the window ledge, kicked free another piece of glass, and lowered myself onto the carpet.

As I knelt next to Wendy I saw blood oozing from a wound just below her neck. I raced to the telephone, dialed 911, shouted 'Ambulance" into the receiver, then rushed back to Wendy.

Her eyes were glassy, her pulse was feint, and my medical knowledge was minimal. Tourniquets were meant to reduce blood flow to the limbs, but how was I supposed to slow bleeding where Wendy had been hit?

"Don't bleed out on me, Wendy," I whispered to her.

My thoughts turned to Korea, back when I was a young, inexperienced soldier. My unit was among the first four hundred American troops to arrive in Korea. We were all twenty years old or younger, had been given eight weeks' training, then sent to face what seemed like the entire North Korean Army. We fought like hell, but we were overrun time and again by battalions backed up by Russian tanks, until we were finally forced to retreat in grand disorder –at least those of us who were still among the living. We were told afterwards how brave we had been in executing delaying tactics until fresh UN troops arrived to replace us. Well, if being scared shitless and fighting for your life count as bravery, so be it.

I thought that we few survivors would be branded cowards. Instead, our commanding general praised us for holding the line. All I could remember immediately afterward was seeing wave after wave of enemy infantry coming at me. Time collapsed into the moment. Pick a target and fire. Then quickly choose another, and another, then another, all the while only hoping my weapon wouldn't jam. Finally I ran out of ammo and played dead. Brave, eh?

I thought of today's college boys being turned into cannon fodder in the name of saving one batch of Asians from being trampled by another batch. Since 1950 I have imagined more than once that I had been killed in Korea, that I had bled out from my wounds, no medic coming to give me enough morphine to allow me to die a painless death.

Waiting for the ambulance, I put pressure on Wendy's wound from both sides to try to staunch the flow. Stupid me, thinking Wendy was safe, home alone, stupid for thinking maybe the gunshots aimed at Wendy were meant for me. Now I had to consider: Who wanted Wendy dead? Jude Crowder and Carmen Armenta were on their way to Mexico. Mary-Margaret and her boyfriend were facing charges in Santa Clara. That left only Sister Melda? Or did it?

Melda, for sure, was part of the conspiracy to kidnap the girls. How many other nuns lived and worked at the convent? Half a dozen? A dozen? Could one or more of them also be partners with Carmen, Melda, and Jude? And what about Mother Agnes? She managed the graveyard next to the chapel. Did she know that Eileen and Melissa might be buried there?

I heard sirens.

"You'll soon be in good hands. Please, don't bleed out on me," I told Wendy, as I patted her arm.

I realized, too late of course, that I should have paid more attention to Sister Melda. That she was competing with Carmen for Jude's attentions did not alter the fact that she and Carmen had obviously agreed to share the phony story about the license plate number on the Woody and both stuck with that false story through the interviews with the sheriff, the chief of police, and the FBI. With Jude and Carmen now on their way to Mexico, that left Melda in the lurch in more ways than one.

What I now realized I might have overlooked is Father Reed Mackinzie's relationship with Sister Melda, and if he was screwing Melda, he might well be involved with the orphan's abductions. Might Melda and Reed have come together, each on the rebound after Jude discovered Carmen had been transferred to Santa Julietta? If so, was Melda sharing with Reed how she was lying about the abduction of Melissa and Eileen? Maybe so. But Father Reed couldn't have shot at Wendy. He was still in jail. However, he could have directed Sister Melda to kill Wendy, supposing that with Wendy dead I would have no reason to continue looking for the missing girls.

If so, they misjudged me.

55

I followed the ambulance with Wendy in it to Cottage Hospital and watched Wendy being wheeled in ER. For the next two hours I alternated reading sports magazines and women's monthly mags while I waited for Wendy's surgery to wind down. At last an operating nurse came out to tell me Wendy was going to live, but that she was far too weak and drowsy for me to be allowed to see her. Morning would be the earliest that she could have bedside guests.

From the hospital I placed a call to Amanda Reynolds asking if Reed Mackenzie had been discharged from jail yet.

"Fletcher, by now you must have heard the phrase 'the law's delay' a hundred times. Well, my getting Father Mackenzie released makes a hundred and one. "

I said, "So the answer is 'No'?"

"Yes. Do you want to see him again? The fact that you saw him eyeing jail matrons started the ball rolling to set him free, but there really is a ream of paperwork to be done. A judge has to meet with someone from the prosecutor's office, et cetera, et cetera."

"Thanks."

"I'll arrange for you to meet him in jail again if you like."

"No. I just wanted to know where he is."

I decided to return to the convent, where I parked my car across the street from the nuns' dormitory. As I turned off my car's engine, Amanda's answer about the law's delay rang hollow. Father Mackenzie was out of jail and back at the convent. The door to the nuns' sleeping quarters was locked so I rang the buzzer. A young nun I hadn't met before came to the door, saw me, and tapped her watch.

I pulled my pen and notebook from my sportscoat and scribbled *Sister Melda* on a blank page, then held it up for the young nun to read. She tapped her watch again and shook her head. I then wrote *I know Father Mackenzie is inside the convent. I want to see him, too.*

The sister's jaw dropped, and she shook her head. I nodded repeatedly with just as much vigor. Next I pulled out my wallet and showed her my detective's ID that included my photo. She unlocked the door and stepped aside.

She said, "Father Mackenzie cannot be here. Because he's not allowed to be here this time of evening."

"Being not allowed doesn't mean he isn't here. I just now parked my car near his," I said.

She replied, "I passed Sister Melda a while ago. She was headed to the chapel and she was alone."

"Father Mackenzie must be waiting for her there," I said.

"That can't be true," she said. "Men aren't allowed anywhere on the convent grounds this late in the day."

"Follow me, Sister."

She flinched and stepped back.

"I'm not going anywhere with you, Mr. Fletcher."

"Very well. I'll walk to the chapel by myself."

"Oh, no you won't."

She took the lead and I had to tell her, "Slow down, please."

She slowed, looked over her shoulder, and said, "It's your duty to keep up with me."

"My duty?" I tried to laugh. "What is your name, Sister?"

"I'm sister Estelle."

"Let's not charge into the chapel like a pair of buffalo," I said.

She stopped and turned. "Are you implying that I am shaggy and fat?"

"Neither one. It's just an expression."

"A poor choice of comparison. Insulting. That's what it was."

I apologized.

She turned and stormed away. I did my best to keep up.

The chapel was empty.

"Hum. Most odd," Sister Estelle said when she came to a halt at the back of the chapel.

"Where might she have gone?" I said.

She raised her left hand, forefinger extended as she took a deep breath.

"Someone has been smoking in here," she said sternly.

I had to concentrate intensely before I detected the smell of cigarette smoke.

"You do not smoke, do you, Mr. Fletcher?"

"I do not." I concentrated again, at last matching a name with the scent. Reed Mackenzie.

So I asked, "Has Father Mackenzie been here lately to see Sister Melda?"

"He's here now. I'm sure of it. The scent belongs to one of those funny little cigarettes he is addicted to. Not marijuana, but it might as well be."

"Could he be with Mother Agnes?"

She put her hands on her hips, glared at me, and said, "How dare you?"

"No. I don't mean that."

She charged past me and went straight to Mother Agnes' office and knocked. When no one answered, she tried the doorknob and discovered the door opened easily. So she peeked in, shook her head, then closed the door gently, as if she feared waking the dead.

"Follow me."

We didn't go far. She knocked louder on the door of the private living quarters of her Abbess. As she was about to knock a second time the door opened.

"Sister Estelle. What do you want at this hour?"

At that moment Mother Agnes saw me standing behind sister Estelle. She gasped. "What are you doing with *that* man in your company? You haven't…?"

"No, Mother. I most definitely have not." She took a deep breath and let it out slowly. "We are looking for Sister Melda. I thought she might be in our chapel, seeking our Lord's forgiveness for her usual compendium of sins."

Mother Agnes said, "I take it you did not find her there."

"We did not. However, we did detect the presence of a vile, familiar odor – from one or more cigarettes."

"Someone has been smoking in our chapel?" Mother Agnes said and shook a forefinger at me.

I held up both palms to object.

"You, Mr. Fletcher, are the source of wickedness engulfing my land. Once again, I must insist you depart, to cease and desist as the Church's attorney would say to you."

"Jude the Kidnapper. Are you in league with him? Right now he and Sister Carmen are running away together to Mexico to avoid local authorities and the FBI."

"You'll leave now!" she shouted.

"What are you afraid of?"

"It is you who have me to fear. Now go!"

I tried to step past her, but she moved to block me. So I turned to Estelle and said, "Keep her here."

Estelle took hold of Mother Agnes's arm and pulled her aside.

"You'll regret this," the Abbess said.

I stepped past her and continued back toward the chapel again.

56

The altar candles had burned down a quarter of an inch, otherwise nothing had changed inside the chapel. So far, the only blood spilled in the sanctuary came from Christ's wounds as he hung nailed on the plastic Cross. I checked the small waiting room on the right side of the altar and found a table with two long tapers and a box filled spare candles.

I moved across the altar to the room on the far side, the door Father Spannard had opened for me earlier. The knob wiggled slightly but the door didn't open. So I searched the room for a hidden key but didn't find one. I decided I could revisit Mother Agnes and ask politely for the key, or I could pretend I was a tough guy and kick the door in

Sister Estelle showed up.

"Mother Agnes is phoning authorities," she said. "You had better go."

I gave her a thank-you smile, kicked the door in, and found a light switch. Ahead of me was a miniature version of the altar in the chapel, along with an upholstered bench to kneel and pray. To the right of the miniature altar was a gold-colored tapestry. Behind the tapestry was another door. It was a sliding door, no turn handle, no lock. I put my ear to the door and thought I could hear sounds.

Sister Estelle came into the room.

"What's behind here?" I said.

"I don't know. I have only been here once to give a message to Mother Agnes.

I pulled the notched handle and stuck my head into the darkness. After waiting for my eyes to adjust, I saw a descending staircase. I groped the wall for a light switch and finally found one. A dim light at the top of the stairs came on.

Voices were replaced by running sounds. I removed the .38 pistol from my waistband and cocked its hammer.

"Follow me or not," I whispered to Sister Estelle.

"I'll stay here," she whispered back.

"If she shows up, do not let Mother Agnes follow me down. Okay?"

"Okay."

I moved quickly down the stairs and at the bottom found another set of light switches. I flicked them all on and found myself in an empty room with a door at the far end. I looked back up the stairway. Sister Estelle looked down at me. I motioned for her to come down and waited for her to join me.

"You've never been down here?" I whispered.

"No. Never!"

I gestured with my pistol that I was going to open the next door.

From Sister Estelle, "I'm scared."

"So am I."

The door opened noiselessly. Ceiling lights illuminated a steel slab in the middle. On a wall to one side were shelves filled with bolts of white fabric. A chill ran up my spine. The last time I had seen such a table was in LA, in the underground labyrinth that led to the forensic pathologists' suite of labs.

> *"...all wrapped in white linen,*
> *Wrapped in white linen as cold as the clay."*

I kneeled and found a black-beaded rosary. Next to the rosary lay a used condom. Sister Melda and Father Mackenzie? I tried to flush the images that came to mind but couldn't. Sex on a morgue slab. Sister Estelle peeked over my shoulder and gasped.

Another door awaited us.

"Let's look," I said to Sister Estelle in a low voice.

"I'm still scared," she whispered.

"Sorry. I don't have another gun to lend you."

She was not amused.

The door, at the right corner of the morgue-like room, was solid and locked. In movies cowboys and policemen shoot at door locks to open doors. I tried it and the reverberating sound was deafening. When I turned I saw sister Estelle kneeling, her headpiece thrown back, her hands to her ears.

Knowing it was cruel to leave her, I pulled her up and held her tight. She whimpered.

"I'm sorry," I whispered. "Stick with me, stay close. We're going to push on."

All she could do was nod, while continuing to whimper.

Beyond the door, in a stack, lay homemade torches and boxes of matches.

I replaced the spent cartridge in my handgun, tucked my gun away, and lit a torch. I then took Estelle by a hand again and turned to look inside what was clearly a cave. I realized that, except for the alleyway that ran behind the chapel, the chapel butted up against a high, rocky hill. Odd, I had never paid attention when standing out in front of the convent. Now sister Estelle and I were standing in a cave hollowed out beneath the ground-level base of the hill.

"Come, Sister." Only then did I notice how cold Estelle's hand felt.

"Light a torch, sister. Then stay close to me."

"I don't want to set you on fire."

"Okay. You go first."

"No!" she shrieked.

So I lit the torch and began to walk ahead of her. Three steps into the cave I stopped, frozen by what I saw.

When Estelle saw what the torch illuminated she gasped, covered her mouth and let out a muffled, "No! Oh, no!"

Along the right side of the cave we saw mummies, stacked two high for as deep into the cave as we could see with the torch's light. All of the mummies were small. My own thought no doubt paralleled what Sister Estelle was thinking: Schoolchildren.

Estelle reached out until her trembling hand gripped mine. We edged forward for a better look at the first mummies. The linen wrappings had grayed but stuck to each mummy was a tag with a name and date. The first one read: Paulie Nordmann, 6/23/1949. From the background material I had read on Agnes Sullivan, she first arrived to take charge of the convent in March of 1949, following the death of the previous Abbess.

Sister Estelle made the sign of the Cross as she looked at the long row of mummies. "There are so many," she cried.

I wondered if the Aztec god and goddess of the underworld, Mictlantecuhli and Mictecacihuatl, might be lurking nearby, ready to protect the souls of these mummified youth against an incursion by infidels.

I said, "Mother Agnes has a great deal of explaining to do. Do you think you can manage to go upstairs and phone the police?"

From behind us came the voice of Mother Agnes.

"Neither of you is going anywhere."

Estelle and I turned to see Agnes pointing a shotgun at us.

She said, "In high school back in Michigan I was an outstanding skeet shooter and dove hunter. On Okinawa I blew a sniper out of a tree as we were setting up a field hospital. Later I helped stop a Japanese bonsai attack on our camp."

My thought of drawing my .38 special on her quickly evaporated.

She said, "Sounds from a blast won't carry beyond this cavern and the walls will withstand the vibrations."

"How could you, Mother Agnes?" Sister Estelle cried out. "These are our children, entrusted to the convent. God is watching. What do you say to Him?"

"He knows that not all children come to us by the grace of God. Some are the spawn of the Devil."

"No!" Estelle shouted. "No!"

In a voice worthy of a psychopath Agnes replied, "Some are brought to us to test us, to see if we recognize the satanic blood that flows through their veins. And when we see these children for what they are, we must strike."

"And what are we to do when we see you for what you really are?" Estelle asked.

"You are blind, Sister, blind. Why God has chosen to blind you, I do not know. He truly does work in mysterious ways."

During the exchange between Mother Agnes and sister Estelle I slid my hand slowly toward my backside, toward my .38.

"I see you reaching for your gun, Mr. Fletcher. Continue on, but when you have it in hand, place it on the floor in front of you."

I complied.

"Sister Estelle, must I remind you of the book of Proverbs: *Foolishness is bound in the heart of a child; but the rod of correction shall drive it far from him.* And also from Proverbs: *He that spareth his rod hateth his son; but he that loveth him chasteneth him betimes.*"

"You equate murder with chastening, Mother Agnes. That is not right," Estelle said.

Agnes' comeback was to quote a passage from the book of Romans: *Slanderers, God-haters, insolent, arrogant and boastful; they invent ways of doing evil; they disobey their parents; they have no understanding, no fidelity, no love, no mercy. Although they know God's righteous decree that those who do such things deserve death, they not only continue to do these very things but also approve of those who practice them.*

Estelle's rejoinder was, "I assume Melissa and Eileen are embalmed here among the other mummies. Do you really think they were slanderers, God-haters, insolent, arrogant, and boastful?"

"There was no question of it, Sister Estelle. Those two were most adept at inventing ways of doing evil. Insolent, arrogant, and boastful? I have never encountered two who were better at those practices. So, too, they were slanderers and God-haters. Both were as atheistic as …as…as Mr. Fletcher himself."

Estelle replied, "I saw them otherwise, Mother Agnes. A tad irreverent, yes. But they were far from qualifying for your passage in Romans. Far, I say."

While the abbess and her young nun engaged in Biblical exegesis I contemplated my chances of dropping down, grabbing my .38, aiming and hitting Mother Agnes before she could send a broad pattern of buckshot at Sister Estelle and me. The odds didn't seem to be too good. But then neither were the odds of not doing it.

Dropping my torch, I dragged Estelle to the ground with me. My Taurus .38 revolver held seven bullets in its cylinder. I wanted to try to center three quick shots toward the center of the woman wearing a bulky black habit, but I only pulled off one round before her shotgun went off.

The cavern echoed with the shotgun's blast. I counted to three before peeking.

"Are you okay, Estelle?" I whispered.

"No. I'm shaking like a leaf," she whispered back.

If I fired again, my muzzle flash would give Mother Agnes a pinpoint of light toward which to shoot.

To Estelle I whispered again, 'Crawl toward the wall nearest to us, and then crawl toward the rear of the cave."

She reached to me and squeezed my arm twice, which I took for, "You needn't tell me a second time."

From somewhere behind Mother Agnes a voice called out. "Melda? Are you down there, Melda?"

Reed Mackenzie.

I yelled, "Call the police, Father Mackenzie!"

Agnes fired her shotgun as I rolled to my left.

"Mother Agnes!" Father Mackenzie called out. Somehow he was now back in the chapel and oblivious of the situation below him.

"Agnes has a shotgun," I yelled as I rolled back to my right.

No blast. I wanted to shoot, but I guessed Agnes was no longer where her second muzzle flash came from. I needed to know where Sister Estelle had crept to, but I didn't want to whisper to her for fear Mother Agnes could zero in on my location. Instead, I gambled on yelling toward the rear of the cavern, hoping the sound of my voice became too diffuse for her to pinpoint the source.

"Sister Estelle, stop when you reach the cave's opening and wait for me! And do not, repeat, do not answer me."

Boom! Agnes fired, while I crept rapidly across the cavern. I heard the buckshot pellets slam into the wall behind me. I saw her muzzle flash, but I didn't shoot at it, because in case I missed I didn't want to give her my own muzzle flash to fire at. Nor did I want to pause in my crawling to Sister Estelle's side of the cave. I had no idea how much sound my under-barbed-wire style of crawling created.

Now I had to crawl quickly along the side of the cave. I kept reaching out in front of me, tapping my hand until at last I touched Sister Estelle's shoes. She jerked away from my touch and winced. Her soft sound echoed in the cave, drawing a shotgun blast from Mother Agnes.

The sun had long ago set, but I could tell we had reached the cave exit from the cool draft of night air flowing into the cave. It was the exit Reed Mackenzie must have used. Estelle lay still as I crawled past her and raised myself on one knee. I tapped Sister Estelle and whispered, "Up and out. Quickly." She moved, I stood, fired a shot in Agnes' direction, then stepped forward, holding Estelle by one arm. Another blast from Agnes' gun erupted and the sound of chips from the cave wall fell just behind me.

I nudged Estelle forward and in the distance I could see a streetlamp glowing. To my left I felt fist-sized branches and smelled the faint scent of oleander. To my right I felt the same. This entrance to the cave was well-concealed. The tall bushes from both sides grew so closely together that even a slender person needed to maneuver sideways to get out.

Suddenly there was a voice just beyond us.

"Fletcher? Is that you?" Father Mackenzie had returned.

In a loud voice he said, "I have a gun, Fletcher. Mother Agnes told me where to find her pistol. If you're there, come out slowly. You, too, sister Estelle. I don't want to shoot anybody, but I will if I have to."

His voice trembled and from experience I knew just how dangerous a nervous man holding a gun can be. I gently pulled sister Estelle behind me and pressed her down to a kneeling position. I knelt, too. I didn't have a plan but knew a standoff with Father Mackenzie put me at a disadvantage with Mother Agnes somewhere in my rear.

Better I should make a move against the padre and do it quickly. I doubted he was skillful with a handgun, but at close range he didn't need to be. And if Mother Agnes pulled the trigger on Estelle and me from close range, well… I envisioned two more mummies being added to the long row of mummies already lining the far side of the cave.

I took two steps back and listened for Mother Agnes, but heard nothing. Where was she? I waited and listened. A flashlight came on and shone at the oleanders. I pressed Sister Estelle to the ground.

Then a voice.

"Turn that light off," Agnes yelled at Father Mackenzie. She was no longer in the cave, but behind the priest. A serious tactical error by the abbess. She should have remained in the cave. She was a greater threat to me there.

"Did they get by you, Reed? Are they gone?" Mother Agnes shouted.

Between the oleander stalks I fired one shot where I thought Agnes stood. My shot was followed by a gasp. Next came a pistol shot. I crouched as low as I could get and fired a single shot where I saw Reed Mackenzie's muzzle flash.

"Flat," I whispered to Estelle. She flattened and I lay on top of her. A shotgun blast erupted, and oleander branches snapped just over my head. I fired two shots at the muzzle blast. In the distance I heard sirens.

57

I waited until the sirens ceased then fired three shots in the air, reloaded, then fired three more. The police were slow in finding a way past the wire fencing. When two uniformed cops appeared, shining their flashlights here and there, one of their lights landed on a wounded Father Mackenzie.

I helped a trembling sister Estelle to her feet and hugged her, as I listened to one of the patrolmen speak into his handphone to call for an ambulance.

The other patrolman said to the padre, "Sir, I'm going to put a tourniquet just above your wound. It's bleeding pretty badly." Father Mackenzie nodded.

I yelled to the cops, "Over here. We're the ones being shot at. When the ambulance arrives I want one of the attendants to check out the nun who is with me."

Bothe cops nodded and one asked, "What's been going on here? Who are you?"

"I've been helping your Lieutenant Hamilton on a murder case." I then explained about finding the mummies and Mother Agnes' finding us and shooting at us with a shotgun.

"This abbess you're talking about. Where is she?" one cop said.

Just then Lieutenant Hamilton showed up. "Hello, Stu. I heard shots."

"Mother Agnes has been blasting away at us. This is Sister Estelle. She's been through a lot just now."

More sirens.

The lieutenant spoke to two uniformed officers behind him. "One of you help the sister to the ambulance and tell the ambulance attendants to bring a stretcher for the priest."

I said, "Mother Agnes was here just a couple minutes ago. She's the one who wounded the padre. She meant to aim at me and I fired when I saw her muzzle blast and I think I wounded her. She dropped her weapon so let's go looking for her."

One of the cops left with Sister Estelle to go find the ambulance. The other cop was tightening the tourniquet on Reed Mackenzie and Lieutenant Hamilton gave me an after-you gesture. So I turned and we both entered the cave, where I asked the lieutenant to shine his light on the far wall.

"Oh, my. Whose handiwork is all of this?" Hamilton asked.

"When I first met Mother Agnes she told me how fond she is of children. What she meant was: How fond she is of mummifying them."

The lieutenant shined his flashlight up down the long rows. "A serial killer?"

I said, "You're looking at nearly all children. A few may have died of childhood diseases, but I'm betting not all of them did. I think you'll find the bodies of Melissa Hargrove and Eileen Sanchez over there somewhere."

The lieutenant shook his head in disbelief. Then, after a sigh, he told me, "I have a piece of news that will warm your heart. Earlier air traffic control for the LA region had an unidentified blip on their screen, heading on a course of 180 degrees in a straight line some twenty miles out to sea.

"Jude and Carmen?"

He said, "We may never know. When the blip approached a line that, by extension, would be the U.S.-Mexican border, the blip vanished. The air controllers dispatched two Coast Guard helicopters and a cutter to the point where the plane disappeared from their screen. The helicopters found some debris, including most of the left wing. The Coast Guard said the wing could easily be off a DC-3. Anyway, they hovered for as long as their fuel permitted. No sign of survivors. Their cutter had just arrived when they made their initial report and broadcast it."

"Goodbye Jude and Carmen," I said.

"I'm declaring this cave and the above chapel to be crime scenes. Let's get a count on the mummies. Have you looked yet? Are there any identifying marks on them?"

"Names and dates."

Hamilton said, "Let's take a count."

While I was looking for Mother Agnes a forensic team arrived and set up klieg lights. We saw that the mummies went on for at least forty yards into the cave.

The lieutenant stepped outside, and I heard him tell one of his uniformed patrolmen to call for a forensic team.

Walking along the row of mummies, Hamilton and I discovered that the nearer to the chapel basement, the grayer the bindings on the mummies. Also, we determined that the grayer mummies' tags bore the earliest dates. Paulie Nordmann had been in the cave the longest. When we reached the last mummies my mouth went dry. There lay the only adult-sized mummy and it belonged to Morgan Crowder. Next to him lay Melissa Hargrove and Eileen Sanchez.

How Morgan died was no mystery. All accounts, written and verbal, said he died from choking on his own vomit after consuming too many alcoholic beverages at a fraternity party on the campus of Santa Clara University in 1946.

Lieutenant Hamilton decided he needed to phone forensic people higher up the administrative ladder to let them decide how to proceed with the mummies. The uniforms outside were gone, making the nearest telephone one in Mother Agnes's office, so we headed there and just as we arrived one of Hamilton's uniformed cops stepped into her office. He was wearing latex gloves.

"Lieutenant, we found a diary in one of the nun's bedrooms. It belongs to Sister Melda Torres. We didn't touch it, but we thought you would want to look at it."

The lieutenant handed the policeman Agnes's phone to call and let the forensic people know about the mummies in the cave. The young policeman looked rightfully puzzled.

"Never mind," Hamilton said and took the phone back. "Go guard the mummies. They're in the cave in the basement of the chapel."

Hamilton laughed a nervous laugh. "We'll pre-date the warrant so it shows we had a right to search the nun's rooms." He then pulled on latex gloves before examining the diary. "My, my. Won't the DA turn a somersault when he sees this."

Another uniformed cop entered Mother Agnes's office. "Lieutenant, we have not been able to find the nun who belongs to the diary."

"No problem, son. Mr. Fletcher will track her down for us, I'm sure."

I wasn't so sure about that but decided to try, using Father Mackenzie as bait. So, I drove to Cottage Hospital, where I was told that Father Mackenzie had already checked himself out, AMA, Against Medical Advice. My next stop was the Pacific Beach Retreat Hotel.

The desk clerk told me, "You just missed them. Mr. Mackenzie and his wife said they were catching a boat leaving San Francisco for Hong Kong."

While checking out, why would Mackenzie announce his destination? I had no doubt he and Melda were going anywhere but San Francisco. I reported what the clerk heard to Lieutenant Hamilton so the coppers could make of it what they chose to.

Anywhere but, left quite a few options.

I checked myself in the PBR Hotel for the night. I decided to let the coppers tie up all the loose ends. But even a long, hot shower failed to wash away the depressing filth I had encountered that day. Room service delivered me a bottle of their house bourbon and I settled into an easy chair next to my bed and allowed the whiskey to seep into the rough edges of my soul until I fell asleep. When dawn arrived, cold and late, I had dreamed of dozens of ways I had slain Boris Karloff, Vincent Price, and Bela Lugosi. But when chasing Father Makenzie and Sister Melda my cop car kept running off the road and plunging down a seaside cliff. I awoke at 10 a.m. with both my telephone and my head ringing.

Hamilton told me, "Your priest and your nun crossed over at Calexico."

My priest and my nun. Right.

Calexico is a border town two thirds of the way from San Diego to Yuma. The town of Mexicali is on the Mexican side of the border there and is much larger than Calexico. The best way to avoid unwanted observation by cops was to drive east on I-10 from LA to Indio, then turn south on State Road 86, passing through Coachella, down through the Imperial Valley to El Centro, finally crossing I-8 into Calexico, where the border crossing with Mexicali is almost always heavy with truck traffic coming into California, almost always light on traffic passing into Mexico. The All-Points Bulletin for Reed Mackenzie and Melda Torres apparently had not reached the Border Patrol in time. Or maybe it had arrived timely, but remained unread until too late.

So Father Mackenzie and Sister Melda accomplished what Jude Crowder and Sister Carmen had not – escaped safely into Mexico. When I asked Lieutenant Hamilton if Mother Agnes had been found yet, he laughed.

"What's so amusing?" I said.

"We hounds were outfoxed by the Vatican. Our APB on her didn't get much attention at airports that have few or no flights leaving the country. The APB was acknowledged by security folks at SFO, but not by anyone at San Jose, even though several flights to Canada and Central America leave from there. Anyway, it turns out we've lost Mother Agnes. She took a flight from San Jose to Denver and from Denver to Dulles. I offer you three guesses where she flew from Dulles."

I said, "To the moon."

"Close, Fletcher. Now think of somewhere safer than the moon."

"Rome?"

"Bingo! You clever gumshoe! I wish I had a mind as sharp as yours."

"Yeah. Right. Just be thankful your pay grade is higher than mine. Money compensates for a lot of unpleasantness in life. If I made as much as you do, Hamilton, I'd be on a flight to Rome myself," I said.

"But you'd be eyeing the ruins of the Coliseum and be exchanging banter with all the flossy tarts, whereas the lady of the blessed Convent of Santa Theresa Ornella is admiring paintings deep within the Vatican."

"What the hell is she doing there?" I asked, feigning ignorance.

"Making herself untouchable to the police forces of the world. Interpol wasn't informed in time to stop her. So now Pope Paul VI can give her a job mumbling prayers to saints and angels," Hamilton said.

"Does His Holiness have a Department of Egyptology?"

"I think Egyptian Christians are not Catholic, Fletcher. Coptic Christians, I believe, are what they call themselves, although I couldn't tell an Egyptian Copt from a Southern Baptist."

I said, "Maybe the pope will give her a job overseeing the teaching of Vatican children."

Hamilton said, "And killing those who annoy her. I took the opportunity to read relevant pages of Sister Melda's diary. Melda claims Agnes killed children who had behavior problems. With the exception of Melissa Hargrove and Eileen Sanchez, no one on the outside of the convent gave a shit about any of the convent kids. They had no parents, no relatives. Not even the CPS checked in on them. Forensics tells me some of the mummified kids died from health issues. But Melissa and Eileen were strangled, being deemed incorrigible by Mother Agnes. The same for other children, too. We're told that Agnes had very little patience. She didn't belong at a convent that had young children. Anyway, whether the children died from pneumonia or from bad behavior, no one knew of their deaths. Wendy Ellen's existence proved to be the abbess's downfall. Wendy cared very deeply about their welfare and hired you."

I cleared my throat loudly.

"Of course, I mean to give you full credit, Fletcher. Wendy's talking you into working for her *pro bono* led to Mother Agnes's slipping up."

On the subject of *pro bono* cases, I needed to check in on the Ledbetter twins. Father Mackenzie may have had knowledge of what went on in Agnes's mummy-wrapping cellar, but he was innocent of the false boy-rape charges brought against him by Tyson and Bryson on a lark.

As Reed Mackenzie's defense lawyer Amanda Reynolds wrote a letter to the dean of students at the University of San Diego explaining how and why her client was being turned loose and suggesting perhaps the Ledbetter boys be chastened by the university while the Santa Julietta DA mulls over whether to charge the boys with obstruction and see what the NCAA hierarchy thought of a school that allowed student-athletes to continue to participate with criminal charges hanging over them. Amanda as yet had received no reply from USD.

Mrs. Ledbetter invited me into her home, treated me to tea and cookies, then confirmed that her sons had returned to collage, that the University of San Diego required their superb basketball skills, that after Thanksgiving the school was counting on her boys to lead the school in conference play. Forgiveness is a celebrated Christian virtue, she reminded me. And thus, the Church, in the form of the university's administration, was quite willing to look upon the boys' accusations against Father Mackenzie as nothing more than a bit of misguided youthful exuberance.

No harm, no foul. No lasting harm would come to the priest on their account,. Thanks to me Father Mackenzie's true sexual orientation was brought to light and exposed in the fact that the priest possessed a nasty penchant for screwing nuns. But the Church insisted that Father Mackenzie's soiled character and immoral behavior cast no darkness on the Ledbetter twins.

Yeah, right!

"You should be ashamed, Mr. Fletcher. My sons told you the truth and you refused to believe them.," said Mrs. Ledbetter.

So much for contrition.

"What truths do you have in mind?" I asked.

"Just because a priest is not a homo doesn't mean he had no evil intentions toward my sons."

"Ah, yes. In your Catholicism if John's intent is to molest Mary, even though he fails to follow through, he has sinned just as much as if he had followed through. Am I right?"

"That is so," she said.

"Now tell me how you came to know Father Mackenzie's intentions toward your sons."

She began thinking so hard that I could hear the gears spinning in her skull.

At last she said, "At summer camp that man had no women to lust after. So his prurient mind turned elsewhere. And my boys…my boys…." She began to sob.

I had no idea whether her tears came from genuine sorrow or were crocodile tears, though I suspected the latter. She was suggesting rather strongly that her sons were worthy objects of lust by either sex, which left open the possibility that a mother could lust after a son. Or even two sons. I had to admit her boys were as handsome as they come. But Wendy Ellen Littleton would not have raised such sons to be liars, ones who thrilled at inflicting wanton sadism toward an innocent man.

From Mr. Ledbetter, "I think you should leave, Mr. Fletcher. You have caused more than enough damage to this family already."

"You sincerely want to believe that you are all the victims in this affair," I said.

"Of course, we are the victims. You obviously do not understand just how much damage you and that vile priest have inflicted on us. You've tried to make my sons out to be some sort of monsters. How dare you!"

Amanda, bless her, managed to put a dent in the Church's collection plates. Her bill to Cardinal McIntyre for defending Reed Mackenzie was a whopper, more than quadruple what she would normally charge for such work. Plus, she even had a line item on her Church invoice that I had only seen twice before, when she was so fiendishly incensed at the client and his backers. This time she charged the cardinal $6000 for ten hours of "think time". That also meant my fee for the work I did was likely going to be much more than she normally doles out to me.

Thanks for being an asshole in Mrs. Ledbetter's mind, Padre.

One of Amanda's office minions, Judy, was a part-time staffer while earning a degree in Classics at UCSJ. That meant she spent a lot of her time honing her skill at reading Latin. To help Judy Amanda subscribed to the Vatican's weekly newspaper published in Latin, and it was there Judy discovered that Mother Superior Agnes Sullivan, a recent arrival in Vatican City, was assigned by Pope Paul VI to work in the Vatican Secret Archives, where she would help examine information submitted by supporters of sundry candidates for sainthood to determine whether such evidence was accurate, relevant, and, in many cases, sufficient to elevate those candidates.

Saints be praised!

58

My last stop before driving home was to see Wendy Ellen. I'm not at my best conveying grim tidings, but I tried not to fumble my account of what happened to her girls. Her reaction was to let out a scream, followed by a flood of tears. She gave new meaning to the phrase *cry me a river*. We sat on her sofa and I held her close until the tears ebbed.

"I just knew that nun was a witch. I knew it, I knew it," she said as she pounded her fists against my chest. "I could kill those women at CPS. They're as guilty as anyone at the convent."

I was not about to dispute that. I was hoping she would not invite me to stay the night. She didn't. She knew that the best cries are a reversal of Hank William's "I'm So Lonesome I could Cry". You cry alone, without feeling lonesome. I promised I would call her in the morning, kissed her on her forehead, and made my exit.

After two beers, a hot shower, and a pastrami sandwich I picked up from a deli in downtown Santa Maria, I was in a better mood. The deli puts pickle juice in their potato salad, just the way my mother used to do. Sated, I was looking forward to a restful night's sleep in my own bed.

I had barely counted a dozen sheep when my doorbell rang. Mary Ann Chase and Germaine Payette stood on my porch, Mary Ann in her bathrobe, Germaine with a blanket wrapped around her. I invited them in. Mary Ann guided Germaine to my sofa, gestured for her to sit, then joined her. I sat in my favorite reading chair.

After tucking the blanket tighter around Germaine's shoulders, Mary Ann said to me, "Stu, here is Randall Crowder's private home telephone number. I want you to call him and ask him to come to Santa Maria immediately. Tell him to pack an overnight bag and to bring several hundred dollars of his father's cash. Tell him Germaine needs him and needs him now."

Never one to question Mary Ann Chase's wisdom or judgment, I did as I was told.

"I'll be there in an hour," Randall told me, his voice even.

When I returned to the women, Mary Ann said to me, "Stu, I'm going to put Germaine to bed in your bed. I'll stay with her while you go see what you can do for Sarah Payette. Use her back door. It's open."

Once again I did as I was told.

I found Sarah standing in her kitchen, staring into the middle distance. Her hands were trembling.

"Sarah? It's Stu Fletcher. Tell me what is going on, please."

She held a napkin and wiped at her nose before saying, "He's in there." She pointed toward the hallway that led to the bedrooms.

In his and Sarah's bedroom I found Fowler sprawled across his bed, blood had ceased to ooze from a small hole in his right temple. He was fully dressed. A handgun lay on the bed. I looked closer and recognized it as Fowler's long-barrel .22, the gun he told me his father had given him, a souvenir from his old man's WWII flying days as a fighter pilot in the Pacific Theater.

I didn't know if Fowler had ever fired the .22. I had never offered to take him to the local outdoor shooting range on the northeast side of town. But someone had now clearly fired it at least once – with a deadly result.

"He had it coming."

Sarah stood behind me.

"Whose fingerprints will the police find on the gun, Sarah?"

She reached over, picked up the gun, aimed it at Fowler's head, and said, "Mine."

"I'm going to phone the police, Sarah. I'd like you to put the gun down exactly where you just picked it up. Okay?"

Zombie-like, she said, "Okay. I will."

"Come with me. We don't need to be in the bedroom any longer."

"Okay."

The first pair of uniformed cops arrived less than three minutes later. Two more squad cars pulled in right behind them. I gestured toward the hallway when the first policeman said, "There's been a murder here?"

I said, "Maybe." I again pointed toward the hallway, putting my arm around Sarah as more policemen arrived. I then walked Sarah into the living room and gestured for her to sit on the sofa. After she sat I joined her there.

One cop returned from the bedroom and asked, "Who is the deceased?" But just then a homicide detective I barely knew, a man named Kirk Streitholm, came through the front door and said, "Stay with the body, officer. I'm fine here."

The detective ignored me and asked Sarah, "Are you related to the deceased, Ma'am?"

"I'm his wife."

"Your name?"

"Sarah Payette."

To me he said, "I know who you are." To Sarah he said, "Anyone else here in the house besides you and Mr. Fletcher?"

"No. My daughter's not here."

"Where is your daughter, Mrs. Payette?"

"She ran away. She ran away." Zombie tones again.

"Where did she run to?"

"She didn't say. She didn't say." Singsong, like a drunk.

"When did your daughter leave?"

"Such a long time ago. Hours and hours."

Streitholm turned to me. "What are you doing here, Gumshoe?"

"I live two doors away. I heard a shot, came looking, and found Sarah standing on her back porch, acting like she didn't know up from down. She muttered something about the bedroom. So I went to take a look and found Fowler. Next I called you."

"Such an upstanding citizen you are, Fletcher," he said snidely. "Although not everyone will vouch for you."

I didn't dare offer him Amanda's name as someone who would vouch for my good citizenship, because more than once Amanda had probably destroyed a case that Streitholm had thought was going to be a no-brainer conviction.

59

When I arrived back at my own house, Germaine was asleep in my bed. Mary Ann quietly rocked in my bedside rocker. I opened a bottle of beer and stood on my front porch, watching for Randall to emerge from a street filled with flashing police-car lights. Ten minutes passed and I went inside to fetch another beer when I saw Randall running up to my back door.

"Jeez, Mr. Fletcher. Is Fowler really dead?"

"Yes, and we need to get Germaine out of town."

"I'm ready to take her. Where do you suggest we go? I was thinking I could drive to San Francisco and from there she and I could hop on a plane to Hawaii."

"Reno is closer and cheaper. Or Las Vegas if you want an Elvis impersonator to marry you."

"Reno it is."

"Okay, but what comes after a quickie wedding? You don't have a job."

Randall laughed.

"A.C. already has my life planned out for me. After a highly paid one-year internship, learning the ins and outs of the *'awl bidness'*, he intends to make me president and CEO of the company, while he and Mom relocate to a large piece of ocean-view property on Maui. The house will be transferred into my name – well, California being a community property state, into my name and Gemmy's."

"What does Germaine think of the two of you reigning as king and queen of the California 'awl bidness'?" I couldn't quite pull off a Texas good ol' boy accent as well as Randall could.

"As long as we're married, I could be a king-of-the-road hobo. Or a Woody Gutherie boxcar hobo. Or so she says."

I said, "She could hone her golf game better if you both belonged to a local country club, don't you think?"

"Yes! And as for Stephanie, A.C. will put up enough cash and stock to endow as many academic chairs as necessary to get her into a top Bay Area medical school. And he'll do the same endowed-chair shtick to get Teddy into Cal Poly as a legacy. So, you see, my parents are looking out for all of us."

"What about your soon-to-be mother-in-law?"

"Is she really going to confess that she shot Fowler?"

230

"She is."

"Is there any way I can help her?" he said.

"There is. You, or your family, or your father's oil company can foot her legal bills. They are going to be substantial."

"Do you know any great defense attorneys?"

"I do. Her name is Amanda Reynolds. She's in Santa Julietta and I'll be seeing her first thing tomorrow morning."

"Who really shot Fowler?"

"I wasn't there. But whatever you do, don't press Germaine for an answer. For now Sarah says she, Sarah, pulled the trigger. Let's wait to see how Amanda makes her plea when she is arraigned. Now come in and we can wake Germaine."

However, Mary Ann already had Germaine up, dressed, and ready to travel.

Germaine was startled to see her fiancé. "Randall, Oh, how I'm glad to see you. Daddy's dead and I…." Before she could finish, Mary Ann put a hand to Germaine's mouth.

May Ann said to her, "What you mean to tell Randall is that your father is dead and that you are very confused about what all happened." With her hand still across Germaine's mouth, Mary Ann said, "Now just nod."

Germaine complied, but I could tell she was eager to tell Randall what really went down.

So I said to her, "Save it for the long drive to Reno."

Her face brightened. "Is that where we're going?"

Randall smiled and nodded.

After Randall and Germaine were gone, Mary Ann asked, "Is there any more I can do for Sarah tonight?"

"You've done plenty already," I said.

"Does that make me an accessory after the fact?"

I opened my palms and shrugged. "Probably. And me as well."

"How much will my bail be? Should I be moving money to my checking account?"

"The judge will likely let you off on your own recognizance. Me? Not so likely."

"Would you like to borrow your bail money? I'm willing to cover it for you."

"Amanda will think of something."

"What possible defense will she think of for poor dear Sarah?"

I put a forefinger to my lips. "Shh. I can almost hear her giving her final summation to the jury. It will sound something like…."

"Ladies and gentle of the jury, the purpose of a trial such as this one is to see that justice is served. No more, no less. Now I want you to consider the possibility that in this particular case justice was fully served even before the judge first banged her gavel, that justice was served in the moment Sarah Fowler retrieved that .22 pistol from her bedroom closet shelf, pointed it at her husband's head, and pulled the trigger.

"If you have been listening closely, observing closely – and I'm sure you have – you will have noted the reluctance on the face of Mr. Edwards to prosecute this case. Oh, he will deny it. In fact, he must deny it. But you know it, I know it, he knows it: Sarah Payette does not deserve to be found guilty of murder. Instead, she deserves to be thanked for seeing that justice was carried out in full. She knew that her husband, for what he did to his daughter, Germaine, no longer deserved to live. She knew he was no longer fit to live in the company of civilized human beings."

"Yes, many who are unfit to live in the company of civilized people we lock away in jail cells until we are convinced they are worthy of our company again. But would a jail cell really fulfill the demands of justice in the case of Fowler Payette? After the crime he committed, how could he ever look any of us in the eye again? He couldn't. He would be condemned to serve the remainder of his life outside those bounds.

"Throw him in a cell and throw away the key. That is the state of California's way of isolating him. Putting him in a box six feet under is another way, Sarah Payette's way. But that is taking the law into her own hands, you counter. And this is true enough. But imagine Sarah Payette in the throes of anger, fear, and hatred imagining a different jury in a different courtroom that turned out to be less perceptive than the twelve of you. Might that other jury find Sarah guilty and thus acquit her husband for whatever soulless reasons they might find? How well do you imagine Sarah could bear life in the months, the years, ahead of her when certain justice was as simple and assured as reaching for a pistol on her bedroom shelf in order to spare the state of California from having to treat Fowler Payette to a cold, gray cell not much bigger than a coffin?"

"My, my, Stu. Maybe you should have gone to law school to become a criminal defense attorney," Mary Ann said when I had finished my impression of Amanda's courtroom summation.

"Bah! The world suffers from a surfeit of lawyers already. No sense in adding one more."

"But there are lawyers and there are lawyers," she said.

"I know. Most of the lawyers I bump into in my line of work spent their years in law school studying phrenology and astrology. For every Perry Mason there are ten sacks of coal masquerading as lawyers. Flat-earth attorneys. Sorry for mixing my metaphors."

"Oh, but you blend them so colorfully. So you really truly believe Amanda Reynolds can get Sarah off scot-free?"

"I do. If you listen closely you can hear the jury foreman tell the judge: 'We find the defendant not guilty. And, if we may add a second conclusion, Your Honor, we unanimously believe Fowler Payette committed suicide.'"

"Really?" May Ann said.

"No. That's a fantasy too far. Too much to hope for. But trust me. Sarah will walk."

"What's next for you? That is, after you arrange for Sarah's defense?"

"There's a young woman in Santa Julietta who needs some help. She's had two children ripped away from her and now those children are dead through no fault of hers. She would like to become a foster mother again, I imagine, but CPS will put a stop to that."

"That is so sad," Mary Ann said.

"I'm not sure of the final body count in the convent's cavern crypt. It doesn't matter. The Church has promised to relocate the mummies to other sacred Church grounds. I told Wendy Ellen I would see to it that the Church also pays for two gravesites at a small cemetery just below Santa Ynez Ridge. We'll bury her two girls there. It's a gorgeous place. Fantastic views.

Next what I'd like to do for Wendy Ellen is to open a daycare center with her in charge. She's great with kids – as long as she can see to it that the children are properly fed."

"I don't suppose her house would work for such a center, would it?"

"No. I doubt if her neighborhood is zoned for that many giggling kids in one spot. The church is closing the convent. But having a daycare center there would surely be too much for Wendy Ellen to bear."

"Stu, I'd be willing to put up some money for such a venture. I can't think of anything better for my money to do. I've been saving half my paycheck since the first day I started work at the public library here. I never did have a goal in mind for much of my savings."

"That's very kind of you, Mary Ann. I'll keep your bankroll in mind."

"Oh, dear. It's after midnight, Stu."

"Not to worry. Cinderella is safely in her coach and off to Happily-Ever-After Land with her prince."

"What next for you, my dear man?"

"I think I'll take the rest of the year off. It's been a grim enough one already. Martin Luther King dead, Bobby Kennedy dead, the Chicago convention, Richard Nixon soon on his way into the White House. Vietnam raging."

"Don't forget an abbess murdering her children."

"No, Ma'am. I will not forget that, even when all else has faded. I'll probably think of Mother Agnes as Michtecactihuatl."

"No, no, Stu. You do the Aztec Goddess of the Underworld a disservice."

"Maybe I do."

"Good night, Stu."

"Goodnight, Mary Ann."

After Mary Ann left I scooped up a pair of blankets and a pillow, took them out into my backyard, and flopped down on my back with my cheap binoculars in hand to stare up at the stars. Astronomy has always seemed too confusing to me. I could never remember the names of the constellations, even with a star chart in hand. Centuries ago a handful of Greeks lay on their backs, stared up, and drew pictures in their minds, assigning colorful names to what they both saw and imagined. And to the *wanderers* in the sky they gave the name *planet*. Arab men, taking as candid an interest in the stars as the Greeks, gave names to the brightest stars they could see. My favorite is Betelgeuse, which today's astronomers call Alpha Orionis, the alpha (brightest) star in the constellation Orion. In Arabic Betelgeuse means *armpit of the great one.* And there it is, in the armpit of Orion, the Hunter.

I didn't suppose it occurred to any of those men that millennia later men, both serious and not so serious, would look up and know the heavens by how those ancient men named and described what they saw. Or maybe it did occur to them. What do I know?

Having been a reference librarian at the local public library for forty-two years, Mary Ann Chase knows all manner of exotic facts, one of which is that the name of the Aztec god Huitzilopochtli means *left-handed hummingbird.* I wonder what she knows about Mayan astronomy? I'll have to ask her.

Meanwhile, I'm just a rough-shod private detective, plying my trade on the Central California coast.